Merry Christmas Papa! I hope you enjoy this gift. You have worked very hard on this, and I thought it deserved to be completed.

Love you always,

Sasha

ONCE A CHAMELEON

James G. Caffrey

James Caffrey

CHAPTER I

Newcastle, England - 1992

Donald stirred in his bed and licked his dry lips. His tongue felt like a zookeeper's boot. He reached for the half-full glass of water on the bedside table. It was warm and tasted awful, but it was wet. As he placed the glass back on to the table, he stretched out to prevent the empty Merlot bottle from falling. For a brief moment he stared at the empty wine bottle realizing he'd drunk too much the night before.

He'd slept well but the feeling of dehydration and a compelling need for a glass of orange juice had awoken him. He lay staring at the ceiling. His thoughts of the previous evening made him linger a little longer in bed. Was it his non acceptance of how they were living and how their relationship had deteriorated year after year which was compelling him to leave? Or was it his lingering doubts surrounding Allison's fidelity which had pushed him over the top?

Donald's focused switched to the open suitcase on the floor. Items of clothing lay around the room waiting to be packed. He knew then he hadn't been dreaming. He really was leaving.

Sooner or later any discussion he had with Allison would end up in an argument. This is how they had lived

3

for several years. They could no longer communicate. What was he supposed to do? He couldn't let things continue the way they were. His decision to leave had been bold yet he felt unsure and isolated. Allison didn't react because she didn't really believe he was leaving. No protest, nothing other than, "go, but you'll be back". Maybe she was in denial or suffering from delayed shock. Soon or later reality would hit. By then he would be gone.

He would have liked to have turned over and gone back to sleep but knew he had to get up.

Slowly he lifted himself up and draped his feet over the side of the bed. He raised his arms above his head stretching his body. At the same time, he shuffled his feet around the floor searching for his slippers. Suddenly he made contact. Using his toes he maneuvered each slipper onto his feet. He stood up and walked quietly across the room. He gently pulled back the curtain to expose the steamed windows soaked with condensation. Moving his fingers in slow circular motions he cleared a small porthole and peered out of the window. Monday morning and it was still raining.

Making his way towards the bedroom door he wiped his wet fingers on the leg of his pajamas. The bathroom door creaked as it opened breaking the stillness within the house. He froze and looked towards Allison's closed bedroom door. He listened for the slightest sound. Everything remained quiet.

He wanted desperately to shower but he knew the

4

noise would awaken Allison, so he washed, cleaned his teeth and then got dressed. Hurriedly he finished packing. He tried to take extra care to be quiet while closing the suitcase, but the keys jingled as he turned them in the locks. Walking downstairs he deliberately avoided the steps he knew creaked. He placed the suitcase by the front door and went into the kitchen and got himself a large glass of orange juice. Gulping down the cold liquid he noticed the travel brochures which were still lying on the table. The thought of yet another holiday in Rhodes had been the trigger he'd need to let Allison know how he really felt.

Stepping outside into the rain he turned to gently close the door behind him. The door got within an inch of closing when he stopped. Just for a brief moment he wondered whether he would ever see the inside of his home again. He'd lived there for over 20 years. It seems strange to be just walking away. He took one last look inside then eased the door closed.

Turning out of the gate he glanced up at the front bedroom window. The curtains were still drawn. He imagined Allison lying in bed asleep. He wondered how she would react when she awoke and discovered he was gone. Even though he no longer loved her, he still cared about her. Maybe one day she would understand why he'd decided to leave. He'd know for a number of years that one day he would.

The rail station was only a short walking distance. He checked his wallet to make sure he had everything.

Passport, driver's license and credit cards. He would pick up some travelers' checks at the airport.

When he got to the top of the road he turned and looked back. All the houses were lined up in neat rows like cardboard boxes. The milkman was making his early morning delivers. Donald stood for a moment listening to him whistling. The tune sounded familiar. The milkman had a spring in his step as he moved from door-to-door, just as he had done every morning for more than 10 years.

His attention switched as he heard a house door open. A pair of arms appeared dropping a cat onto the wet pavement. As the door closed the cat stood in the rain with its back hunched. It looked around trying to come to terms with the reality that it had been rudely awakened and dumped outside. It lifted each paw off the wet surface shaking them one by one. The cat raised its head slightly tilting it to one side and stared at the closed door. Donald smiled second guessing the cat's thought, "I didn't really want to come out today, it's raining. But then again, I guess I get put out every morning at this time."

Donald knew then he'd made the right decision. He turned and walked in the direction of the rail station. He looked a lonely figure in the rain and early morning mist.

The rail station was deserted except for the ticket clerk and an old woman selling newspapers. He purchased his ticket and pushed it into the top pocket of his jacket. The clerk had indicated it would be 20 minutes before the next train. He made his way along deserted platform and found a vending machine. As he sat down on a cold wooden bench hugging a hot cup of coffee with both hands his thoughts began reflecting upon the events of the previous the evening.

The sound of the rain dancing on the roof of the garden shed seemed to ease the pressure and anxiety Donald felt burning inside of him. It was early evening. He'd left his Sunday dinner only half eaten. Allison knew he looked forward to a nice Sunday roast dinner. He couldn't help thinking that maybe this was the why she'd picked her moment to discuss the planned holiday to Rhodes. It wasn't that he didn't like Rhodes. The problem was a lot more serious.

For several years now he and Allison had been living together as what appeared to be a happily married couple. Yet as each day went by, he felt more and more like a lodger in his own home. There was no affection in their relationship. There was no love in their life. Their friendship had died a long time ago. Why do so many people mistake contentment for happiness he thought?

He was living his life as the person she wanted him to be. The persons she'd created. Deep down inside he knew over the years of their marriage he'd changed. The difficulty he was struggling with was the need to discover the real person trapped inside of him. He had to get away, but the challenge was taking the first step then accepting the consequences of his actions.

Their arguing had become a lot more frequent. The periods of not speaking were getting longer. Sometimes they lasted for weeks. On so many occasions their disputes were over things small and insignificant. He took a big sigh.

She'd known for months how he felt about their holiday, yet she'd gone ahead again and booked to go to Rhodes. He was fed up with the place and who wouldn't be after six consecutive years? Even the airport immigration officers now knew them personally, hugging and kissing Allison each time they arrived. There was a whole world out there he wanted to see. He'd made several suggestions that had been ignored. It wasn't as if they couldn't afford to go to the Far East or South America, financially they were now quite comfortable.

The time was right, he'd had enough, and he needed to leave.

Where would he go? How would he live? It wasn't the loneliness that cast doubts in his mind; he'd been lonely for many years. Maybe it was the thought of the unknown and starting over. There was also the fear that after a few weeks he may return home begging for forgiveness. Wherever he went he'd have to find a job. This thought would have really scared him a few years ago, but not now.

Having been made redundant after more than twenty

years service with his company he felt hurt and disappointed, but in reality, it had turned out to be his springboard to freedom. He'd been fortunate and found work quickly as an Engineering Consultant. He enjoyed being his own boss and having the opportunity to travel and work away from home. The bouts of freedom had helped him to be more independent. The timing was right he had to take the initiative and follow his heart.

It wasn't as though he'd never loved Allison. In their own adolescent and innocent way, they'd fallen in love and married when they were teenage sweethearts. Within a few years Richard was born. The years flew by and now Richards was grown up and in his final term of University.

He gathered himself together before going back into the house to face Allison.

No matter what she says or does I'm not giving in he thought. I have to be firm and put my foot down. It's time I told her how I really feel and what I've decided to do with my life. He felt a deep sense of commitment as he turned and walked back into the house.

The noise of the backdoor closing brought an immediate response.

"Is that you Donald?"

The tone of her voice indicated she was acting as if

nothing had happened. This was Allison's way of handling and controlling the situation after they'd argued.

"No it's the milkman." replied Donald.

Who does she think it is, he thought? She always does this pretending as if nothing has happened and everything in the garden is rosy. He knew if he reacted she would start playing the offended martyr.

"Well then, do we feel a lot better after our visit to our little garden sanctuary?" Allison inquired in a condescending manner.

"I don't recall seeing you out there. Where were you, hiding under a plant pot?'

Donald paused before he continued.

"Why is it Allison that every time we have an argument you have to treat me like a small child and talk to me in your schoolteacher tone of voice? Does it make you feel superior or the feeling of being in charge? Is that why you do it? "

He was desperately trying to suppress the irritation he felt inside. He needed to stay calm. He could feel the discussion beginning to build up into another argument. He mustn't let that happen, that's what she wanted. This was how she took control.

Donald turned and started walking into the living room. A delayed response came from Allison.

"Now there's no need to get like that Donald,"

Allison followed Donald into the living room continuing the conversation.

"Now you've got all that off your chest and your feeling better let's just get this thing about our holiday sorted out. We've gone to Rhodes for the past six years and you loved it every time. What's the big problem this year?"

"Okay. I'll tell you what the problem is. Yes, I like Rhodes. Yes, I enjoyed visiting there but I told you months ago, I wanted to go somewhere different. There is a whole world out there but no you went ahead and booked Rhodes because you like it there. You wanted to go back. Didn't you stop for one single moment and think about where I would have liked to have gone? No, I guess you didn't, but you never do so why did I expect you'd act different this time."

Allison stood with her mouth half open. Slowly pools of water began to appear in her eyes.

Here we go again he thought but I won't let her get away with it this time. I have to tell her.

"It's always what you want Allison. It's always been

11

like that, always, but not anymore,"

His voice was firm as he decided to continue. This was the moment. The right moment to open up and let her know what was in his heart.

"You think you can herd people around from field to field like cattle whenever it suits you. You do it to me. You do it to Richard. You even done it to the friends we used to have. No one ever calls and visits us anymore. They all feel they have to be invited. Most of the people we knew as friends are now long gone. I don't have a best friend and neither do you. Don't you see this all because we've shut out the rest of the world. We've created this Alice in Wonderland environment and view the rest of the world through a looking glass. I'll take my share of the blame for letting it happen but enough is enough. Don't you want to see what's out there? Don't you want to step back through the looking glass and experience real life?

There was no response from Allison.

"No, I guess you don't do you? Your happy playing Alice and always will be."

She continued gazing out of the window as if in a trance. Occasionally she reached up and fiddled with her hair. Donald continued with his head bowed tracing the swirling pattern on his tie with his finger.

"People feel uncomfortable around you Allison, including me. Everything has to be done just how you like it. You cannot find it in yourself to open up your heart and accept people for what they are. You're suspicion of everyone's intentions keeping them at a distance. Trust and love have disappeared from your heart. I'm sorry Allison; I can't go on living my life like this. I'm sorry but I've had enough."

Donald felt uneasy as Allison turned away from the window to face him. As he looked into her eyes, he could see feelings of doubt whirling through her mind. He felt a little guilty, but this was overcome by a feeling of relief as if something trapped deep down inside had finally erupted.

"What's happened to us Donald?"

"We used to be so much in love when we were younger. We really cared about each other and enjoyed each other's company so much. Where did we go wrong? Why is it so different now? What changed so much whereby we can hardly stand being with each for more than a few hours before we're at each other throats?"

She wiped her eyes. Donald stopped fidgeting with his tie and looked at her.

"In love Allison? when was the last time we made love? I mean really made love with feelings and tenderness"

13

"Oh, about six weeks ago. It was after we got home from Dawn and Roger's Anniversary Party. I thought it was quite nice actually. I always enjoy our love making."

Donald responded with a mixture of anger and desperation in his voice.

"Perfect, bloody perfect. You see Allison to you that is what our lovemaking is about. Quite nice, thank you very much!"

There was a long pause before he continued.

"We don't make love Allison; we have sex that's what we do. We go through the physical act of satisfying our animal lust. When we are finished, within minutes we both turn over in opposite direction of the bed, back to back and go to sleep. Not even our legs or feet touch. It's so clinical and cold, there's no tenderness or feelings. Many nights I have lain in the darkness of our bedroom with a deep knot twisting inside of me. The distanced which separated our bodies might well have been a mile. I got used to sleeping alone a long time ago".

His voices trailed off as he looked up at Allison and realized he was not getting through to her. She was again staring out of the window. Only his silences made her turn and look back in his direction.

"Tell me what you want Donald? Tell me where you

want to go on holiday, and we'll do it?"

"You see what I mean Allison. Have you understood one word of what I've been trying to say to you?"

He poured himself a glass of red wine and walked into the front room taking the bottle of wine with him. After a brief pause Allison followed. Entering the room, she was about to say something then hesitated and changed her mind. They both stood in silence until finally she turned and sat in the large armchair by the fireplace. Donald stood in front of the window watched the rain, occasionally taking a gulp of wine.

Allison sat staring at the back of Donald's head thinking it was about time he needed a haircut. Suddenly she realized what an odd thought to go through her mind at such a serious moment.

Donald continued gazing out of the window. His mind drifted as he thought why it does always seem to rain on a Sunday. It was one of those days where people read every piece of print in the newspaper and go to work the next day sounding super intelligent, I say did you read that article in the Sunday Times about the plague in India? Started in Surat you know five hundred dead. Bodies everywhere. The media always appeared to give the biggest headlines to tragedy and suffering. Maybe that's because people don't really like hearing about people being happy. There are so many lonely and unhappy people in the world he thought.

15

Slowly he turned and looked at Allison. He walked towards her and placed his glass and wine bottle on the coffee table. He then sat on the floor in front of her. He reached up and took hold of her hand. His mind searched for the right words to express the feelings in his heart.

"Being in love is about tenderness. It's about affection, consideration and sincerity. Two people in love have fun together. They share feelings of pleasure because they've done something special for each other that's made them feel great. Love isn't a state of mind. Love is a gift from the heart. It's a spontaneous gift given unconditionally. The foundation of everlasting love is friendship. The person you love has to be your best friend. Without that bond of friendship love cannot survive. When we are apart, even during a normal day, has either of us ever felt we could hardly wait to get home to see each other? Can you truly put your hand on your heart and say we've ever felt that way about each other? Have you ever felt like that Allison?"

Allison searched for words to respond.

"Why didn't you tell me how you felt." she said in a teary voice.

"I love you in the only way I know how Donald and if that not enough I don't know what to do about it."

Donald continued.

16

"I am lonelier with you, than I am without you Allison. Can you understand that? Can you understand how I feel deep down inside? Sometimes we're alone in this house for hours and even days and we hardly find to two words to say to each other. We struggle to make even polite conversation so we can   break the embarrassing silence. We never go out for a meal together, just the two of us. That's because we no longer know how to talk to each other. We no longer have anything in common. Over the years we have just drifted apart. Don't you think that's sad Allison?"

The immediate response Donald hoped for never came. He hesitated a little longer. As he got up from the floor he reached out and picked his glass and wine bottle and walked back to the window. The silence in the room was uncomfortable as he waited for a reaction from Allison.

"So, what do you want to do about the holidays then? Does this mean you want to go on your own this year? Is this what all this is about? Why don't you just come out and say so instead of going on about love and friendship."

Donald turned unable to control his anger as he screamed at her.

"You see Alison, even now you haven't heard a single word of what I've being trying to explain. This is a

17

typical example of what I am talking about. You haven't a clue of what I am trying to say, do you?

I'm not just wasting my time; I'm wasting my life by just being here with you.

Allison didn't respond. She was afraid to utter what was going through her mind. She felt if she didn't respond it wouldn't happen. Donald couldn't possibly be thinking of leaving her. Oh God! What would the neighbors think? She would have to make up a story they would believe. He's gone away on a business trip to the Middle East for three months. He's an engineer and he often goes away on business trips. That's it! That's what she'd tell them. Her thoughts were racing though her brain. He wouldn't walk out and leave her just like that. It had to be something else!

Suddenly she started screaming at him.

"It's another woman isn't it? I know it is. You enjoy the comforts of home too much to just walk out the door. You have another woman! You've being cheating on me. Where did you meet her, during one of your business trips?"

"Don't be stupid Allison. There's no other woman now and there never has been. Why can't you accept what I've being trying to explain? We're just not good together anymore. If we stay together, we'll drift further and further apart and end up hating each other. We'd become more unhappy as each day went by. I have to do what I

18

feel is in my heart. I don't mean to hurt you but somewhere out there is real happiness. There's no nice way to say this but there has to be more to life than the way we are living."

She stood biting her white knuckles.

"I want to go back Allison. I want to go back through the looking glass."

"Where will you go Donald? What will you do? Who'll take care of you?" she asked with concern and emotion in her voice.

"Why didn't you tell me before how you felt? Have you lived all of our married life with these hidden feelings? Has our married life been a total pretense a waste of time? What about my life?"

The pools in her eyes broke sending tears rolling down her cheek.

"I've felt like this for a very long time. I tried many times to talk to you about my feelings, but it was always difficult and awkward. People don't talk with you Allison; you talk at them. You never give anyone a chance to express their thoughts or opinions. That's just the way you are. You'll never change. You're happy to live in Alice's world for the rest of your life but I'm not!"

He stood for a brief moment looking down at her

then walked into to the hall with his glass in one hand and the bottle of wine in the other hand. On the stairway he stopped and called.

"I'll leave early in the morning. I'll call to make sure that you're all right and let you know where to contact me. That is if you feel you want to. I wish there was a right way to do this Allison but there isn't, I am sorry for all the disruption I am about to cause in your life. You've been a good mother and always kept a good home for the family. Please don't mention anything to Richard if he calls tomorrow. I'll give him a call and try to explain what's happened."

He never heard Allison's response as she yelled.

"Go ahead if that's what you want to do. Why don't you get out tonight? All this stupid talk about Alice and the looking glass! You're going crazy; you're out of your mind. Run. Run as fast and as far as you can but you'll be back. I'll give you a month and you'll be begging my forgiveness. Just wait and see."

Chapter II

Miami, Florida, USA.

Donald didn't mind flying but found long flights boring and therefore got restless after the first few hours. It wasn't that he was afraid he just got bored and restless after the first hour. In between napping his thought had constantly reflected on events of the previous day. The telephoned conversation from the airport with Richard had been difficult with lapses of silence that seemed to last forever. He'd given his son a brief account of what had occurred. The noise of the public address system added to the difficulty of trying to talk to each other. There wasn't a great deal of response from Richard and this worried Donald. Maybe Allison had already talked with Richard.

He tried to rationalize the situation by attempting to put himself in his son's position. How would he have reacted if his father had called to inform him that he was leaving his mother? It was difficult to imagine because his large family environment and upbringing of open love and affection. He knew he needed to give his son time to absorb the reality of the situation.

If he hadn't already done so, Richard would also be hearing his mother's version of events. She would be playing the deserted wife and blaming everything on Donald. Well if putting the blame on to him helped her to handle the situation better, that was fine. They had been together for over 25 years and although he no longer loved Allison he did care and worry about her well being.

As he got into the taxi at Miami airport, Donald gave the driver the name of the hotel he had obtained from Tourist Information. He'd asked for medium priced place to stay and as the cab pulled up outside the hotel, his initial reaction was that he was pleased with the selection.

The hotel receptionist handed Donald a pen as he picked up a registration card.

"Will you be staying long Sir?"

"Two or three nights, I'm on my way to Venezuela"

Oh! Didn't that sound good, he secretly thought to himself? He handed back the completed registration form and his credit card. The receptionist completed the check in formalities and handed him back his credit cards and his room key.

"Your room is on the sixth-floor sir. If you need any assistance, please give me a call. Will there be anything else Sir?"

"Oh Yes. Does the hotel have a bar?"

"Yes Sir. We have a lounge bar on the roof top;

Happy Hour is from 6:00 PM until 9:00 PM. We have live music and dancing."

Donald spent the early part of the evening unpacking and getting a shirt and a pair of trousers pressed. He showered and wrapped himself up in the large fluffy robe he found hanging in the bathroom. As he lay on the bed, he started surfing through the numerous TV channels.

Why does American TV have so many TV Channels? He thought. They can't possibly watch them all at the same time. He loved the old shows like The Lucy Show. In fact, some of the older shows were now quite refreshing. He was also amazed at the talk shows and all the personal and secrets people were prepared to tell the world about.

He had a couple of cold beers from the mini bar which made him feel good. By 9:30pm he was ready to go and check out the roof top lounge bar. Riding in the elevator he looked at himself in the mirror. He felt good. Crisp and clean. The elevator door opened straight into the area of the lounge. The band was playing a tune with a soft Latin beat. As he walked towards the bar, he secretly twitched his hips. He sat down on a vacant stool where a very attentive bar lady was waiting to serve him.

"What can I get you to drink Sir?"

For a moment he stared at her. She looked and

sounded just like Victoria Cannon from The High
Chaparral TV series. One of his favorites.

"Excuse me sir, would like a drink?"

"Emmm! ...... Oh, sorry beer please. Nice and
cold."

As she placed his beer in front of him, he
anticipated she was going to ask him a question.

"Are you English Sir?"

"Yes I am. Sorry I mean I'm British."

Although his reply sounded a little hesitant there
was a hint of pride in his voice.

The bar lady smiled. "Oh..... I just love your
accent; it sounds so polished and cultured."

Donald returned her smile politely but was a little
relieved when she turned to attend to another customers.
The place was beginning to get busy. Looking around he
noticed that many of the people were of Latin appearance.
Then he realized this was what Miami was all about.

People really do dress up to come out over here,
he thought to himself. Not like back home at the local
pub. Who wants to get dressed up for a game of darts,
dominoes, and a packet of chips and a few pints of beer

eh? He swung his stool around towards the bar and ordered another beer. He was beginning to get a buzz on. Through the large mirror at the back of the bar he noticed an extremely attractive young lady laughing and joking with a group of her friends. She looked to be in her mid twenties and had the most gorgeous smile he'd ever seen. He continued watching her through the mirror as she joked and laughed with her friends responding. As she stood up Donald briefly looked away. Slowly his eyes returned to watch her. After taking money from her purse she walked towards the bar. He discreetly continued to look at her as she walked in his direction and stood next to him. She had a gorgeous aroma about her. Not perfume but more like a discreet smell of fresh flowers.

The bar lady appeared and motioned to serve Donald another beer. He reacted quickly by making a gesture in the direction of the young lady.

"Please serve the young lady first; I don't mind waiting a few more minutes."

The young lady turned and smiled acknowledging his gesture, she then proceeded to order her drinks. When she had finished ordering she turned to face Donald.

"Thank you. That was very nice of you. You're a gentleman and they're not too many of them around these days."

"No problem the pleasure is truly mine."

"You're not American, are you? I cannot quite place your accent but it's nice and refreshing.

What's it is? I'm sorry; I mean where you are from Ireland?"

"No, I'm British." Donald replied.

She smiled nodding her head in a gesture of understanding. She'd noticed him swaying in his seat to the beat of the music. She decided to bold.

"The music is good but why are you not dancing?"

"Yes, the music is great but I'm not dancing is because no one's asked me." he jokingly replied.

She was puzzled by his response but decide to pursue their line of conversation.

"The man is supposed to ask the woman, yes?"

Donald had a slight smirk on his face as he responded

"I didn't know that there was a set of rules."

"But it is always the duty of the man to ask the woman. That's just the way it's done."

She was still puzzled as she paid for her drinks and walked back to join her friends. Donald couldn't take his eyes off her. Watching her through the mirror the thought "She's beautiful. Everything about her is perfect.

When she got back to the table her girlfriends were eagerly awaiting to find out what had been going on. As she talked to them, they would occasionally look back in the direction of the bar. Donald concluded she was telling them what they'd been talking about. The sounds of their giggling and laughter could be heard even from where he was sitting. Ten minutes had elapsed when suddenly Donald felt a tap on his shoulder. He didn't need to turn. He lifted his head and through the mirror he saw the young lady had returned.

He swiveled his stool turning to face her.

She looked him boldly in the eye. "Okay senor, come on let's go."

Although he knew exactly the lady's intent, he decided to play dumb.

"I'm sorry?"

She decided to repeat her request but in a more persuasive manner by swinging her hips back and forth to the beat of the music.

"I said okay senor, come on let's go?"

"I'm sorry?" he reiterated continuing the pretense.

"So, you like to play games? Well we shall do this the formal way."

With a slight hint of a curtsey and a devilish look in her eyes the young lady decided to continue her pursuit in trying to get Donald on the dance floor.

"Excuse me sir, please would you like to dance with me?"

Donald struggled trying hard not to burst out laughing as he also decided to continue their little game not knowing where it would lead.

"Dance, oh I'm sorry but no thank you. Maybe I'll dance with you later."

The fury in her eyes said it all as she turned and strode away. She was definitely not amused. The wild look on her face made Donald think he may have taken the joke too far. Even in anger she was stunning beautiful. During the rest of the evening she continued to glare back in his direction occasionally with a puzzled look in her eyes. Each time she got up onto the dance floor, she would look in his direction to make sure he was watching. Dancing she wriggled her torso with a sexual shimmer as if to remind him of what he was missing.

Watching her dance was exciting. Donald tried not to stare but he could help himself. He'd never seen anyone move their body in such a sensuous manner. In fact, all the couples on the dance floor were great dancers. It was exciting to watch. Although the music was very fast, as they twisted and turned their bodies never moved very far apart. At times they appeared to be so close that they looked as if they were dancing as one person. The combination of the music, dancing and the short tight-fitting dresses the girls wore made it difficult not to stare. The whole exercise was extremely sexual and in a strange sort of way hypnotic.

It was now close to midnight and Donald was feeling guilty of his rude behavior towards the young lady. He felt a little strange, trying to pick up enough courage to go and apologize by asking her if she would like to dance with him. He didn't know where to start. He was out of practice when it came to wooing ladies. He got off his seat and started walking towards her. Suddenly he sensed her movement and as if by telepathy, she got up and began walking towards him. In reality she had been watching him most of the night and sensed his mood changing, mellowing with each drink. They never spoke as he took hold of her hand and led her to the dance floor.

Although he wasn't familiar with the Latin music the band was playing, he felt was this girl could dance like no one he'd ever danced with before. She made them both look great as they twirled around the floor. She made him feel great as his heart pounded with excitement.

29

One dance after another they seemed to improve and get better. Throughout their dancing they never spoke, but their obvious enjoyment vibrated from them both. Finally, the music stopped, and they walked hand in hand towards the bar.

Victoria, the bar lady, placed two drinks in front of them. She'd been watching them dancing and had this look of expectation on her face. They picked up their drinks and clicked glasses gulping eagerly to relieve their thirst. Victoria stood watching them. Finally, she walked away sensing they needed to be alone.

Donald held up his glass again. "Cheers."

Their glass touched again as she replied, "Salute."

"What's your name?"

"Leela, and yours?"

"Donald " he replied quickly.

Leela watched Donald's eyes as he checked her over. She didn't mind, in fact she felt flattered and took the opportunity to do the same to him. Donald couldn't stop staring at her, she was so beautiful. She had long black curled hair that glistened with cleanliness in the lights from the bar. Although her skin was light, he detected a hint of Latin blood in her complexion and features. The texture of her skin looked so smooth and soft with hardly a sign of any body hair. She had the most beautiful big dark brown eyes he'd ever seen. She really was quite stunning.

Leela, he thought, even the name fits perfectly. He could hardly believe where he was and who he was with. After having swept him off his feet on the dance floor, she was sitting next to him enjoying a drink. It was difficult to comprehend it was all actually happening to him.

He watched as she took a sip from her glass leaving a slight trace of lipstick

` "Where did you learn to dance like that?" she asked.

"I never did, in fact I never knew I could, you made it so easy for me. I guess we looked pretty good out there, people were staring at us. I must admit it felt good. You made me feel great. What were we dancing?"

Leela was now beginning to appreciate Donald's sense of humor. With a big smile on her face she answered.

"It was the Salsa."

A humorous puzzled look appeared on Donald's face. "Salsa, I thought that is some kind of sauce."
She was now laughing and placed her hand over

stomach in a mocking gesture.

"It is, but also it's a dance. I'm beginning to understand your sense of humor, although I must admit, I didn't think the British had one."

Now it was Donald's turn to laugh. He like her. In fact, his instincts told him he liked her a lot.

"Yes, does it look that obvious? I'm here for a few days, I'm on my way to Venezuela."

A mischievous gleam appeared in Leela's eyes.

"Oh, why Venezuela, have you been there before?"

"No, I haven't, and actually this is also my first visit to the United States."

They both sat looking at each other for a few moments not talking. Suddenly Donald broke the embarrassing silence.

"Look about what happened before when you asked me to dance, I was fooling around and didn't mean to be so rude. I have to admit I was amazed you had actually come over and asked me to dance. Anyway, I'm sorry I hope I didn't offend or embarrassed you in any way? I guess my sense of fooling around backfired eh?"

James Caffrey

" That's okay, no problem. I just didn't understand your sense of humor at the time, but it's okay now we are friends. Yes?"

"Yes sure, we are friends. You know I never realized there were this many Latin Americans here. Also, they play Latin music on the radio everywhere, in the taxis, even in the elevator, it's just played everywhere."

With the hint of a frown Leela asked. "You don't like the Latin people?"

"No....No.. It's not like that. I think they are nice people and the music is great. All of the Latin people seem to give a high priority to enjoying life. That's why I can hardly wait to get to Venezuela, I'm really looking forward to it. I don't know quite what to expect other than what I've seen on the Travel Show on television back home. It looked a great place."

Leela smiled. "Oh! I love your accent, it's so cultured and perfect. I could sit here all night just listening to you talk. It gives me, how'd you say, goose bumps all over."

What is it with these folks he thought, they all go barmy about my accent? Strange, funny people......

As they drained their glasses Victoria miraculously appeared. "Same again?"

33

Donald responded for them both hoping he was not offending Leela "Sure, why not, a nightcap eh, one for the road?".

Leela reached for her purse. "Yes, but please let me get these ones okay. I insist."

The powers of her persuasion were very effective, so Donald agreed. He was also tickled by the idea of a beautiful lady buying him a drink. Once Victoria was out of ear shot, Donald leaned over and quietly asked Leela.

"Did you ever watch a TV Show called The High Chaparral? It was about an American rancher called John Cannon; he had a son called Blue. They had this huge ranch somewhere in Arizona or New Mexico. The Indians were Apaches. Anyway, this bar lady looks and speaks just like Victoria, John Cannon's Mexican wife in the show."

Leela started laughing. She didn't know what Donald was talking about and he was getting a little drunk and looked funny.

"No, I'm sorry I never watched the show but if you say she looks like Victoria then I guess she does. By the way she's not Mexican she's Cuban"

Donald was still laughing when Leela caught him off guard.

"Are you married Donald?"

"Yes " he replied sheepishly but honestly.

"I'm separated from my wife" He bit his tongue as it came out wrong. He wasn't trying to justify why he was on his own in the company of a beautiful young lady. There was no reason for him to feel guilty. Leela seemed to read his thoughts and smiled at Donald as he continued.

"There wasn't any traumatic breakdown in my marriage, more of a gradual breakup in the relationship. We stopped being friends, it was as simple as that. No one was really to blame, it just happened.".

Looking into his eyes, Leela sensed that Donald was a nice guy but a very lonely person.

At the same moment Donald's instincts were telling him that Leela was a nice young lady. He liked the way she'd said they were friends. Unconsciously he gave a loud sigh and Leela knew it was time to call it a night.

"Listen Donald, are you free tomorrow?"

"Free, No. But I'm reasonable."

His joking made her laugh out loud. She was still giggling as he continued.

"I've checked my busy calendar for tomorrow, and I guess I can fit you in. What do you have planned?"

"My girl friends brother has a boat and we are meeting to have lunch. Would you like to join us? It will be fun, lots of dancing and Latin music." she teased.

"It sounds great to me. What time and how do I find the boat? There are tens of thousands of boats in a multitude of marinas"

"We shall come to the hotel and pick you up before noon. Is that okay?"

Leela leaned forward and took hold of Donald hand and kissed with gently on the cheek.

"Goodnight Donald. I need to go. My girlfriends are giving me a lift home. I shall see you tomorrow. It's been so nice meeting you. I can't remember laughing so much for a long time. You are a nice person."

"Goodnight Leela. I had a great time to. I can't remember having such a good time as I've had with you tonight. I enjoyed your company so much, especially our dancing. Take care. See you tomorrow. It's past my bedtime as well."

They got up from their bar stools and went through the motions of gently kissing each other on the cheek.

Walking back to his room, Donald had a definite spring in his step. He felt he'd come alive. As he put the key in the door, he heard the phone ringing. He was puzzled because he wasn't expecting a call. In fact, no one knew where he was staying. He picked up the receiver and waited. After a brief silence he heard Leela's voice.

"Hello, hello. Donald is that you? It's me, Leela."

"Oh, hi Leela, sorry you surprised me, I didn't expect a call. No one knows where I'm staying, and I don't know anyone in Miami accept yourself. How did you know my room number?"

"Oh, it wasn't difficult. Anyway listen, I wanted to remind you to bring your swimsuit tomorrow. We usually just roll up in shorts and tee shirt. Is that okay?"

Yes, that's fine. I'm looking forward to it."

"Goodnight Donald and sweet dreams. See you tomorrow lunch time."

"Goodnight Leela. I'll be there."

Donald continued holding the telephone until he heard the dial tone purring and realized he needed to hang up.

He got up early the next morning and decided he would call the airline and confirm his flight arrangement to Aruba. During his breakfast all he could think of was the wonderful evening and his lunch date with Leela. He then realized he needed to go out and buy some decent shorts. Maybe he would spoil himself and get a nice sports shirt as well. I wanted to look good when meeting Leela and her friends. He couldn't believe he was going on a boat for lunch. This only happened in the movies.

Coming out of the coffee shop the receptionist called him over and handed him a message. It was from the airline giving him a number with a request to call immediately. He scratched his head and found the house phone and called the number. He listened as the lady explained that his flight to Aruba following day had been canceled. He had to be at Miami airport within the hour as he was now re-booked to leave today. This was the only seat available within the next four days. He hung up the phone not wanting to believe what was happening.

How would he get word to Leela? Although they'd only met, he didn't want to leave without at least giving her a message. Just my luck, he thought. She was so gorgeous.

He quickly packed his bags and went down to check out. While he was waiting for his bill, he scribbled a note to Leela apologizing but he had to leave urgently. He didn't know how to contact her, so he decided to leave the note with the receptionist. She promised she would make sure Leela got the message when she came to pick him up. He gave the receptionist a ten-dollar bill for her help. He felt really bad about the whole situation. He had no forwarding address to leave. In the taxi on the way to the airport he wondered if he would ever see her again.

CHAPTER III

Aruba, Dutch Antilles

During the flight to Aruba Donald couldn't stop thinking about Leela and the events of the previous evening. He'd really had a great time, especially the dancing. He'd never really been a person who danced a lot, but this was different. It felt different. He hoped the receptionist had remembered to give Leela the message. He glanced at his watch, it was 1:30 PM. Leela and her friends would now be on the boat having lunch. She seemed to be such a nice girl, with a great personality. She gave the impression that she came from a very good family. He kept thinking about how beautiful she looked.

His mind drifted to back home to England and Richard. I wondered how he was handing everything. He hadn't really had enough time to explain to him over the phone why he was leaving. He needed the opportunity to express how he felt during all those years of being married to Allison. His mother would be bending Richard's ears telling him she'd always been a good wife and a good mother. Donald agreed she'd had been a very good mother, but she had also been a very difficult person to live with. Maybe one day he would have the opportunity to tell Richard how he felt in his heart.

A twinge of butterflies in his stomach reminded him he was now on his own. He was looking forward to experiencing his freedom. After his encounter with Leela he realized he was a totally different person.

Leela had thought him to be witty, charming and a great dancer. She had made him feel good. His only regret was that he would have loved to have spent more time with her. Who knows where it may have led to? Snapping him out of his thoughts, the captains voice on the intercom announcement they were about to land in Aruba.

He cleared immigration and customs then made for the hotel reservation desk. They quickly found him a place to stay and he was on his way from the airport to downtown. For the price range he had requested, the hotel was a lot better than he had thought it would be. The high tourist season hadn't yet started so accommodation prices were still a little cheaper. Donald had a warm feeling for Aruba. It looked clean and tidy and the people at the airport were friendly. As the taxi pulled into the hotel driveway he looked up at the sign, The Anchor Inn. Very nautical he thought.

The hotel registration card required details of his entry visa. As he searched though the pages of his passport he stopped at the page with the visa. His attention focused on the entry visa stamp. "Bon Bini Na Aruba " he whispered to himself.

The receptionist overheard him and smiled.

"It means have a happy stay in Aruba. We are

41

known as the friendly island. Our whole economy
revolves around the tourist industry. We have an
obligation to welcome every tourist in a special way that
will want them to return."

Donald smiled and took back his passport,
collected his room and key and walked towards the
elevator.

Once he had finished unpacking and cleaning up,
Donald decided he would venture out to see if he could
find an inexpensive place to eat. He'd noticed the hotel
Coffee Shop on the way in but thought he would find
better value outside. He wanted to have a good look
around anyway.

It was early evening and still light. Walking down
the main street, he noticed that nearly every other shop
appeared to be a Tee Shirt shop. He had never seen so
many, not even in Rhodes. He heard music coming from
a small cafe and stopped to look inside. It appeared to be
homely, neat and clean. There were a number of people
eating and drinking. He scanned the menu, chicken,
hamburgers, hot dogs, steak and salad. The smell of food
cooking finally tempted him, so he ventured in and sat
down.

Finishing off his chicken-in-a-basket he signaled
to the waitress to bring him another draft beer. The first
one had gone down quickly and was exceptionally cold,
which felt great in the warmth of the early evening.
Picking up his drink his attention switch to the loud

laughing of a group on a table close to him. They were really having good time. He'd unintentionally being eavesdropping on the conversation during the course of his meal.

One of the young ladies in the group switch her attention as she noticed Donald was listening and watching. He started to turn his eyes way, but she raised her glass in his direction in a friendly gestured. He smiled back reciprocating her friendliness. It was obvious from their accents that the two guys were Australians and the two girls Americans. They all seemed to be getting into the spirit of the occasion with their laughter getting a little louder with each round of drinks. They were not being offensive to anyone but just enjoying life. He ordered his third beer and the same response came from the same young lady, only this time she called over.

"If you're on your own and would care to join us please feel free."

Donald hesitated but then thought, why not. He got up from his table and as the waitress came over, he settled is bill. He ended up giving her a bigger tip than intended but he didn't want the group to think he was tight fisted. Being from England, where tipping wasn't the norm, he was never really too sure of how much to leave. Moving around to join the group he pulled up a chair and sat down.

"Thank you for the invitation. It was nice of you

to ask we. Was I sitting there looking like a little lost puppy?"

They all laughed then the elder of the two guys start introductions.

He held out his hand welcoming Donald. "Hi. I'm Scott. This is Pete....."

"I'm Donald " he replied shaking each of their hands

Before anyone could proceed further with introductions, the friendly girl jumped in. "Hi, I'm Julie and this is my friend Donna." Julie had a warm honest smile.

"So, are you here on holiday?" asked Scott.

"Well sort of passing through on my way to Venezuela."

Julie interrupted, attempting to relax Donald a little and making him feel a little more comfortable.

"Enough of the twenty questions guys, okay. Let's get another round of drinks."

Everyone agreed including the waitress who'd overheard the conversation and was already at the bar pouring the beers.

Donald didn't immediately get involved in their conversation but was content to listen and watch. Most of the talk revolved around boats and diving. Gradually Donald began to get a feel for each of their individual characters.

Scott was the sailor of the group; he'd spent most of his life from early childhood around boats. Pete was a lot quieter and although he wasn't as well built as Scott, he looked a lot stronger. He was the fisherman of the group, hook, line or spear gun, he had several years of experienced in all methods of fishing. It was strange, because when Scott talked, his conversation became just a sound in the background. Yet when Pete had something to say, it was more interest and said with a lot more thought and feeling. Pete had a stabling influence on Scott which seemed to balance things out between them. Two totally different personalities, yet good friends. Donald enjoyed watching people and loved being around them.

Julie and Donna had a different kind of relationship. They'd grown up in the same hometown and went through high school together. They both loved the life of traveling, sun and surf and met up with the two guys in Bonaire while diving.

With the exception of Pete, Donald reckoned that they were all in their late twenties or early thirties. It wasn't easy guessing Pete's age. Apart from the fact he was very tanned, which can some make people look younger, he acted with a lot more mature. His maturity was more evident in his mannerisms than in what he actually would say. He had this confident air about him of being a world traveler.

The rounds of drinks rolled in one after another. He thought the British could hold their beer, but had to admit, these two Australian drank beer like a camel who had just crossed the Sahara. He could feel himself beginning to get buzzed. He hadn't intended to get into a boozing session but now it was too late. He'd accepted the invitation so the best thing to do was to just enjoy himself. The jokes were starting to come fast and thick and getting a little raunchier each time.

As Julie placed her glass back on to the table, she reached over and touch the back of Donald's hand.

"Your sitting there nice and quiet Don."

Don. He thought to himself. I liked the way she said that, it has a good ring about it.

"Oh, I'm just listening to you all talking and enjoying your company."

Julie's didn't remove her hand but with a wicked gleam of excitement in her eyes she asked bluntly.

"Do you gamble Don? Or what is it the British

say Do you like a little flutter?"

Donald laughed at her attempt of a British accent.

"Yes, I like a little flutter now and then mostly on a Saturday afternoon when there's horse racing on the TV."

"But do you win Don? That's the important thing. The thrill of winning is the whole object of playing the game." Donna added with a wicked giggle in her voice.

"I suppose I don't do too bad. But then again I only gamble for a hobby."

With his elbows on the table and his head between his hands, Pete with a serious frown on his face commented.

"Don't you think life is gamble? If you want to achieve something great, something different, there's always an element of risk. That's what makes it life so interesting and exciting. It's not our life span that's important, it's what we do while we're alive that people remember us for. We all start getting old from the moment we're born, one year old...two years old...three years old. Nobody ever gets younger. No one ever says one year young, two years young if you have an opportunity, always take the chance to live your life to the full before it's too late. Within the blink of an eyelid, an opportunity has gone."

Donald related to Pete philosophy more than any
of them could have realized. The mood of laughter and
jokes died away. For a brief moment there was silence
among the group. In fact, the whole cafe was silent. Scott
broke the lull jumping in where Julie had left off.

"The reason Julie asked if you gamble Don, is that
when we finish here, we are going over to the Sonesta
Hotel Casino to have a game of blackjack or roulette. You
can even play the slots of you want. Are you game for a
laugh Don?"

They all cheered and roared with laughter
breaking the spell Pete had briefly woven over them with
his philosophy on life. They finished off their drinks and
settled the bill by going Dutch. Soon they were on their
way heading for the Sonesta. As they walked both girls
put their arm through Donald's arms, one on either side.
This made him feel good. Just before they entered the
hotel Casino Julie pulled Donald to one side.

"Listen what we usually do is get a bunch of
quarters and split them between us then go and play the
slot machines. The secret is while playing the slot
machines the waitresses will come around serving free
drinks. As long as we are gambling, the drinks are free
and keep coming, so drink as many as you can okay? At
the main bar the drinks are at least three to four dollars a
pop, this way we get buzzed real cheap."

Once they got the quarters shared out, they went their different ways to chance their luck.

Donald was quite excited listening to the sound of the slot machines spouting out winnings. It was a great sound which seemed to ricochet from all direction. Everyone looked as if they were in a trance just standing pumping money into the machines. Some people had several machines going at the same time. He wondered how they kept track of what to pull or push. Suddenly the sound of a machine paying out a

good size win made everyone look around to see who the lucky winner was. Rapidly spouting out quarters, the machine appeared as if it was paying out thousands of dollars when in reality, it had paid out twenty-five dollars, that was the limit on the quarter's machines. Anyway, a win is a win and the thrill is still the same.

Donald had played for about half an hour and had lost four dollars, which wasn't too bad he thought. He rationalized this was how the machines were programmed. They let you win a little back at a time just to keep you playing. But in the end, you lose all your money.

The noise from the Craps table was getting louder and the crowd getting bigger. He never could understand that game. He found it even more difficult to understand where the name came from, Craps? He chuckled to himself imagining in his mind a big loser reacting. Oh shit, I 've crapped. Walking towards the roulette table, he was stilling laughing at his own private joke as a small chubby

49

lady looked at him funny. This made him laugh more. He had played roulette only once. It was back home at a small casino after a bachelor party with the guys from the local pub football team. He was drunk and had played rather recklessly. He recalled one of the croupiers had cautioned him because he was flicking his chips in the air, watching them land at random on a square or number on the table. They only got upset because he was winning.

A familiar voice behind him made him turn quickly.

"Winning anything?" As he turned, Donna was standing with her bucket of quarters in her hand.

He looked into her small bucket. "No not really, what about you? You look as if you have won a little."

She had a pleased look on her face and shaking the coins around in her bucket.

"Oh, I am up about seven or eight dollars. Do you fancy giving it a break for a while and going out by the pool? What we will do is get another drink then take it outside with us. Is that's okay with you?"

He agreed without much thought. "Yes, that'll be fine."

They sat on the terrace overlooking the main street with the harbor water in front of them. Across the

road Donald could see an Italian restaurant. A, red neon light flashed on and off, Mama Mia's" A large viewing window from the pavement looked into the busy kitchen of the restaurant. People passing stopped fascinated as they watched the chefs and kitchen staff preparing meals. The strong smell of garlic and basil floated into the night air through two large exhaust fans. Eventually a number of the onlookers would go in to eat, tempted by the combination of what they were seeing being prepared and the powerful aroma engulfing them. Even from a distance, everything in the kitchen looked so spotlessly clean. Beyond the terrace of the restaurant Donald could see rows of large motor launches and yacht
anchor along the dockside. Many had colored lights and flags strung from their masts Their reflection on the water lite up the harbor area. It all seemed exciting yet sleepy.

Donna sat looking at Donald, watching his eyes flicker from side to side absorbing the scene around them. The look of wonder and excitement she saw in his eyes reminded her of a small child at her Christmas when the tree lights are turned on for the first time. She didn't want to break the spell, but her curiosity got the better of her. She decided to be bold.

"So, what is it your running away from Donald?"

He was caught unaware by her frankness, yet it was more of a statement than a question. The way she'd asked felt warm and friendly. His reply was immediate and just as honest.

"Loneliness. Years and years of loneliness. I don't suppose you could every understand what it feels like. As each year goes by you get more and more lonely. Your soul starts to die the gradually your heart begins to wither."

There was a brief pause before Donna responded. His reply had taken her be surprise.

"Strange, I thought you looked the married type. I would have never taken you for one of those guys who decided to go on a Caribbean holiday to find himself a wife."

Donald smiled and turned looking Donna in the eyes. "I'm already married and that's what I'm running away from. I'm not really looking for anyone other than myself but before you say anything and start being judgmental."

He stopped when he saw the look on her face. He knew she wasn't about to make any form of judgment. Donna never asked him any further questions. They sat absorbing the warm night air. The silence only being broken by the sound of the ice cubes floating in Donna's drink as she nervously twirled her glass around.

Suddenly the band in the night club started playing. They both turned looking into the club through a large window. It was still early so there were no guest. The first few numbers the band played sounded like they were just waking up and starting to stretch and yawn. There was no real feeling in their music. The emptiness didn't really encourage the musician.

They finished their drink and simultaneously got up and started walking back inside.

Julie watched them as they entered. She'd noticed they were not around and had tried to shrug off the feelings of jealousy she was experiencing. She wasn't normally the jealous type. Hell, they had only just met the guy. Julie also knew from way back in high school, she and Donna always had this little secret competition going when it came to winning the attention of a guy, they both liked. It was something which occurred occasionally, but they never talked about it. This time it felt strangely different. The stranger they had met was different. She couldn't put her finger on it but there was something so gentle and comfortable being around him. They both came walking towards her.

Donna had a beaming smile on her face. "Hi Julie, are you winning?"

"Yeah. I'm winning about fourteen dollars so I am just about to cash in my. You want to come with me Don? Donna you can go and look for the guys then we can get the hell out of here. Maybe we shall have a nightcap on the way home eh?"

Donald didn't reply but followed Julie as she began walking away. He also cashed in his quarters. When they'd finished, he turned to walk back but Julie caught his hand.

"Come on we'll meet those guys outside, they know where we're going. We have a favorite watering hole where we go to have a nightcap, or even breakfast, depending on what time we call it a night, or day."

Donald followed Julie's lead and they walked out hand in hand. They strolled along the Harbor Town area watching the reflection of the lights on the dark black water. The fresh salty smell of the sea was invigorating. It was now past midnight and apart from the occasional reveler, Aruba was beginning to go to sleep.

"Listen Julie do you mind if we stop and have a cup of coffee? I guess I am beered out."

"Sure, there's a nice place a little further on that stays open late. It not too far. I could do with a nice cup of coffee myself."

Within a few minutes the reached to cafe.

Donald watched the waiter as placed the coffees on the table and walked away. He was trying to work out whether the waiter was Filipino or Indonesian. Julie broke the silence.

"So, Don, what do you think of Aruba? I know you've only been here for a short time, but what are your first impressions?"

"It's great. Well what I mean it's great for a brief holiday, I am not too sure if I would like to live here all the time. Too many tourists and also it's not cheap here is it?"

"No, I guess you're right. Donna and I couldn't really afford to live here on what we earn from serving tables, even though the tips are good. If it wasn't for Donna and the friends she's made in Aruba, there's no way we could afford the rent on our apartment. I think Donna's parents also help her out a lot financially, she always has
  money. Not like me, I go from one paycheck to the next. So, Don what's your next stop from here?"

"I don't really know; I have no firm plans other than I am heading for Venezuela."

"How are you going there? By boat or are you flying? You can go by boat, but probably the best bet is to fly to Las Piedras on the Paraguayan Peninsula. It's only about 15 minutes flying time and I think it costs about forty dollars for the flight."

"How do you know so much about Venezuela?" Donald asked with a grin on his face.

"Donna has made a couple of trips over there.

55

She fell for this guy a few months ago, I mean hook line and sinker. I'm not sure whether he's Venezuelan or Colombian. They had this thing going and he kept inviting her to go to Maracibo. He would call her up and then send her the ticket. It was strange because he didn't really love her but spoiled her with luxury gifts. Anyway, she enjoyed herself. I thought of going over with her on one of her trips, but her boyfriend wasn't too happy for some reason. I never went but I will one day."

"When did you meet up with Scott and Pete then? Did you meet them here in Aruba?"

"No, we met them in Bonaire on a diving trip last month."

Donald hadn't realized the girls had only know Scott and Pete such a short time. He'd assumed they'd been together for quite some time as they appeared to be very friendly and affectionate with each other.

"No, we haven't slept with them." Julie said interrupting his thoughts.

"Oh! I wasn't thinking you had." He wondered how she'd read his mind.

With a lovely smile Julie started teased Donald.

"Yes, you did, you thought we were a number and had teamed off. Well this is one time when four is not made up of two and two. We are enjoying our holiday and like each other's company, that's it. Don't get me wrong, I have nothing against sex, especially if it's with someone I really like. However, in this day and age you have to be so careful, even with safe sex, if there is such a thing. I got to get to know a person really well to be sure he has clean personal habits. Cleanliness is important in a relationship; don't you think so Don? Donna think sometimes I too careful and particular?"

"Oh no, I agree."

It had taken him a lot of effort not to stutter his reply. He was totally bowled over by her frankness in talking about relationships and sex. He'd never experienced this type of conversation, not even with Allison during all the years they were married. They never talked about sex and only did it when the urge came over them.

"I agree with you totally." he reacted, becoming a little more confident.

His mind drifted as he thought, I wonder how many guys Julie has had a relationship with? He'd always been totally faithfully to Allison. She was the only woman that he'd ever been with. He didn't know whether their sex had been great together or whether it was just average. they never talked about it. Fidelity between partners is important especially if you have decided to spend the rest of your life with someone.

The thought of wondering whether Allison and Kevin had really had an affair started nagging in the back of his mind. Should he have confronted Allison for the truth before he left? How much did his pride effect his decision to leave?

What would he have said to her, So Allison was Kevin a good fuck? How many times did he screw you? Was he better than me?

Kevin and his wife Glenda were once their best friends, but as the years went by Donald and Allison drifted away from them. If what Arthur told him was true, Allison and Kevin really kindled the flames of their affection for one another. Arthur was drunk the night he let the cat out of the bag, he possibly didn't even remember the next morning that he had told Donald. It was strange because he should have been shocked and hurt but he wasn't.

Julie's voice broke his chain of thought.

"Are you divorced Donald?"

"No not divorced but separated from my wife. After more than twenty years of marriage we were just existing. We were so content we rarely found the time to communicate never mind having time to make love. To us having sex was like a prearranged telepathic understanding. We both knew that if we had been invited out to a party and consumed enough alcohol, we would have sex when we got home. We never talked about it or discussed it yet we both knew. It was strange."

Julie sat in anticipation of Donald continuing his story.

"It was so clinical and quick. When it was over, we'd never know or even asked each other how it felt. Did you like it? Was it good? Was I good? Nothing was said, absolutely nothing. We just finished then went to sleep, both turning over in opposite directions of the bed. Sometimes I had to control the simple urge of putting my arms around her and to cuddle. Once I picked up enough courage and placed my arm around her waist. She politely brushed me aside saying, "Now you've had your little bit of pleasure dear, so let's just go to sleep."
An important part of love making is affection. The feeling of wanting to hold and gently crush the person you've just made love to, gives as much pleasure as the Physical act of love making."

Donald suddenly he realized what he was saying and was overcome with embarrassment. He'd never talked to anyone so openly about how he'd felt.

Julie had sat listening intently, catching hold of every word he'd uttered. She'd never met anyone who displayed so much open tenderness. She felt the pain in his heart.

"You really have been a very lonely person haven't you Don. How'd you manage to go on knowing you had all those feelings hidden inside you? Did your wife not know? I mean, I don't want to judge but she must have either been blind or a fool. Couldn't she see you had so much to give and so much love in your heart? I've only known you for a short time but one the thing which attracts me to you is you have this innocent honesty about you. It shines like a beacon signaling, 'I'm a nice guy' . They're not too many nice people around Don. Honesty and sincerity are very special qualities in a person. I can see you have had so much to give but no one to give it to. That's sad!"

This was the first indication from Julie that she liked him and was also attracted to him. He hadn't really given it much consideration. She was a friendly, nice girl who was also smart and attractive.

Julie picked up her coffee cup and put it to her lips. Donald sat looking at her, the longer he looked the more attractive she became. Her hair was naturally golden, bleached by the sun and it hung down across one side of her face. She had beautiful pale blue eyes.

When she realized he was looking at her she smiled with her eyes, without moving the cup away from her lips. There was a long silence as they sat looking at each other both their minds whirling with secret thoughts.

Donald got up out of his chair, indicating it was time to call in a night.

. "Listen I am going to have to take a rain check, as you Americans say. How about I walk you back to your apartment. Maybe we can all meet tomorrow and spend some time on the beach?'

Julie followed his lead as she gathered up her purse.

"Sure, but I guess it's just you and me for the beach. The other guys are going off on a diving trip somewhere, that is unless you want to go with them?"

"No " he replied as they started walking. "Spending the day with you sounds great to me. I enjoy your company a lot, your an easy person to talk to. I hope I didn't go on too much about my personal life?"

"Not at all, you're a very interesting person Don and you're also a nice person. I like you very much. I'm really looking forward to our day out tomorrow"

Soon they arrived at her apartment. She was about to say something but before she could, he kissed her on the cheek. His kiss was soft and gentle.

"Goodnight Julie and pleasant dreams. See you tomorrow morning, between ten thirty and eleven." He turned quickly and began walking away but stopped as he'd not heard her move. She was standing watching him.

"Please go inside. I want to be sure your inside safe and sound."

She waved and turned walking into the apartment block.

While Julie was getting ready for bed she stopped and looked at herself in the long mirror in the bathroom. She examined the shape of her body, the roundness of her hips, waist and breasts. Her body was shapely and firm. She wondered if Donald had thought about her sexually. She gave a little chuckle to herself assuming he hadn't. This is the first guy I have ever met, she thought, who isn't after a quick thrill. In fact, he isn't after anything other than my company. I like that a lot, it makes me feel he respects me. It makes me feel good about myself.

She got into to bed and lay awake for a while thinking about Donald. The look in his eyes when he was talking about being lonely haunted her. Maybe they're many married couples who live their whole life together just being content. With these thoughts going through her mind she fell asleep. It was a very deep and content sleep. She never awoke even when Donna arrived in the early hours of the morning, stumbling around in the dark getting ready for bed.

Donna had a strong urge to awake Julie. She wanted to find out where the hell she'd gotten to with

Don. What she really wanted to know was had anything happened?

The walk back to Donald's hotel was a lot further than he realized but it gave him time to reflect on what had happened during the past few days. It was as if his life had switched from starring in a black and white movie, to the Technicolor world of cinema scope vision and surround sound.

Me a nice guy he thought? Me an attractive person? In the darkness of the night he wanted to scream and shout out loud and tell the world how good he felt about himself. At the end of the day he thought, it really doesn't matter who or what you, are or even what you look like, it's the person you are inside which makes the difference. Strange as it may seem, he hadn't one single regret over what had   happened since his departure. He truly believed in his
heart that he took the only decision. Come hell or high water, he'd made his bed and he was going to lie in it.

In the past few days he'd met three lovely ladies, relaxed and enjoyed their company and been himself. Most important of all though, was the ladies had enjoyed his company. He'd talked openly about love and sex like he'd never done before. How was it he thought, that I can meet complete strangers and open up the way I have?

He went to sleep that night with a tingle and a glow inside which felt good.

Once a Chameleon

The next morning, he was prompt in arriving at the apartment to pick up Julie. She was finishing her breakfast and looked fresh and radiant. She had a big slice of toast in her hand which was smothered in black current jam. She beckoned him to sit next to her and continued to eat. He sat down in silence happy to just watch her. Julie smiled but continued eating. Eventually as she digested the food in her mouth, she greeted him warmly.

"Hi! how are you? Did you sleep well?"

"Like a log, what about you? Did Donna wake up you when she came home?"

"No way, I was out like a light. I felt really good when I got into bed and thought about our day together and our discussion. I hope I'm not going to embarrass you Donald, but I need to say something. Meeting you has been one of the good experiences of my life. Being with you, being around you, makes me feel good. There I've said it okay? Now I've got that off my chest I'm really looking forward to our day together."

Donald never ceased to be amazed by her pure honesty. If she'd something on her mind, she got it out in the open. It was very refreshing. He looked at his watch.

"Come on then, stop feeding your face and let's go. How many more pieces of toast and jam do you

64

need?"

"I can't help it, I'm absolutely starving, and I feel so good. I feel as if I got laid last night."

He took her free hand lifting her out of her chair. Julie scrambled around the table with her other hand grabbing a quick mouthful of orange juice and getting a last bite of toast. Walking out of the apartment they were still laughing at her comment. They were both looking forward to the rest of the day and knew they were going to enjoy themselves.

When they arrived at the beach and began settling down, Julie took off her shorts and tee shirt and lay down on the towel. It was only then that Donald noticed and realized what a beautiful body she had.

She noticed him looking and felt self-conscious. He saw the look on her face and now he felt uncomfortable.

"Oh, I'm sorry for staring, please forgive me, I'm being rude. I just never realized how beautiful you are."

His own boldness surprised him.

Julie quickly realized he was paying her a compliment. She was the kind of person who wore tight fitting clothes to show off the curves of her body. She preferred something which was more comfortable and loose fitting. She reached over and squeezed Donald's hand to reassure him everything was okay. .

Once they'd settling down, Donald began to feel the heat of the mid day sun beating down on his back. Compared to the other folks on the beach with their beautiful tanned bodies, he looked like a bottle of milk.
Julie sat up and reached over into her beach bag.

"Shall I rub sun lotion on your back Don? You'd better take precautions, or you burn yourself."

He never answered as she began rubbing in the lotion. Her touch was soft as hands moved over his back and down his legs. It felt good. When she'd finished, she lay back down on the towel handing the sun lotion to Donald. Her pale blue eyes reflected the color of the sky overhead.

"Now it's your turn to put the lotion on me. Go ahead, don't be shy."

He looked at her and didn't know really where to start. She felt his shyness and whispered.

"Start on my tummy, then my legs, arms and shoulders ".

He started off very nervously but gradually got more confident as he moved his fingers over her skin. She didn't move or make a sound, but he could feel her responding to his touch. He deliberately took longer than necessary but, in the end, had to stop.

"There, does that feels better?"

"It feels great Donald. You have a gentle touch and very soft hands for a man. Listen I thought about something last night. I'm going to call you Donald. Don sounds to American and doesn't go with your British accent."

He smiled laying back down. They both stretched out soaking up the ultraviolet rays with their minds wandering in silence. Eventually Julie broke the long calm.

"So, tell me more about yourself Donald?"

"What do you want to know?"

" Well I know you are married but do you have any children? What about brothers and sisters?"

"I have a son Richard. He is in the final term of University or College as you know it. I have three brothers and three sisters, a real big happy family."

They both laughed.

"No really, my brothers and sisters and I are very close. Sometimes our spouses accuse us of being too close. This was one of the big hang ups my wife couldn't

67

handle. Being an only child, she found the hurly burly of a big family too much to take. We had many rows over this. When I look back and think of the days of preparation, I had to go though picking up the courage to tell my wife I'd invited my mother to tea on a Sunday, it makes me sick in my stomach. I'll never forget it. I regret this whole episode of my life; it was such a waste. I missed many family get together, and in doing so I missed a great part of my family's love and affection. My son Richard hardly knows his grandparents. My mother loved her grandchildren as if they were her own children. She was a great person with a real instinct for human needs and feelings. I was just getting to know her as a person and not as my mother, when she died. She was only sick for about six weeks, then she was gone. We were all devastated. No one had died in our family for nearly thirty years, so we all had a hard time accepting her death. Fifty-seven is no age at all and definitely too young to die. I think about her a lot. Maybe my feelings of guilt were one of the factors that pushed me over the edge in my decision to leave. Who knows?"

"What about you?" he asked, changing the subject.

"Oh, I have a sister, older, married with three kids. When I go home and see her with her children sometimes, I really envy her. Other times, when I see the stress she goes through trying to hold the family life together, I am happy that I am not tied down and have the freedom to move around as I like. The difference between you and I Donald is deep inside you know what you are searching

for. You've made a bold decision and decided to go out
and try to find a new life. I know it can be quite
frightening and lonely starting out on your own. The
hardest part is having the courage to follow your
convictions. I suppose the rest comes with time. I don't
have your courage, instead I just live in hope that one day
someone will come along and change my life for me. I've
taken the cowards way out."

A very nice girl he thought to himself.

He felt his back beginning to burn so he turned
over. Julie saw his concern and suggested that they move
further up the beach and find a tree with some shade.
Soon they had settled down in a shaded area. lying on
their backs gazing up into the clear blue sky through the
gaps in the palm leaves. He turned to look towards her,
but she was already looking at him. They didn't speak. He
reached out and touched the back of her hand, she
responded by turning it over and placing it into his palm.
They both felt good, it was a warm comfortable feeling.
Gradually they both began to drift off to sleep.

Julie stirred, awaken by the sound of a ski boat
close to the shoreline. She looked at Donald, he moved
but continued to doze. He was now drifting in and out of
a light sleep, half hearing what was going on and half
aware that Julie was sitting looking at him. It was such a
lovely feeling floating in and out on the edge of being
asleep and being awake. She sensed he was conscious of
what was going on and began to tease him by gently

blowing in his ear.

"Hey, don't do that. I mean it's nice but in England when a person does that to someone it only means one thing which is very suggestive and sexy."

She continued her giggling and gentle blowing

"So, what does it mean Donald? Come on, tell me what I am supposed to be wanting to do to you?"

They wrestled around a little, giggling and laughing then both fell back on to their towel in a mock gesture of exhaustion.

Donald sat up slowly looking at his watch.

"What time is it? Oh, its after four thirty. How about we have a quick dip to cool down and then go and wet our whistles? By the time we dry off and clear up here, we can walk along the beach and shall just be in time for Sundowners. What do you say?"

"Sounds good to me, maybe we can have a snack or have an early dinner? I'm absolutely starving."

"What about the others? Shouldn't we try to meet up with them? I mean I don't mind, their your friends, what do you think?"

"Oh, they can take care of themselves. We shall

70

probably meet them later this evening. Aruba is a very small island, like a village."

They made their way down the beach heading in the direction of one of the large hotels. Soon they were seated at the beach bar of the Holiday Inn Hotel deciding which of the exotic cocktails they should order. Julie was feeling good about how they'd spent the day and with and air of adventure she asked.

"I feel like being a bit of a devil, how about you? Why don't we try the Rum Punch Cocktail it's very good and has a kick like a mule? I fancy a bit of horsing around, don't you? For the next two hours it's happy hour, so it's buy one get one free."

They were both still laughing when the waiter went off to mix their drinks.

Over their drinks, they munched on a Club Sandwich and French Fries. They thought they enjoyed the nourishment of their meal, gradually the Rum Punch began to give them a warm glow inside. It was strange for Donald feeling relaxed so relaxed and at ease with Julie, especially as they had only known each other for two days. There were moments when he felt he had known her longer. The open intimacy of their conversation had brought them a close. He was a little worried as to where their friendship was leading. He didn't want to get into a situation where they'd both end up feeling full of regret and embarrassment. That would break the spell they'd

71

woven. He really wasn't looking for anything other than her friendship and company and he hoped she felt the same. At the moment his life was in too much of a turmoil for him to make a fool of himself in some poor attempt at a sexual escapade. Deep down inside he felt very inadequate when it came to the opposite sex. Not knowing how to start, what to do. That's the secret he thought, how to start. Just suppose...for one moment he felt like trying it on with Julie. Where does he begin, how is he supposed to let her know? Here they were, sitting drinking exotic cocktails in a really romantic setting. The sun was going down and the sky just beginning to turn a beautiful golden orange and red in

Excuse me, can we go somewhere so we can be alone?. What for she'd ask? That's when he would be dumb struck, feel stupid and freeze up. It wasn't that he'd never developed a technique when dealing with the opposite sex, truth was he'd never had any reason to practice.

" Did you ever have an affair during your marriage Donald? "

There it was again, the open candor he loved so much. Candor really formed a great part of her character. What you see is what you get, without sounding rude or offensive.

He never even stopped to think as he answered.

James Caffrey

"No, never. I suppose the secret recipe for infidelity is a combination of having the desire and the opportunity at the same time. I've never had either. Funny as it may seem, even now as we are sitting here, I feel a sense of obligation to my wife. No, it's not guilt, it feels more like there's still something in my life that's only half finished. As if I'm waiting for permission to start living my own life. It's not just having to be honest with myself, but also any other person who I may meet or get involved with. I know it sounds old fashioned and corny but that's the way I feel."

" You made a bold and courageous decision in making the break." she said

Donald played with the cocktail stick in his drink, twirling the little umbrella around and around. After a short silence he looked up at Julie who had been watching him.

"Have you ever been in love Julie, I mean really in love? I'm not talking about a high school sweetheart or even an affair you may have had. What I mean is, have you ever experienced the feeling of wanting to spend the rest of your life with one special person?"

There was a long silent pause as they stared into each other's eyes.

"This is the kind of feeling I'm searching for."

"Wow! That's a difficult question to answer. I mean each of us have our own ideas of 'being in love. Starting in our early teens, we experience our first feelings of infatuation and we think we're madly in love. Then, as we grow older and become more mature, our values change. I suppose we also become more afraid to recognize and accept love for the fear of being hurt and let down. This is the great danger when we open up our heart."

Julie could see she had roused a sleeping tiger as she watch Donald's eyes dance around excitedly.

"Yes, what you're saying is correct. The failure of the system makes it difficult for us to identify the difference between infatuation and real love. That's why many people get married to young. The environment of family traditions expects us all to meet a nice partner, fall in love, get married, have children and live happily ever after. Where it all falls apart is the 'Living Happily Ever After. Most marriages start out like a fairy tale, but very few have a happy ending."

Donald gave a deep sigh.

"Anyway Julie, enough of this serious stuff. We need to change the mood and get a little livelier. Let's have another Rum Punch, they're just beginning to warm the cockles of my heart."

She began laughing and loved the British

expressions that Donald kept coming out with. She wanted to ask what the cockles of my heart meant but didn't want to spoil the magic of the moment.

The rest of the evening went by very quickly as it does when one's enjoying themselves. As they got up to leave, Donald discovered what Julie had meant about the potency of the drinks. They were not fully aware of it while they were sitting, but they knew the Rum Punch had crept up on them. Making their way back to her apartment they laughed and swayed holding on to each other as they walked. By the time they arrived Julie was a little worse for wear than Donald.

It was probably a combination of her persuasive ways and the effect of the drinking, which resulted in him ending up in her apartment. They both sat on the bed with their legs crossed facing each other. An opened bottle of white wine was floating around in an ice bucket. They raised their glasses toasting their friendship, then friendship and then friendship again.

Although nothing had been said or intimated, he felt he would just let things take their course. If something was going to happen, there was no reason to feel uncomfortable about it. Suppose Donna walked in! What would she think? Well, after all they were just having a drink. He was so wrapped up in his thoughts he failed to notice Julie had passed out on the bed in a deep sleep. He couldn't help but smile looking at her lying there. She looked so vulnerable and innocent. Her hair hung over her face. As Donald went to push her hair back, she stirred and although asleep she took hold of his hand. After waiting until he felt she was asleep again, he took his hand away. He sat for a while watching her, she looked so beautiful.

Slowly he managed to get her comfortable and laid her head on the pillow and pulled the top sheet over her. Turning to walk away he stopped and bent over kissing her gently on the forehead and saying softly. "Sweet Dreams my lovely lady."

On the way back to his hotel he decided he would get up early the next morning and go to the airport to see if there was a seat available on the early flight to Las Piedras. The hotel porter had told him it was the low season, so there was a very good chance of getting on the flight.

Aruba airport started to stir as the early morning passengers began filtering into the departure lounge. Donald looked around watching passengers and airline staff drifting in. Everyone still looking half asleep, making him wonder what he must look like to them. He managed to find a small snack bar with hot black coffee. He didn't have a hangover but felt a little rough. His tongue felt like the bottom of a bird cage. The bottle of water he'd drank before he went to sleep, had prevented too much dehydration. He wondered how Julie was feeling, probably not yet awake. He also wondered what her reaction would be when she realized he'd left.

It was all for the best and he hoped she would understand.

CHAPTER IV

Las Peidras, Venezuela.

The Avensa flight time from Aruba was twenty minutes. The Las Peidras airport consisted of one small terminal, which was crowded with people. Through the open door of a tiny room, Donald handed the Immigration Officer his passport. The officer examined the passport taking out the visa form which Donald had completed on the flight. Donald stood watching the officer as he flipped through the pages of his Passport. He waited anxiously hoping he had completed the details on the form correctly. The problem he'd encountered when completing the documents was giving an address in Venezuela. He'd decided at the last moment just to put the Hilton Hotel in Caracas. After a short delay he was clear of Immigration and Customs and began searching for a taxi.

The airport was even smaller than he thought and didn't have a Tourist Information desk. He would have to rely on the taxi driver to find him a decent hotel. As he left the airport terminal, he was immediately besieged by more than a dozen taxi drivers, grabbing at his luggage and hustling for his fare. Only to prevent a mini riot, he picked one, more by instincts than anything else. The man had a nice face, an honest face. Once he was in the taxi, he began asking the driver about a reasonable hotel and this is where his problems started.

" No Habla de Ingles."

This was all he could get out of the driver as they proceeded in the general direction of a large petrochemical plant. In the distance a large lonely mountain peak could be seen, it looked like an extinct volcano. The taxi driver noticed Donald looking out of the open window of the taxi. Lifted his arm and pointing in the direction of the mountain he called.

"Santa Anna, mountain, Santa Anna!"

Donald nodded his head indicating he understood.

Donald sat on the front edge of his seat in the taxi. His eager eyes were searching hoeing he would see a sign in English that he would recognize. Suddenly he pointed towards an arrow indicating there was a hotel, Judibana - Hotel

Donald shouted pointing his arm across the front seat and under the nose of his driver.

"There, hotel! Senor, over there, hotel, see?"

"Si Senor." came the calm reply from the taxi driver as he abruptly turned in the direction of the arrow.

Donald looked back wondering whether any

vehicle had been following behind, the taxi driver had not given any indication he was about to turn right. He would learn later that this was the norm when driving in Venezuela.

Within half a mile, they entered a small town which Donald presumed to be Judibana. They were traveling on the main street of the town. The taxi stopped and the sign read Hotel Jardin. The hotel porter grabbed Donald's bags. He reluctantly let go realizing he needed local currency to pay the taxi fare. He quickly cashed a travelers check with the receptionist and paid the taxi driver.

The hotel was small but clean and had an Andalucian flavor in the decor and style of the furniture and fittings. His room rate was good value, considering what it had cost in Aruba. Once he got to his room he realized why. The room was very basic but again it looked clean. He examined the bathroom, okay he thought, I have to remember where I am, and this is what I came to see and experience.

After unpacking and cleaning up he went for a walk to explore the town and discovered that Judibana was really a small village. Most of the houses were villas which were painted white, with large red tiled roofs and an abundance of tropical vegetation growing around them.

There was a small supermarket 'Cadre'. It was well stocked, but Donald didn't recognize many of the brand

names of the products. The fresh fruit looked good and
the beer and hard liquor were cheap. Leaving the
supermarket, he discovered a bakery, news stand,
pharmacy and a barber's shop. A large sign advertised the
Banco de Venezuela. The rest of the shops appeared to
be boutiques displaying an array of colorful clothes. A
number of the shops had outside speakers playing loud
Latin music, it sounded good and added character and
flavor to the place. There was also another smaller hotel
at the far end of town called Luiges which had an Italian
ambiance about it. He had noticed several cafe's and of
course a Cantina. Judibana was small, the length of the
main street being only a few hundred yards.

In the center of the village was a large square
which was dominated by a huge white stoned church. The
park had an abundance of beautiful colored flowers all in
full bloom. A number of people sat resting on benches
which had been strategically positioned under the large
trees. Under a large tree a man lay sleeping, his dog lying
next to him. As Donald walked past the dog, it cocked its
head to one side but continued to stare at him. Browsing
through a few a of the shop he quickly discovered no one
spoke English. It was something that had never crossed
his mind. Not being able to speak Spanish was going to
be a problem. He'd wrongly assumed everyone would
speak English. They did in Spain and in Greece.

When he got back to his hotel, he realized part of
the complex was a shopping mall. He spotted a small
restaurant with tables placed outside under the shade of

trees, it looked inviting. Even though it was early, he thought he would try a nice cold beer. As he sat at down a table, a young boy approached. He wasn't dressed as a waiter; therefore, Donald was surprised to find out he was waiting tables.

"Hola senor"

"Hello. Beer please"

"Si Senor. Sevesa, Polar!" he said walking away. understood. Polar, isn't that a bear? He was about to discover one of the best kept secrets of South America! The boy arrived with the beer which had chunks of ice and frost stuck to the bottle which made it slip around in the waiters' hands as he attempted to remove the cap. He poured half the beer into the glass and placed the bottle on the table. Donald took a drink, it was ice cold and to his surprise it tasted great, one of the best lager beers he'd ever tasted. As the ice and frost began to melt and slide down the bottle it was then he saw the name of the beer....Polar!

Ordering another beer and a sandwich, he sat watching the activities around him. Although busy for the time of day, there was an atmosphere of sleepiness about the place. There was no hustle and bustle of a tow, everyone seemed to take their time in whatever they were involved in. Totally laid back.

He sat relaxing when a tall dark-skinned man

came out of the cafe towards him. Greeting Donald in English, he approached with his hand outstretched

"Hello Senor, how are you?"

His handshake was firm.

"Hello, how are you?" Donald replied in a friendly manner, glad to find someone who spoke English.

"Fine." said the stranger sitting down in the chair next to him.

"Have you just arrived? Working for the American company doing the construction in the refinery are you?"

"Yes, I've just arrived, and no, I'm not working in the refinery."

At least it was a relief to hear there was other expatriates around.

"Are there many Americans working on the construction project?"

"Yes many, each night they come here to drink beer, many beers and eat good food. This is my cafe, my business. Fernando makes great food and has a clean place."

"Oh, you're the owner eh? Please to meet you Fernando my name is Donald."

"So, Donald, if you don't work in the refinery, why do you come to Venezuela? You come for a holiday?"

"Yes I'm on holiday and staying in the hotel. Nice place, clean and comfortable, very good."

Fernando took a long draw from his cigarette. "You come here tonight, have a good time, party every night and plenty of pretty girls. You like Venezuelan girls? They are the most beautiful girls in the whole world. Many times they win beauty contests. Miss World, Miss Universe, they win many times. In Caracas there is a special college just for beauty queens."

Donald nodded his head as Fernando talked. He had to admit, many of the girls he'd seen since his arrival were very attractive. They all appeared to wear the tightest and shortest skirts and dresses he'd ever seen. It was difficult not to stare but they appeared to enjoy the attention.

Fernando left Donald's table to greet a friend who had arrived. Donald paid his bill and as he walked passed Fernando he told him he would be back in the evening. He began to realize that the Venezuelans were very friendly people. I think I am going to like it here, he thought. Maybe it was the heat and humidity and the few

beers he'd drank at lunch, but Donald found himself
wanting to take a Siesta. Judibana went quiet just after
1.00pm.

Donald was awakened by the sound of laughter
coming from the courtyard below. He looked out of the
window then realized he was directly above Fernando's
Cafe. It was starting to get busy with the construction
workers coming from the job site. He decided to shower,
get ready and go down and have dinner.

As he walked into the small courtyard a number
of the construction workers were already well into a bout
of drinking. Obviously very thirsty from working out in
the heat and sun all day. He sat eating his mixed grill and
his polar beer. He watched as some of the workers wives
appeared and sat down to join their husbands for a
'Sundowner'. Gradually as more people arrived, they
moved several tables together and, in the end, there must
have been around twenty people all drinking and laughing.
Speakers hanging from the trees piped out loud Latin
music.

There were only three or four tables not being
utilized by the large group and most of these were
occupied. A man and his young lady arrived and they
stood looking around trying to find a place to sit. After a
few minutes Fernando spotted them and gestured to lead
them in the direction of Donald's table. When they
arrived, he asked Donald if he minded sharing his table.
Donald had no objection and the couple smiled at him in

a gesture of friendliness.

The man ordered drinks. Donald sat listening discreetly as the couple began conversing in Spanish. He was hoping to catch a word or two which might give him a clue as to what they were discussing. He was totally lost. It was going to be difficult not being able to speak the language.

After about ten minutes the young lady stood up and walked in the direction of the toilet. When she'd left the man suddenly spoke to Donald in English, gesturing in the direction of the construction workers.

"You don't sit with your friends?"

"Oh no, I don't know them. I don't work in the refinery I am here on a visit."

"Oh, I see, so you are new to Venezuela eh? You plan to visit many places like a tourist, no?"

"Yes, I guess so, but I'm not quite sure of my travel program yet. I need first to get my bearings."

"You should think about getting off the Peninsula. There is little vegetation here and it's arid and parched. Oh sorry, let me introduce myself my name is Marco and my wife 's name is Nevis, she will be back in a little while. As I was saying, once you get beyond the Medinas and the other side of Coro the vegetation's a lot lusher and

86

agua that's where you need to go, it is beautiful up

"That sounds just what I am looking for. I want
to see as much of the countryside as I can. I don't want to
go to the usual tourist spots, I want to see how the
Venezuelans live. Are there any small hotels in the
mountains you can recommend where I could stay for a
while?"

"Yes for sure. There are several but the one my
family and I like is called the Golden Falcon. It's located
on the top of Falcon Ness. That's around two hours'
drive from here to Coro, then another hour up the
mountain. It's very nice, quiet and green with many
Orange Groves. You'll like it, I know you will. Everyone
who visits there always goes back. The food is good, and
the accommodation is like a motel, reasonably priced as
well. The owner is Dutch. He came here to work more
than twenty-five years ago and married a Venezuelan girl
and decided to stay. He is our friend of ours, his name is
Hans. If you go, give him our regards and tell him we sent
you. He and his wife will take good care of you."

" That's very nice of you. Thank you "

Donald spotted Marco's wife returning to the
table. As she reached their table, she started waving her
arms around talking very quickly. Although Donald didn't
understand, he caught the word telephone and knew

87

there was some sort of urgent problem. Marco politely apologized advising Donald they had to leave.

Meanwhile, the expatriates party was really beginning to warm up. He could tell from the different accents that many of them were of mixed nationalities, American, British and a couple of Scandinavians. He ordered another beer then went to the toilet. When he returned, he was surprised to find that his table had been moved to form an extension for the party. Fernando was standing there with a big smile on his face.

"Senor Donald, hola. I hope you don't mind but we invite you to the party. Is this okay? We want you to enjoy your first night in Venezuela."

Donald smiled. "Sure, no problem."

Fernando started introducing the group of people using their first names. Donald tried to remember each person's name as he shook hands but, in the end, gave up. He was seated next to a married couple from Nottingham, Len and Doreen. They were typically British and a lot of fun. Everyone was drinking at a tremendous pace and were starting to get drunk. As if by magic the waiter appeared with the bill and everyone started throwing bolivars into the middle of the table. Donald reached into his pocket and grabbed a handful of bolivars and threw them in.

The group started to leave, singing and dancing as

they did. Donald was informed by Len and Doreen he'd been invited to a party. Suddenly, his arms were linked by two of the ladies who proceeded to gently tug along. They all piled into a number of cars and trucks and drove a short distance to a housing complex. Within no time at all the party was in full swing.

Donald had been asked to dance a couple of times but felt a little uncomfortable, he didn't really know anyone. He took a beer from a large cool box then walked outside onto the patio. It was a warm clear night. The only sound which could be heard were the crickets. There was no wind, which was strange as he'd felt a strong breeze most of the day. He heard movement to his right and turned to see a man and woman dancing very close to each other. They were obviously extremely drunk as they swayed around and around on the same spot. He looked away not wanting them to notice he had been staring. He spotted a young lady sitting on her own in the corner of the yard. When she saw him she smiled.

"Hi, how are you? I hope you are having a good time? Things can get really wild around here."

"Yes I have noticed."

Donald responded, looking back in the direction of the couple dancing. They were now starting to get down to some heavy petting. He walked towards the young lady and she moved making room for him to share the wooden swinging chair she was sitting on.

"Would you like to join me? I haven't seen you around here before, are you new?"

Donald followed her encouragement and sat down next to her. The chair continued to swing gently back and forth.

"Well I'm sort of new, I'm only passing through. I don't work here, I'm just traveling around seeing the country. My name is Donald, how do you do?' He reached out and shook her hand.

"Oh I'm sorry. My names Bonnie, I live here. This is my house and that's my husband Joe you probably saw passed out in the bath. This situation is normal, so no need to look concerned, I'm kind of used to it by now. I just hope his boss continues to be as understanding. If he fails to turn in to work just one more time, it's a one-way ticket for us out'a here."

Donald never reacted; he didn't know what to say.

"It wasn't always like this. When I met Joe, I was sixteen and he was my hero. The knight in shining armor who rescued me from the small Midwest town where I was born. It's funny how time can change things. At the time I thought I truly loved him. I guess he was my bus ticket out'a there but I'm not sure if I want to stay for the whole ride. The only problem I have is I could get hurt jumping from a speeding bus."

Donald sat listening to Bonnie. Suddenly she rolled her eyes indicated he should look over towards the couple who had been dancing. He turned and saw they were no longer dancing.

The man had the woman pressed against a large slopping palm tree. One of his hands had lifted up her dress which was now raised around her waist. His other hand frantically trying to loosen his belt. Donald couldn't believe what was happening. Were they actually going to make love there right in front of them? He quickly glanced at Bonnie who was trance fixed. He couldn't resist and turned to look back at the couple who had now started making love.

Bonnie had a strange intense look on her face as she gently bit into her bottom lip. She continued rocking the swing back and forth. The couple's love making had started awkwardly, but as they became more aroused, it became more physical and passionate. Their tempo of their love making increased, Bonnie's moved the swing keeping time. Suddenly the lovers bodies started twisting and jerking as they lost control. In the brief moment of a shudder, it was over. Donald was flabbergasted, but Bonnie appeared to take it in her stride and continued to keep the swing moving.

Bonnie saw the look of amazement on Donald's face. Teasing him further she flippantly remarked.

"Don't look so shocked. The guy's wife's a lesbian and gal's husband screws every woman he can get his hands on. That includes the bar girls in Punto Fijo and Coro. She's just getting some of her own back on him. Sometimes I've had her around my place in tears terrified she might have caught some form of sexual disease from her husband"

Bonnie took a large drink and emptied her glass. She could still see the look of disbelief and embarrassment on Donald's face. There was now a hint of a drunken slur in her voice.

"Look don't be too concerned about it, okay! This is how we live here. If we didn't have a little excitement, we would go crazy, right! You don't know what it's like. Nothing to do, bored out'a your brains. The booze and sex keeps us all sane. The first time Joe asked me if I would like to start switching, I was disgusted. He kept asking, then there was party after party and all the heavy drinking. In the end when it happened, and I was so drunk I never even knew who the guy was. When Joe later pointed the guy out, I started to get embarrassed until I realized he never remembered either. What really made my day was when Joe boasted to our friends that this guy's wife was the best screw of his life. Once you've switched, it's expected of you. Variety is the spice of life."

A lonely teardrop clung to Bonnie's eye lash, suspended in defiance of gravity only by her will, not to show weakness.

"I hate this place; I hate this life. I guess I hate Joe for the part he played in making me what I am today, a drunken whore. But most of all, I hate myself for letting it all happen."

Donald searched for the right words to respond but was totally stunned by the raw intimacy of Bonnie's conversation. He had never experienced anything like it.

Bonnie cleared her nose with a soft sniffle. "We're you staying Donald, at the Hotel Jardin?

Donald nodded his head indicating she was correct.

"Listen Donald, I know you don't know me, but you seem to be a decent guy, a nice guy. Well right at this moment, I need to feel good about myself. I need to be treated nice you know, like a lady should be. I'm sure you can do that. In fact, I kind'a fancy you. So how about you and I get out'a here, right now and we could go back to Judibana to your hotel? We could have a few drinks and give each other a nice time? I know I can give you such a good time that it would make your toes curl. What do you say?"

Bonnie was an attractive woman in her mid thirties with a wild sexy aura about her. He also knew he had to be careful in how he reacted to her approaches. She was trouble with a capital " T ", and he knew he had to get out of there with the least fuss and bother. He

93

would have to plan his escape quietly. Suddenly lady luck smiled his way. A bunch of Bonnie's friends came outside and started dancing around to the loud music coming from the party. Bonnie was grabbed by a passing hand and whirled into the dancing by one of the guys. Donald ceased his opportunity and made his move. He glanced back over his shoulder and saw Bonnie's gazing eyes eagerly searching for him.

Walking back to the hotel he could still hear the loud music coming from the party. He couldn't believe he'd encountered, two people making love right in front of him. Bonnie was another issue. What a poor lonely existence she lived. Deep down inside he felt she was a decent person who'd drifted into the life Joe had created for them. She was living like a chameleon and responding to her husbands contrived sexual demands and fantasies.

Donald got up early the next morning and had a light breakfast of coffee and toast. The coffee tasted good, so he had several cups. During conversation with one of the waiters he asked about arranging transportation to take him in the mountains to Falcon Ness. Before he knew it, a deal was done whereby the waiter's brothers would drive him there for twenty dollars, plus tip. Somehow, he felt that the tip may work out to be more than the fare, anyway he agreed and soon he was on his way.   The drive across the Peninsula was boring but as they approached the outskirts of Coro, they passed a large group of sand dunes. The driver pointing at the dunes calling. "Medinas, Medinas".

Donald nodded his head not understanding what the driver was trying to tell him. After a few more miles they entered Coro. The town was busy with the early morning traffic. Many of the buildings were old of Spanish architecture and painted white but the color had faded to a dirty cream over the years. There were several really old churches. Coro looked like an interesting place which Donald planned to come back and see more of at a later date.

Once they had left Coro, the mountains ahead began getting closer. In no time at all the vehicle was struggling against the steep twists and turns up the mountain road. One thing Donald had noticed about Venezuela was many of the cars were the old American vehicles like Chevrolet, Buicks and Fords. Most of them looked as if they were about thirty to forty years old and appeared to be falling to pieces. It was amazing they were still in working order.

Each twist and turn in the road took them higher up the mountain. The vegetation had now become more tropical and thicker, dominated by wild banana trees. Looking down over the edge of the road was scary. There was a shear drop of hundreds of feet and no barrier to prevent a fall. When they reached the top, the view was spectacular. A vast valley lay in front of them spread out across a sunken plateau. It was lush and green and in the distance were numerous cultivated squares of land which had been developed into orange groves. The driver stopped the vehicle and disappeared into the bushes relieved at the opportunity to empty his bladder. Donald took advantage of the rest and got out of the car. There was also a cool gentle breeze blowing which gave the air a rich freshness. He stood with his hand over his brow as the sun beat down on him. What lay before him was breathtaking. He'd never seen anything like it before. And Allison wanted to go to Rhodes again, he thought.

The driver returned, got back into the car and they started on their way. Passing through a number of small villages, the poverty of the indigenous population was evident. At many of the simple dwellings, laundry was hanging on trees and fences. He had also observed women constantly sweeping the area outside the main door to their homes. The local people were poor but appeared to be clean and proud. He'd also noticed they had different facial features to the Venezuelan he'd seen at the airport and in Judibana. The local people looked more like the South American Indians he'd seen in a television documentary on the Amazon. Each village was similar in as much as they all had a small village square, dominated by a large church. Most of the buildings gave the appearance they'd not changed for hundreds of years. Donald waved back at the young children as the played by the roadside.

Immediately after passing through one of the villages, the driver suddenly swung the car on to a dirt track road. Donald looked back trying to work out where they were going. He caught a glimpse of a sign that said,

"Golden Falcon Hotel." It was so small if he'd blinked, he would have missed it.

Driving up the steep narrow track, they passed through orange and lemon groves until they reached the front entrance of the hotel. The place was well positioned on top of a prominent hilly area overlooking the valley below. It was similar in appearance to the Andelucian hotels he'd visited in the mountainous areas of Spain. Two young boys came running out to greet them grabbing at his baggage.

The checking in was quick, with room key in hand, he decided to look around the place. Off the small reception area was a large lounge dining room. The bar was located at the far end of the dining area with a large fireplace dominating the room. A small piano was situated at the far end of the bar. The decor of the hotel had a rustic flavor which was complimented by the bare brick walls and large black beams stretching the width of ceiling. The floor was a dark highly polished slate with large rugs generously scattered around. The place felt warm and homely.

Donald turned his head looking in the direction of the noise of clattering dishes. Through the kitchen door emerged a large tall man with a jolly face. Spotting Donald he walked towards him, put out his hand in anticipation of a handshake.

"Hello, how are you? My name is Hans, I'm the

owner of the hotel. We have a nice place here, so I hope
we make your stay pleasant. We are hidden away in a
beautiful valley on the top of the mountain. Considering
how high up we are, we call this our little bit of heaven on
earth." he joked.

Donald instincts clicked in, he knew Hans was a
very likable and friendly person.

They both laughed and began walking towards the
bar. A number of stools were lined up as if they had been
placed in military fashion. The aroma of freshly brewed
coffee filled the room. Hans didn't ask Donald if he
wanted a cup, he just assumed he did and poured two
cups. He handed one to Donald and they both sat down
on the bar stools.

Hans held his cup to his mouth but did not take a
drink. He tilted his nose up slightly, savoring the aroma.

"South America has the greatest selections of
coffee in the world. This is Colombian, it's beautiful. It's a
pity that Columbia is more well know for drugs and not
it's coffee. You know there are other hidden treasures to
be found in South America, for example the Chilean
wines. They are much nicer and cheaper than the French
wines you must try some while you are here"

Donald took a drink. "Yes I will. The coffee taste
great."

"So what are you doing in this part of the world,
sightseeing, on holiday?"

Donald shrugged his shoulders. "Probably a bit of both. I've always wanted to come to Venezuela and now here I am, I can't believe it."

With an air of expectancy in his voice Hans asked.

"How long are you going to stay, in the hotel I mean? Will you need your room for over two weeks? I can give you a reduced rate for longer stay period.?"

Donald thought about it for a moment, not sure whether to jump in and accept the offer. He really had no plans.

. "Can I let you know tomorrow, after I've had a chance to look around?"

"Sure, take your time, no hurry."

They exchanged small talk and finished off their coffee. When they arrived back to reception, one of the young boys was waiting to show Donald to his room. Once inside his room, he gave the boy a tip as he left. Donald started checking around. The room was pleasant, good with the basic furnishings which looked as if they had been made locally. He liked the large rugs they had around the place, including the one in his room. He moved across to the balcony and looked out at the valley stretched out before him. He was knocked over by the view of the valley as it stretched out before him.

Everything was so lush and green. The areas cleared for cultivation give each field its own individual shape and shade of color. In a way it reminded him of a patchwork quilt with all the different colors, sizes and shapes. Each field had row after row of neatly placed trees lined up like tin soldiers.

That evening he enjoyed dining alone and found it relaxing after the journey from Judibana. He smiled to himself recalling his escapade with Bonnie the previous evening. He sipped his coffee and as he twirled his brandy glass, the sound of the piano attracted his attention. He quickly recognized the song being as 'Evergreen', which he liked a lot, in fact he thought it was one of the most beautiful songs Barbara had ever sang. He got up and walked into the bar. A young man was playing with a lot of feelings and as Donald sat down, he smiled. Donald sat and soaked up the atmosphere and ambiance of the occasion,

watch the pianist fingers as they floated over the keyboard. Two more melodies followed before the playing came to a halt.

The young man looked over in the direction of Donald.

"Is there anything you would like me to play for you Senor?"

Donald didn't have to think twice as he replied. "Yes, can you play Where or When?'

The young man didn't reply but started playing Donald's request. When he'd finished Donald softly applauded and nodded his head in a gesture of approval. Then he decided to retire for the evening, as he got up to leave, the young man politely called.

"Goodnight Sir, it was nice meeting you."

"Goodnight and thank you. You certainly know how to play. I really enjoyed your music. It was beautiful, finished my day off perfectly, goodnight."

Walking back to his room Donald started whistling Evergreen, now he would have the song on his mind for days.

The following morning Donald was awakened by the sound of voices outside of his window. He drew the curtains and saw Hans with three men who appeared to be workers. They were deep in discussion and even though they were speaking Spanish, Donald could tell by the tone of their voices there was some kind of problem. He quickly got showered and went to breakfast. When he'd finished eating, he wandered outside. Walking around the side of the hotel he saw an extension under construction. The workers he'd seen worked for the building contractor. Hans was still in deep discussion with them and when he saw Donald he waved, calling him over.

"Donald, I need your help."

Donald was puzzled and wondered what help he could possible give as he didn't speak the language. As he got nearer to the group, Hans started to explain the problem.

"These people are already three weeks behind schedule, if they don't make up the lost time, the extension will not be finished for the high tourist season. I have many bookings so I must have the rooms available on time. Donald are you an engineer? Can you help me?"

Donald paused for a moment, looked at the half finished building then asked,

"Do they have any drawings or layout sketches? Let me look at them, also any specifications and material take off will help?"

Hans translated Donald's request to the workers. The person who appeared to be in charge went to get the drawing. Donald was watching the carpenters as they were pulling the old concrete from a recent concrete pour. The man returned and after a few minutes examining the drawings, Donald asked.

"The twelve rooms you are adding, they are all the same design and dimensions, yes? So, for a start we can save a lot of time by developing sets of concrete from work which can be re-used without having to take them apart each time you pour. Also, you should look at the possibilities of pre-casting some of the concrete beams and posts."

The men looked at him with a blank look on their faces. Donald suddenly realized they hadn't understood his English. Hans responded enthusiastically to Donald's suggestions.

"Yes. That's a great idea, great."

Hans proceeded to translate Donald's comments to the workers, they in turn kept nodding their heads, saying the occasional, "Si." When he'd finished talking, they all laughed and started shaking Donald's hand. He felt good and as he turned to walk away, Hans caught up with him and asked,

"Are you an engineer Donald?"

"Yes I'm a Civil Engineer." he said laughing.

"Listen, it's very important for me and my family that I have this extension finished in time for the high tourist season. I've got a lot of bookings for tourists coming over from Aruba on three-day package deals. I have a contract with one of the big hotels over there"

Hans paused and then continued more sheepishly.

"Look, I don't want to offend you but if you do intend staying around for a while maybe you could help me by supervising the work crew and hopefully, we can get the project finished on time?"

Before Donald could answer Hans continued.

"Free room and board for a few hours supervision each day. How does that sound?"

Donald smiled and put out his hand. "Okay boss when do I start."

They both roared with laughter which made the work crew stop and look up in their direction. The workers then shrugged their shoulders and continued working.

Over the next few weeks, progress on the extension was visibly apparent as each day went by. The crews worked hard and responded well to the many suggestions put forward by Donald. He was enjoying himself and it was more like a working holiday. He'd been there for over a week before he realized that the lady who kept supplying him with cool lemonade, was in fact Hans wife Carla. She looked in her late forties but was still very attractive for her age. Whenever he saw her around, she was always actively involved in the day to day needs of running the hotel. She only spoke a little English, therefore every time he was in her company, she just smiled and let Hans do the talking. Today however he sensed she was excited about something and was in a real good mood. Donald watched her as she laughed and joked with the hotel staff. Hans noticed Donald watching her.

" Carla's a real happy lady today. It's because our daughter is arriving on the afternoon flight from Aruba. We are going to the airport after lunch to collect her. She's been studying at college in Florida for the past three years. Now she's finished and, on her way, back home! We can hardly wait to see her."

Donald felt touched by the emotion shown on Hans face and even spotted a little tear in the big fellows' eyes. Later in the day he heard them drive away in the jeep. His thought drifted to back home and his son Richard.

When he finished work, he showered then went to dinner. He was really comfortable with the working arrangement he had with Hans, at least for the time being. He'd decided he would stay and complete the construction on the extension. When he finished eating, he made his way to the bar. He'd really 'taken a shine' to the Polar Beer and even though Hans had Dutch and German Beers, he preferred the local Polar.

The noise of the jeep returning and the noises of excitement in the reception area, told him that Hans and his family were back from the airport. He listened as the group made their way to their living quarters located in the rear of the hotel. When the commotion had died down, he continued reading an old copy of a Time magazine he had found. He felt relaxed, enjoying his cold beer, when suddenly he heard a familiar voice.

"Hi Donald, so this is where you have been hiding?"

He was absolutely dumb struck. The silence seemed to last and eternity. Eventually, managing to close his mouth, as he stuttered.

"Leela! My god, what are you doing here?"

"I live here Donald this is my home. When Mama and Papa told me they had a nice English guy helping them with the construction, I never thought for one moment it would be you. Although I must admit I was a bit curious to find out who it was."

"You're Hans and Carla's daughter? I can't believe it! I just can't believe it."

CHAPTER V

Leela walked over to Donald and shook his hand, giving him a gentle kiss on his cheek. She sat in the chair next to him. He still had a total look of amazement on his face. Carla and Hans walked into the room with big smiles on both their faces as Leela and Donald got up to greet them.

"Ah! you two have met, good."

"Yes Papa we have met." Leela replied with a huge grin on her face.

After a few drinks, including a bottle of Champagne that Hans had saved for this special occasion, Donald thought it was appropriate to leave and bid them all goodnight. He knew they all wanted to be together to catch up on family news. Hans with a nice polite gesture, made a feeble attempt for Donald to stay but he declined. He knew they were eagerly waited to spoil their daughter with their love and attention.

Walking away, Donald turned looking back at them. Leela looked ravishing. They were preoccupied to hear him as he called to say goodnight.

Once in his room, he lay awake for a long time thinking about Leela. He couldn't believe they'd met briefly in Florida and now fate had brought them back together. Was it a coincidence or was it destiny? There was always a reason why events happened. He lay awake for a long time, tossing and turning with his imagination running away. Eventually he fell asleep.

The next morning, he got up as usual and went to breakfast. The place seemed quieter than normal. He never found out why, until the waiter informed him "today and tomorrow is a holiday" If he'd have known, he would have probably stayed in bed a little longer.

It was a beautiful morning, so he decided to go for a stroll. As he walked he was deep in thought. It's the warm weather and sunshine which makes all the local people happy everyday. The weather really does affect our moods and attitudes that's for sure.

Donald' s mind drifted back home that rainy Sunday when he'd decided to leave. He wondered how Allison was managing since his departure. He had called twice and left messages on the answering machine. He sensed Allison was still bitter over his decision. He got to the bottom of the hill close to the outskirts of town. In the distance he saw a lone figure of a person jogging towards him, waving their arms above their head. It was Leela. He stopped and waited until she caught up.

She was a breathless as she approached.

"Hi, wow it really is much hotter here than in Florida."

Her tee shirt was wet with perspiration. The sweat made her hair a mass of small tight black curls. Even with the sweatband around her head and perspiration covering her skin, she looked great.

"Do you jog every day? You look in really good shape, young, fit and beautiful".

His own boldness surprised him, but he felt relaxed with Leela. She smiled and placed her arm around his waist.

"Young and fit yes, but beautiful, no way. Do you jog or workout Donald? You look as if you're in pretty good shape?"

"No not really. I enjoy walking and used to do it quite a lot some years ago. I loved walking in the Lake District of England. I'm afraid an old man like me is not up to jogging, especially in this heat. I used to swim regularly but the weather back home doesn't encourage people to go swimming. At least not in the North Sea. It's absolutely bloody freezing"

They both laughed and continued walking in the direction of the hotel.

"You're not old Donald. How old are you about forty, forty-five?"

"Oh I like you. Keep talking and you'll be my

friend for life. What a way to start a day by being complimented by a beautiful lady."

Leela laughed with an innocent look of embarrassment on her face. They walked up the drive towards the hotel, their joking and laughter attracted gazing eyes.

Carla watched as they approached. She was puzzled because for complete strangers they'd quickly became friends. They appeared to be so relaxed and comfortable with each other. She hadn't heard her daughter laugh so much since she was a young girl. Leela looked radiant. Carla lingered tried to eavesdrop as Leela and Donald stood talking in the entrance to the hotel.

"Listen Donald, would you like to go out for lunch? I don't think you've really experienced the flavor of local cuisine. I know a great place where the food is fantastic. Great lobster, prawns and an incredible view of the lake. What do you say?"

"Sounds great to me. What time shall we meet? Does around noon sound okay?"

"Wonderful, now I shall restrict myself to only one piece of toast for breakfast and save my appetite for lunch. I'm going to shower and clean up. See you later Donald."

Carla continued her work in the kitchen,

preparing lunch. She sensed her daughter liked Donald a lot. Although Leela had changed during the period she had lived in the United States, she'd never been as outgoing and relaxed with men as she appeared to be with Donald. She wasn't too worried though and felt comfortable with the situation. Carla knew her daughter was a levelheaded girl. She had also noticed how Donald had enacted with the construction workers, so she knew he was a good person. Hans was a good judge of character, he liked Donald a lot and she respected his judgment. What's important was she was pleased to see Leela so happy and full of life. She had grown up to be a very beautiful young woman and was showing signs of strength in her character similar to her father.

Donald went back to his room and decided to clean up for his lunch date. As the water cascaded from the shower head soaking his hair, he watched as the lathered ran down his arms and legs and disappeared into the drain. His thoughts drifted to Leela. She was probably doing exactly what he was doing, taking a shower. His imagination began running away. He closed his eyes and lifted his head to facing the thrusting power of the water. He thought of her tight curled hair lathered in soap, then saw the white suds gliding down over her olive skin as she rinsed herself under the water spray. She wasn't just beautiful; she was a nice girl and his instincts told him he liked her a lot.

Leela had borrowed the jeep from her father and as they drove along the mountain road, Donald was on top form with his repertoire of jokes. Although she hadn't

understood his sense of humor when they'd first met, she
now enjoyed the way he made her laugh. They drove
through a number of villages, each with groups of
children waving excitedly as they passed.

Cresting the brow of a hill, Lake Coro could be
seen in the distance below. The view was spectacular. It
was as if they were looking from the window of an
aircraft. His initially route to Falcon Ness had taken him
up the back side of the mountain, therefore he'd never
realized how high above sea level they were. He guessed
they must have been several thousand feet. For the rest of
the journey they didn't speak, they were content to enjoy
the view. The cool breeze felt good as it blew through
their hair. Halfway down the mountain, Leela signaled
and turned left down a narrow dirt track.

They ended up in a small village, with about thirty
houses making up the whole community. Leela parked
the jeep on a strip of waste ground opposite a row of
small houses. They got out of the vehicle and began
walking across the road in the direction of the houses.
Donald looked up at saw a sign hanging above one of the
doors, "Casa Miquel".

He turned to speak with Leela who was now talking
to an old man. Donald had now become used to the
waving of the arms from the local people as they talked.
He couldn't understand what was being discussed, but
knew it was something to do with the jeep. Eventually he
realized that the old man was the restaurant security guard
who looked after the vehicles and was requesting a small

fee. Once Leela had assured him he would be rewarded when they came out, they made their way into the restaurant.

Entering through a narrow doorway, Donald was amazed at the decor. It was deceiving from the outside because the building was made up of two small houses joined together with a courtyard in between. It was beautiful, perfect for their first date. They were promptly shown to their table by a well-dressed lady, who just by her presence and ambiance, let them know she was the owner. No sooner had the lady left their table, when two pretty young girls dressed in sailor costumes appeared and started making a fuss of them. Donald was pleased with the choice of table which was located under a tree in the courtyard area. Leela could tell from the look in Donald's eyes that he liked the place.

They both started nibbling at the snacks the young girls had left on the table. Suddenly their attention was attracted by loud squawking birds. Looking up into the tree above their heads they saw two large beautifully colored birds with huge yellow beaks. The birds continued squawking loudly in an agitated state bouncing up and down on their perch. Leela and Donald laughed at the bird's antics. After a while they eventually began to quieten down and slowly their eyelids began to close.

The noise of a chain being dragged made Donald and Leela switch their attention. Under the tree next to them was an old boat which made up part of the decor.

Sitting on the edge of the boat sat a small monkey staring at them. It cocked its head from side to side then looked up at the two birds who were now dozing. Suddenly, the monkey leapt into the air making a grab at the tails of the birds. The birds jumped and both start squawking all over again. The whole episode was repeated over and over and continued like a show at a circus. Donald and Leela were totally absorbed and couldn't stop laughing. It was hilarious.

The lady of the house returned to their table shouting and yelling in Spanish at the monkey as it scampered away underneath the boat. She had a large blackboard in her hand upon which the menu was listed. Holding the board in front of them she began explaining the specials of the days speaking very quickly in Spanish. When she'd finished, she left to give them time to make their selection. Leela explained to Donald that the restaurant was owned by the lady and her brother, who was the chef. Their names were Anna and Miquel. She went on to explain Miquel had previously been the head chef at the Tamenaco Intercontinental hotel in Caracas, but he had now retired to start up the restaurant with his sister.

Donald explained that he felt a little helpless as he didn't understand a word of what Anna had said regarding the specials and the menu. Leela smiled and suggested they both start with fresh lobster tails in a seafood bisque cream sauce. This would be followed by the main course of a large fish baked in crusted salt. It sounded great and Donald nodded his head in agreement, licking his lips.

The lunch was as good as Leela had promised. The lobster tails were generously sized and topped with fresh, white, fluffy meat. A cream wine sauce containing small shrimp and scallops, chopped roasted garlic was sprinkled over the top of the dish.

When the baked fish arrived the preparation and serving was a ritual. A large mound of hard salt on an earthenware platter was wheeled in front of their table. Anna appeared and began beating the hard salt mound using the back of two spoons, as she did, the salt cracked. At this point, she proceeded to pour brandy over the cracked area and with the strike of a match, the whole dish was in flames. When the flames died down, she began peeling away chunks of the hard salt exposing the crusted and seared skin of the fish. With the skill of a surgeon, she peeled back the skin and spooned out the steaming hot white fish on to their plates. Donald's and Leela's mouths were watering in anticipation.

Everything was perfect. Throughout the meal they had limited conversation. Occasionally Donald would look towards Leela and as she caught his gaze, he would quickly look away. He still couldn't believe he was actually in Venezuela, eating dinner with the most beautiful girl he had ever seen.

The baked fish turned out to be exquisite. It was

also Donald's first introduction to Chilean wine. He found the wine to be as good, if not better, than the wines of France which are so expensive and overrated. When they'd d finished the first bottle, Donald instinctively ordered a second.

Putting down his knife and fork he lifted his napkin and wiped his mouth.

"Leela that meal was superb, absolutely out of this world. I cannot believe in a little village like this we have just had a meal fit for a queen."

Leela lifted her glass in the direction of Donald. "For a King and a Queen."

Donald blushed a little and quickly changed the subject.

"You have many churches here in Venezuela. Nearly every village has a church. Are most of the people here Catholic?"

Leela took a drink of wine and dabbed her mouth with the napkin.

"Yes, in Venezuela religion is a very important part of our history and culture. One of the first churches built in the whole of South America was built in Coro by Christopher Columbus. It is still standing; I shall take you to see it."

Donald smiled and took a gulp of his wine. "Even though I lived in England, religion was a very important part of my culture as well. My family were strong Catholics. In fact, my grandfather was a religious fanatic. In his bedroom he had a small prayer area, like an alter where he used to spend hours everyday kneeling in pray, he had sores on his knees. There were Holy pictures everywhere. When my brothers and sisters and I went to my grandparent's house, we had to bless ourselves with holy water as we entered. When any member of our family was sick, my grandmother would bathe our heads with Lourdes water. Each Sunday after my brothers and sister and I returned from attending Holy Mass we would be rewarded by my grandmother giving us chocolate for attending Holy Mass."

Donald paused feeling Leela wanted to say something. She had a look of concern on her face.

"You sound a little bitter about your childhood?"

"No not bitter Leela. I loved my grandparents and my family. When I look back the one thing that probably left the most scars was the school I attended. I suppose this is where I rebelled against teaching methods of the Catholic Church."

Donald lean forward placing his chin onto the palm of his hands.

"I shall never forget one of my form teachers, Miss Cane, she was a Jabberwocky if ever there was one. She used to make all the pupils in the class keep a Holy Diary where they had to record the number of times they went to Holy Mass, Communion, Confession, Benediction. Even though I was only young, I protested in my own way by refusing to keep the diary. When she started checking and found out that my book was blank, she went hysterical. She called me a wicked boy and accused me of not going to church. She went even more crazy when I informed her that what went on between God and I had nothing to do with her."

Leela was smiling. She was dying to ask him, what's a Jabberwocky? But didn't as it would have broken the flow of his conversation which she was enjoying. She felt comfortable and was getting to know Donald.

"Every Thursday afternoon everyone in the school had to attend Benediction. We all walked two by two through the school grounds, a thick wooded path which led to the Church. During this period, I had a newspaper delivery job after school. Anyway, to cut a long story short, I started hiding in the bushes on the way to church. When no one was around I would then climb over the wall and go to deliver my newspapers."

Leela waited as Donald continued his story.

"Playing truant from the church service continued

for several weeks until one Friday morning. I arrived at
school and Miss Cain was waiting for me. As I walked
into the classroom, she took great pleasure in informing
me she knew what I'd been doing each Thursday. I was
then instructed to accompany her to the Principals office.
I had to wait outside the office for some time before they
summoned me in. With a stern look on his face and in a
loud voice, the Headmaster proceeded to lecture me. He
kept repeating I was a wicked boy, until he advised me, I
was to be beaten for "the sins I'd committed". With a
wicked grin on his face he took pleasure in telling me that
even though I was being punished, God would never
forgive me for what I'd done. Without hesitation I looked
him straight in the eye and advised him that if he beat me,
I would never go to Church again and God would never
forgive him. He and Miss Cane were dumbfounded and
had a look of total amazement on their faces"

Leela was now laughing as Donald proceeded.

"Suddenly, in a panic, they informed me to wait
outside. After few minutes I was called back into the
office. This time I was informed I wasn't to be beaten but
that my name would be put in the 'Black Book'. Well after
this episode I knew my card was marked. Several weeks
later, our class had a Jesuit monk who had been assigned
on a training program. Well one morning he was walking
around the classroom talking about faith. He was
explaining to us that faith is believing in what we cannot
see, touch, or prove. When he asked the class if any of us
had a problem with our faith? Up went my hand bursting

to ask him a number of questions. I decided on one particular aspect of the Holy Bible which had really puzzled me."

Donald paused and took a drink from his wine glass. Leela was now totally absorbed by his story as she eagerly asked.

"Well what was it? What did you want to know?"

"We are told that the first man and woman on the earth were Adam and Eve and they had two children, Cane and Abel. Cane killed Abel, then went out into the wilderness and found himself a wife! My question was, where did he get her from?"

Donald paused long enough for Leela to start thinking about his question. He watched her eyes knowing her mind was now whirling, then he continued.

'The Jesuit thought for a moment, then putting his hand on my head he replied, "God provided my son." After a brief pause and with the whole class on tenterhooks I replied, "Great, well I hope he provides for me." Everyone in the class erupted into laughter. The Jesuit was not amused."

Donald and Leela were now both laughing out loud. Leela was trying to control her laughter and had her hand across her stomach in a gesture as if it was hurting her. Eventually she managed to comment.

"Even as a young boy, you had a mind and a will of your own, didn't you? Just like you have now. You must have been a little terror!"

"Yes, I suppose I did, but it just wasn't right to brainwash children with religion, not when they are so young. Don't get me wrong Leela, I believe in God and prayer, but I wanted to love and communicate with God on my terms. Pray and faith are very personal and private issues."

Leela reached over the table and touched the back of Donald's hand.

"Yes, your right Donald but things have changed for the better now and the Church is not so dogmatic in teaching and applying their doctrine. Here in Venezuela there is a lot of poverty. When you are poor as many people here are, you need something to believe in, something to feel good about. Anyway, enough of all this serious talk, let's have another glass of wine."

They finished off the bottle, most of which Donald drank. Walking out to the jeep, he hadn't really thought about the drinking and driving laws in Venezuela. He was about to have a lesson, not only in the social habits of the locals but also their driving habits and not from Leela. They'd only gone a little distance when a very old dented pick-up came towards them on the wrong side of the road. Donald began to react but as the truck got closer it suddenly swerved away. The driver was hanging out of the window with a bottle of rum in his hand waving it around and spilling half of the contents in the process. Donald was quite alarmed but Leela took the whole thing in her stride as if it was an everyday occurrence. Later he would learn it was a regular practice.

"Don't the Police enforce the laws for drinking and driving here?" he asked.

"I don't know whether you've noticed Donald, but you don't see too many traffic police around. The salary is so low they cannot recruit enough people into the police to enforce law and order. Most of the people who drive, don't even have a driver's license. Venezuela is famous for Angel Falls but it is also just as famous for not stopping at red traffic lights. If you stop your vehicle at a red light, the cars behinds you will start honking their horns in anger and frustration. Here, no stopping at red lights, you could cause an accident.

Before she could finish, she pointed to an old man on a very small donkey galloping down the road towards them. The old man was so drunk he could barely hang on to the donkey's rein. It was a miracle he managed to stay on the donkeys back. They both roared with laughter, it really was very funny.

It was close to 5.00pm when they got back to the Hotel. Leela had advised Donald she had to help her Mama prepare the dinner. Her brother was coming from

Caracas for the holiday weekend. When he commented they'd only eaten lunch, Leela smiled and advised Donald by the time they served dinner he would be hungry.

He pecked her on the cheek with a gentle kiss, thanking her for a great time. As he did, Leela caught the faint aroma of Donald's after shave. She felt a twinge of sexual excitement as butterflies fluttered in her stomach. This was the first time Donald had shown any sign of affection. Pulling herself together she informed him he'd been invited to dine with her family at 8.30 pm. He would soon learn that 8.30 pm in Venezuela really meant 9.30pm. Punctuality was not a strong characteristic of the Venezuelan.

Back in his room, Donald lay on his bed thinking about how much he'd enjoyed being with Leela. The feelings of enjoyment were different from anything he'd ever experienced before. The conversation and humor they shared together had been spontaneous and natural. He'd talked freely about his childhood, religion and his family. He rolled over on to his side and his eye lids began to get heavy. Dozing off, his thoughts were of Leela. His instincts told him she liked him. The thoughts he was having scared him a little. Slowly the amount of wine he'd consumed took its toll and he fell asleep.

He was awakened by the sound of someone banging on the room door. It was Leela.

"Donald, Donald, wake up its after nine."

Once a Chameleon

He jumped off the bed and groped around to put on the light. He then quickly opened the door and Leela walked into his room.

"I'm sorry I must have dropped off. The lunch and the wine made me sleepy. Give me ten or fifteen minutes I will have a quick shower and will be ready in a jiffy."

He walked towards the bathroom and turned as she casually commented.

"Oh, it's okay, we have plenty time. I only knocked on your door as I saw your room light wasn't on and everything was in darkness. Just take your time. We won't be eating for another hour at least; I shall wait for you.".

Wait he thought? I have to get ready; I can't just walk back in there in my birthday suit and say. "oh, what a lovely surprise, fancy meeting you here"

Leela heard the shower running and walked to the bathroom door and called.

"Do you want me to scrub your back Donald?"

He couldn't believe what he was hearing. He wasn't sure whether she was joking or not so he called back.

124

"What was that you said?"

He heard her chuckling as he started to lather himself.

While he was drying off, all he could think about was how was he going to get ready with Leela sitting on his bed. All his clean underwear was in the dresser. He realized in hindsight he should have taken what he intended to wear into the bathroom before he had his shower. He finished drying himself and began putting cream on his face and neck. When that was done, he applied his after shave. 'Want to smell nice tonight, Karl Lagerfeld always does the trick.' he thought.

Suddenly he stopped and listened. There was no sound. She's very quiet he thought.

"Leela? You're being very quiet."

He peeked out around the bathroom door and then walked into the room. Leela was gone. Oh the little devil he thought, teasing me and having me on like that. He saw the funny side of her prank and a smile came on his face as he went about getting ready. The little devil, he thought, she really has got a sense of humor.

Donald was introduced to Leela brother Albert and during dinner he kept looking at him think he'd seen him somewhere before. He racked his brain trying to remember. He shrugged it off thinking sooner or later it will come back to him. He also discovered that Leela had been right about being hungry again at dinner. He looked at the clock, it was 11.40 pm and they were sitting down to eat a great big meal. Usually if he'd eaten this late back home it was because he had just come out of the pub and gone for a Chinese or Indian take-away. "Alcohol stimulates the appetite, he thought."

When dinner finished Carla and Leela got up and started clearing dishes away. Hans motioned to Donald.

"Come on let's go to the bar area and have liqueur. I've got some good brandy which I keep for special occasions, just like this. It's not too often we have both our son and daughter at home together."

They sat down at the bar and Alberto walked over to the piano and began playing. It was then the penny dropped. Donald felt embarrassed.

He reached over and put his hand on Alberto's shoulder in a gesture of familiarity and friendliness.

"I'm sorry. I knew we'd met before, but I never realized. You were the young man playing the piano the first night I arrived here. I'm sorry if I appeared to be rude Alberto. Really I am so sorry."

"Don't concern yourself, we only met for a brief moment. If I recall, that night you were sad and lonely, homesick maybe."

"Sad, maybe, but homesick, I'm not too sure about that. I still remember how beautiful you played though."

"Thank you and yes, and I also remember the beautiful song you liked."

Alberto began playing the first few bars of Evergreen.

Carla and Leela returned and joined them for a drink. Carla cuddled up closely to Hans on one of the big couches. Donald thought they looked so comfortable and happy together. He was sitting at the bar as Leela sat down on one of the big rugs on the floor, propping herself up against the large cushions scattered around. Everyone looked so relaxed as Alberto continued playing.

Donald sipped his Brandy relaxed and content just to be there. Leela was an added bonus. He didn't want to appear rude by staring at her. The last thing he wanted to do was to offend her parents. He had a great amount of respect for them. Every now and then, Donald and Leela's eyes locked on to each other. They lingered just long enough to quietly stimulate their feelings for each other.

Leela sensed the mood and began patting her hand on the rug, she called over to him.

"You look so uncomfortable sitting there Donald, come over here and sit close to me"

Donald looked over towards Carla and Hans. He was asleep with his head lying in his wife's arms. Carla didn't move or speak but just smiled as if to say, "Go ahead it's okay." He smiled back, picked up his glass and made himself comfortable on the rug next to Leela.

Alberto continued playing one song after another from Bach to the Beatles, he really was an accomplished musician and so versatile. He began playing "Unchained Melody" and Donald began to sing the song very softly so as not to awaken Hans. As the two of them played and sang, Donald saw a look in Leela's eyes he'd never seen before. She noticed him looking and shyly smiled and turned her eyes down.

When the song finished, there was a brief silence until Hans muttered.

"Gentlemen, that was beautiful. Alberto you are extremely talented, you take after your father"

They all laughed and when the laughter faded, Carla and Hans got up and bid them all goodnight. It was as if Alberto took a queue from them as he also got up and closed the piano lid. He leaned over a squeezed Leela hand.

"See you in the morning. It's been a long day, but

nice day. It's good having us all back together as a family again. Goodnight"

"Goodnight Alberto " they both said in harmony.

When Alberto had left Leela turned to Donald.

"You really are full of surprises, aren't you? Whatever can I expect from you next! I never knew you could sing like that; you really are good, very professional."
Donald ginned and lifted himself up from the floor. He reached down and collected up the empty glasses and headed for the bar.

How about a night cap? He started singing quietly as he walked. 'Just one for my baby, and one more for the road"

Leela noticed Donald mood as she responded.

"Okay, just a small one. No Donald, what I mean it you sing very well, very professional. Have you ever sung in public"?

"Oh I used to sing and play in a rock band when I was younger. The good old days of Rock 'n' Roll. I really enjoyed it. I could have made a decent living out of it, but it was not too be. Allison my wife, was my fiancée at the time and she didn't like it. She couldn't stand all the attention I got while playing, especially the girls that hung around. Anyway, after a lot of heartache and anger, I gave it up. I suppose I gave up several things I enjoyed during that period in my life. I guess it was all part of believing that consideration was an important part of a relationship. The only problems was, no matter what I give in to she always seemed to expect more. It was strange because it didn't happen all of a sudden as a conscious decision. It was more of a gradual process that developed over the years. Eventually, I just gave in, to keep the peace. When I look back, I realize this was probably the beginning of the end."

He walked back over to where Leela was sitting. She hadn't spoken and continued to listen, hanging on to every word he uttered. He sat down next to her and put their drinks on a small table. She reached and took his arm and nestled it around her then she shuffled her body to get closer to him. When she had made herself comfortable, she turned and kissed him on the cheek. Her touch was so gentle that unless he'd been watching, he would have never felt the touch of her lips. It felt good and he sensed she also felt the same. It was a totally new experience for Donald making him feel a little giddy, that together with the wine and brandy. Well whatever it was, he liked it and wanted a lot more of where it came from.

They lay there not doing anything or saying a word. They didn't need to; it was so nice just soaking up the closeness of each other's bodies.

Was this what he'd been searching for? Was this what he'd missed all those years he'd been married to

Allison? He felt confused but knew it felt so different from anything he'd experienced in the past. He wasn't used to the closeness and affection. He looked into Leela's eyes and whispered.

"I don't know where our relationship is heading Leela, but what I do know is it feels good and I don't want it to end."

He kissed her on the forehead. She had closed her eyes as he gently kissed each of her eye lids, one at a time.

Leela's body began responding to Donald touch and affection until spontaneously they both moved apart. It was as if they both sensed the time was not right for things to go any further. He got up and reached down help her up.

"I guess it's time we called it a night. Come on love, I'll walk you to your door."

They got up and as they walked, Leela was deep in thought. She was trying to sort out her thoughts but was distracted as her imagination ran away with her. She hesitated, afraid to speak for fear of breaking the spell they'd woven. Eventually when they arrived at her door, he kissed her tenderly on the cheek.

"Goodnight Leela, sweat dreams and see you in the morning. I had a great time. One of the best nights of my life. Thank you."

Leela stood watching as he turned and walked back to his room.

Even though she'd gone to bed late, Leela woke early the next morning. She changed into her jogging kit and set of on her run. Traveling along her route her mind drifted back to the previous evening. Other events which had occurred flashed through her mind. The first encounter with Donald in Miami. Her boldness when asking him to dance and how he'd refused. Although they'd only been together one night, she hadn't forgot him. There was just something about him that attracted her. Then low and behold, fate had brought them together again in Venezuela, and at her home. He'd talked so instinctively and honest during their lunch date. He seemed such a nice person. So shy and tender when he touched her. She sensed he was a little reluctant in letting anyone get too close to him. How could someone with so much sincerity and tenderness end up being so lonely?

She pondered trying to sort things out in her mind. The difference in their ages was real, but it didn't matter, not to her. She did however feel Donald was more sensitive to it. Why was she thinking like this? They'd only known each other for a short period. They'd not embraced nor kissed each other passionately, never mind making love. Yet there was this inner glow which made her feel good when she thought of him. She felt comfortable in his company. He was the only man she'd known who hadn't immediately tried to seduce her. In fact, he'd kept himself at a distance. Maybe she would never be able to get close to him? This confused her even more.

Leela arrived back home and as she walked into the kitchen Carla was preparing the breakfast for the guests.

"What's for breakfast I'm thirsty and starving, I could eat a horse. The problem with consuming a lot of alcohol the night before, then going out jogging the next morning is you sweat it all out and dehydrate even more. It's like self inflicted pain."

Carla continued moving around the kitchen, occasionally nodding her head.

"I'm going for a shower; I feel all sticky and sweaty. Maybe the shower will waken me up more and make me feel better"
She finished off the remains of her orange juice and as her mother hadn't responded, Leela felt as if she was talking to herself.

Carla had in fact been listening all along as she went about her chores. She smiled secretly as Leela left to take her shower. She couldn't help thinking how happy and healthy her daughter looked. Maybe she's falling in love, she thought with her smile getting bigger. She wasn't too sure how Hans would react. Donald is a gringo, but then again, she'd married a gringo and they'd been happy with their life.

Donald and Leela had arranged to meet early
morning to go for a walk down to the village. Leela told
her parents she needed to do some shopping and it would
give them opportunity to do some sight-seeing. Although
Donald had driven through the village several times since
his arrival, he'd not experienced the flavor of the village
life. Walking through the streets Donald enjoyed
absorbing the culture and character of the place. Many of
the streets were very narrow. Some so narrow that even a
small car couldn't have been driven through them. The
level of poverty was apparent everywhere, yet the people
all looked so happy, smiling and enjoying life.

They sat under a tree savoring the juicy fresh fruit
they'd purchased from a small street stall. When they had
finished eating, they visited the Church situated in the
center of the town square. For a village that appeared to
be so poor and so small, the church was in a very good
state of repair. It had well cultivated and cared for
gardens. Inside the church the walls were painted pure
white with a scattering of holy pictures around the walls.
A large crucifix was hanging from the back wall where
three women were kneeling in prayer. Although the place
was not air-conditioned it was strangely cool, considering
the temperature outside.

When they came out of the church, Leela linked
her arm through Donald's arm as she had been doing
most of the day, only this time it felt more natural to

them both. They laughed and joked as they walked and the local people stared at them, not in a rude way but more out of curiosity.

Donald and Leela spent more and more time with each other as each day went by. Having dinner together in the evening and going away for the days at the weekends. It really made a difference seeing the country as a "Local" and not as a tourist. She took him everywhere.

One evening as they were finishing dinner, Hans asked Donald if he cared to join him for a drink at the bar. Although he'd dined with the family on many occasions, Donald felt tonight was different. During the meal he'd sensed a little tension as if it had been planned or orchestrated.

Hans finished pouring their drinks and handed one to Donald as he asked.

"So now you have seen a lot of Curimagua, what do you think? Do you like Venezuela? Is it what you thought it was going to be?"

Donald felt self conscious as he attempted to respond.

"It's great, really great. It's more than I ever hoped it would be. Of course, you and your family have made it all so much more enjoyable for me, I mean being able to stay here. You've made me feel as if I'm one of the family. I hope in some way my contribution has indicated my total gratitude. I enjoyed working on the extension and I'm glad we got it finished in time. When do the first tourist start arriving from Aruba?"

Donald felt a little more at ease as he switched the conversation.

Hans sensed the nervousness in Donald and followed his queue.

"Two weeks this Friday. I have a booking for four. We're going to be very busy around here, I'm glad we have Leela here to help. It's a pity Alberto has gone back to Caracas. We miss him. Even as a small child Alberto was always selective in picking his friends, but I know he likes you a lot."

Donald was being sincere, but he was feeling a little awkward as he knew Hans was going to get back on track with their original discussion.

"So what's your plans Donald? Where do you go after here? Oh that must sound awful. I didn't mean we want to see you leave. It's just that the construction is over, and I know you came to see the rest of the country, Angel Falls?"

Hans wasn't doing a very good job of what he'd intended to talk to about so Donald decided to break the ice.

"Hans, I know you and Carla love Leela very much and you care about her happiness. I also care about her happiness as well. I can't remember ever being as happy at any time in my life, as I've been during my stay here. You and your family have made me so welcome. I arrived as a stranger you knew little about. Who was I; Where did I come from. You knew little about me and still do, but this didn't stop you from opening up your heart and accepted me. Although you may not know it, what's happened this past few months has changed my life. It's changed me. I've started discovering the person I always felt existed inside me, the person I've waited years to find."

Donald paused and reached out putting a hand on Han's arm.

"I know you and your wife are both concerned about the relationship which has developed between Leela and I. I'm not concerned but a little afraid because I'm not sure where it's leading us to. I know in my heart that it feels good, for both of us. Leela's a very beautiful young lady with a heart to match her beauty. I think and care for her so much, yet every now and then something inside tells me to walk away. Maybe I should leave and let her meet a nice young guy her own age, get married and have a family. It's a natural instinct for parents to dream of their grandchildren. I tell myself this would be best for Leela. I know the difference in our ages is something you must be concerned about, it's quite natural. I also think about it and this is where I become confused. We seem so right when we are together. Like soul partners."

There was complete silence between them. Donald continued to pour out his feelings.

"Maybe I'm being selfish in wanting to hold on to this happiness I have found. But who wouldn't? I never knew I could be so happy as I am now. When a person finds something that's really special, they never want to let go. When I'm with Leela I get a warm glow deep down inside of me. When I do something nice for her, it makes me feel great. When she hurts, I want to hurt for her. Whether it be for a day, an hour or even for a moment, I want to be with her. I don't know if this is love. I do know I want to find out, I really do. Hans you say the word and I shall do the honorable thing and walk away. But before you do, what you have to ask yourself is this what Leela wants?

"Donald, I don't." Hans stopped when he realized Donald hadn't finished.

"Hans you're my friend, Carla is my friend and Leela is someone with a very special place in my heart. I have the deepest respect for you, your family and of course your daughter. That respect hasn't been violated in any shape or form. I'm a married man who is separated from his wife. I know in my heart I shall never go back to my wife, but I still have strings that need to be cut, and this process is already underway."

Leela stood motionless in the hallway not daring to move. It wasn't as if she was eavesdropping. She'd stopped walking into the bar area when she'd heard Donald and her father talking. Now she was stuck in limbo. She couldn't walk in on them, nor could she walk back for fear of being heard. She decided to stay put. Leela was surprised to hear Donald's expressing his feels so openly. She couldn't stop feeling a tingle of excitement when she heard Donald's remark about cutting the ties. She'd never asked him about his wife and the relationship he'd had. She listened when he felt like talking about it. She waited in anticipation or Donald to continue.

"I have more feeling in my heart for Leela than I've felt for anyone. I don't know whether it's love or not. Whatever it is though makes me feel great. You may think this strange coming from someone my age who's been married for many years. But in the end, all I have to compare this to is the many years of loneliness I endured until I finally broke away. I know Leela likes me. I also feel she enjoys being with me, but I don't really know how she feels in her heart. When the time is right, if there is anything there, she will tell me. Until then I think we should let things take their course. I'm not going to hurt Leela, I could never do that, never."

Hans smiled as they both shook hands, then full of emotion they put their arms around each other's shoulders. As they strolled away, Donald asked Hans if he would say goodnight to Leela. He'd an early start next morning with the painting crew, who were scheduled to arrive early.

When he got back to his room, he felt hot and sweaty and decided to have a shower hoping it would help him sleep better. The wind had died down and it was now very humid and sticky. He came out of the shower, lay on the bed with his towel wrapped around his waist.

He reached over and turned out the light. His mind was in a whirl thinking through the conversation he'd had with Hans. He tossed and turned, rolled over two or three times before he eventually fell asleep.

Floating in and out of his shallow sleep, Donald could hear the perpetual sounds of the crickets ringing though the night air. It was annoying when he first arrived, but now he'd gotten used to it. In fact, it was quite soothing. For a moment, his ears picked up as he heard a different sound from outside, then relaxed when he guessed it must have been a small animal. He quickly drifted back into a deep sleep. His body jerked and twitched reacting to his dreaming. Leela was touching his body with soft gentle circling strokes. He felt the movement of her body next him. As their bodied touched, she curled one of her legs around his waist, thrusting her hips against his. Her kisses started on his stomach and gradually moved up his body, over his nipples, under his chin, around his neck. Oh, it felt incredible. He tried to respond but found he couldn't move. Even his arm wouldn't move as he fought to wrap them around her. It was as if he was paralyzed. Leela was now kissing his ears, slowly moving her tongue around them in gentle movements. Oh God, I want her, I want her. Donald searched deeply for the energy to make one superhuman effort to respond.

His body jolted upright from his pillow. His eyes searched the darkness of the room. Sweat was dripping from his body. He'd been dreaming. He listened intensely anticipating the sound of movement within the room. Everything was still, yet his instincts told him he wasn't alone. The moonlight filtered through the window casting shadows around the room. Slowly his eyes became accustomed to the darkness and the outline of a dark image began to appear. Donald strained to focus his eyes. Slowly the shadow in the corner became clearer. He wasn't seeing things.

"My God Leela, what are you doing here? If your mother and father found out you were here they would be upset, especially after the talk your father and I had tonight. How long have you been there? How did you get in? Did I forget to lock the door?"

"You were dreaming Donald. I'm sorry if I've disturbed you but I need to talk to you. There is so much I want to say. Please may I sit down? We need to talk."

Donald moved over on the bed, making room for Leela as she sat next to him. He reached over to turn on the bedside lamp but the touch of her hand on his arm changed his mind. There was a brief and slightly embarrassing silence before she began.

"First of all, I want to clear my conscience. I overheard you talking with Papa tonight. I didn't mean to eavesdrop but when I heard you talking, I was outside and was about to come in, then I froze. I tried to walk away but I couldn't, I stood listening. My heart was pounding, and my knees were all weak. I guess I needed to know how you felt in your heart. It was so important to me"

Leela paused for a moment and rolled her eyes as she took a deep breath.

"When I was eighteen, I had a boyfriend, Jose. We stayed together for four years. We got engaged and we were to be married. Three weeks before the civil marriage ceremony, I called of the wedding. I talked with my parents and told them I wasn't sure that I loved Jose and couldn't make the commitment to spend the rest of my life with him. I told them that if I really loved him there would be no doubt in my heart. Mama and Pappa were very supported even through the terrible row which developed with Jose's family. We had to cancel the church ceremony and the reception. Months of planning was thrown away. When it was all over, it felt like I'd used a damp cloth on a blackboard and wiped part of my life away. It felt good but strange."

Donald was now sitting crossed legged on the bed listening to Leela story.
"You see Donald, at first I thought I loved Jose, if only a little. I mistakenly thought this is what love is all about. You know like planting a small seed which grows and grows eventually into a beautiful flower. This illusion made me believe that as we lived our life together, I would love him more and more as each day went by. That's where I made my mistake. I now realized there is no such thing as a little bit of love. You either love

142

someone or you don't, it's as simple as that."

Donald was a little taken aback by what Leela had told him, yet he had come to admire her open simple honesty. He felt embarrassed that she'd overheard his conversation with her father.

"Leela I don't know what the future has in store for us but I think we should let life take its course. I know that in my heart I feel we are more than just friends. I think what's holding me back is that I have to get my personal affairs sorted out back home. Until I take care of these issues, I feel reluctant to even think about any form of commitment. I can tell you honestly, I'm a little scared at the moment because I feel so happy, like I've never felt in my life. Meeting you, living here in Falcon Ness, it's like a dream and I don't want to wake up. I promise you one thing Leela, I will never do anything that will harm or hurt you. Oh! I'm saying this all wrong, but I hope you understand what I'm trying to say?"

Leela reached over taking both of Donald hands and cupping them into hers.

"Of course, I understand what you're saying. I shall be patient and wait because I know in my heart, we were meant for each other."

They both reacted spontaneously hugging and kissing each other. Their embraced wasn't passionate but was full of tenderness and sincerity. As they broke away,

Leela thought the timing was right to spring her surprise on Donald.

"I was going to wait until tomorrow to mention this but next weekend I am meeting a group of my cousins and their friends in Moracoy. It's really beautiful there, with fantastic beaches among the many islands. I was wondering if you would like to go. It will be a fun weekend".

"It sounds great to me." he replied enthusiastically. He moved away and stood up. Leela reacted moving off the bed and stood next to Donald. He stepped forward and wrapped his arms around her giving her a big hug.

"You'd better go love. I don't want your parents to come looking for you.

"Okay." she answered in an unconvincing tone. Leela reached up putting her arms around Donald's neck.

Donald leaned forward to kiss her on the cheek. Leela reacted quickly tugging him forward and in one quick movement she kissed him passionately on the lips. For a brief moment their kiss lingered until just as quickly she broke away.

Leela had a devilish grin on her face.

"I've been wanting to do that for a long time."

"So have I Leela, it was nice, but you better be careful because I have sweet, soft, sexy tender lips."

They both started laughing, trying to muffle the sounds of their giggling. When they'd gotten themselves under control, he walked her to the door and kissed her goodnight.

During the next few days they discussed their plans for the weekend trip to Maracoy quite openly, even in front of Leela's parents. He sensed they'd have no objection to them going off together. It was obviously because they were meeting up with other members of the family. He was looking forward to going and was getting quite excited. He hadn't had the opportunity to see other areas Venezuela. His plans had changed a little.

His excitement built up as he began imagining himself in the hotel bedroom with Leela. She was standing wearing only a white towel wrapped around her body. The contrast between the pure whiteness of the towel and the smooth olive skin of Leela made the hairs on the back of his neck stand up. He was lying waiting for her on the bed holding out two glasses of bubbling champagne in her direction. As he pulled himself together, he chuckled comparing himself to Billy Lair. Now there was a guy with a vivid imagination.

CHAPTER VI

Maracoy, Venezuela

They left Falcon Ness around noon traveling down the Lake Coro side of the mountain. There was something about Fridays that makes it different from any other day of the week. Donald always felt good on a Friday and especially this week. During the drive along the coast road, little was said about their discussion the previous weekend. Leela and her parents had all been their usual friendly selves. Hans was pleased when Donald told him the hotel extension was going to be ready on time. He and Leela had gone walking together on number of occasions and during their discussion he found out just how much Leela loved Falcon Ness. The week had gone by quickly.

The road to Moracoy was the main highway running from Caracas in the east across the northern coastline of Venezuela to the Colombian border. It wasn't by anyone's stretch of imagination a superhighway; in fact, it wasn't even a dual lane highway. At times it was scary, especially the way they drove in Venezuela. Leela was a competent driver so Donald felt comfortable with her at the wheel.

Apart from a brief stop for coffee and a snack, they made good time and reached Chi Chi Rivichi by early evening. Driving into the entrance of the La Garza

James Caffrey

Hotel, Donald began wondering about the room arrangements. He hadn't had the opportunity to discuss this with Leela before they left. By the time they were on the road he never felt comfortable about asking her. He felt shy about the whole thing. He hoped everything would work out and luckily it did. Walking into reception they were greeted by her cousin Marie and her husband Jorge. The third member of the party was Marina another cousin. Donald immediately noticed the likeness of Leela and her cousins. They all had striking classical features in their looks which must have been passed down through the generations of their family.

First, they greeted Leela hugging and kissing her. To his surprise they also greeted him like long lost family friend even though they had never met. He sensed they knew quite a bit about him, and he was relieved to find they all spoke good English. While they were registering Donald overheard Marina indicated to Leela they were roommates. She had already checked in so Leela could go straight to her room and unpack. Donald was relieved to find things worked out as they did and felt very comfortable with the arrangements. They all agreed they would meet in the restaurant at around 8:00 PM, which Donald knew meant 8:30 PM at the earliest in Venezuelan time. Collecting his key, he went off to find his room.

When he walked into the restaurant at around 8.20pm he was surprised to find they were all there. He walked towards them with a look of amazement on his face pointing to his watch and making gestures of being

147

surprised, they all started laughing.

"What happened? I don't believe it you are all here and I'm the last one to turn up? This is Venezuela isn't it?"

Again, they laughed out loud. The evening had begun on a lighthearted noted and continued throughout dinner. He lost count of how many bottles of beautiful Chilean wine they consumed. The band was playing with people dancing and singing to the music. It was turning out to be a great night and Leela's cousins were fun people. Donald discovered that the Venezuelans knew how to party better than any of nationality he'd know. He also found out they had this enthusiasm to live their life to the full. He liked them a lot. The band broke into a salsa and right on cue Leela stood up and doing a little curtsey she said very formally to Donald.

"Excuse me Sir. May I have this dance with you?"

The rest of the group looked surprised. After a brief pause Donald got up and placing his arm across his waist, he bowed smiling at Leela.

"It would be my pleasure madam."

As Donald and Leela walked to the dance floor, Marie turned to Jorge and Marina.

"I wonder what that's all about. It's obviously

some private joke they have between them. He seems a nice guy doesn't he Jorge? They look good together. What do you think Marina?"

"Oh, I think he's nice, very nice and also very handsome."

She had a mischievous gleam in her eye as she continued.

"Leela looks so comfortable with him, even though he is a lot older than her. But then again, I also prefer older men. They know there is only one way to treat a lady and that's like a lady."

Their attention had now switched to the dance floor as they watched Leela and Donald dancing. Several other people in the restaurant were also looking at them. Most of them were wondering how on earth a "gringo" learned to dance so well. They couldn't help but admire how good Donald and Leela looked together. When the music finished the room filled with a soft ripple of applause.

A little after midnight Marie and Jorge decided to say goodnight. Jorge placed a number of Bolivars on the table as they left. Marina suggested the rest of them finish off the remaining bottle of wine topping up their glasses before they could respond. She then turned to Donald and asked.

"Do you want to dance with me Donald?"

He was a slightly taken aback and as Marina was now a little drunk, but he thought he would do the honorable thing. Leela indicated her concurrence though the movement of her eyes.

After a short time, Donald and Marina were dancing around the floor but it felt totally different to the way he and Leela danced. Marina was a lot more physical, which made him feel a little uncomfortable. He was pleased when the music stopped but as he was about to walk back to the table, the band started playing a slower tune. Marina had not let go of his hand and pulled him back on to the dance floor immediately pushing her body close to his. During their dancing, Marina began to get sexually aroused, pressing her hips into his body and stroking the back of his neck with her hands. Donald controlled his basic instincts and didn't respond. He continually turned his head in the direction of Leela search for a hint of understanding from her. When the music eventually stopped, he heaved a sigh of relieve. Even though Marina wanted to stay and dance, he gently led her off the floor. He'd had enough and wanted her to know it.

When they returned Leela did not say too much. The silence was eventually broken by Marine who leaned over to Leela and whispered.

"What's he like in bed?"

She said it loud enough so he would hear and as she'd not spoken in Spanish it was obvious, she wanted him to understand. Leela glared at her with clenched teeth and did not respond. The fire in her eyes emphasized her displeasure and rage. Donald didn't want things to get out of hand, he thought, if Marina wants fun, she shall have fun. He leaned over the table and Marina responded by leaning forward. With his mouth close to her ears he whispered.

"You know, a lady once asked me if I could make love five times in one night. At first, I was a little shocked, but when I got my thoughts together, I answered, I didn't know I was supposed to stop and start again."

Marina was speechless and just rolled her eyes. Leela tried hard not to burst out laughing and was having difficulty in controlling her reaction to the clever response Donald had injected. He felt a little apprehensive as he wasn't too sure whether Marina would appreciate his sense of humor. The twinkle in her eyed warned him he had talked himself into deeper trouble.

Leela and Marina then got into a heated discussion in Spanish with a lot of motioning and waving of their hands. The looks on their face told him it was time to leave. Leela was beginning to get angry with her cousin.

Marina was now very drunk and starting to

wobble even in her seat. Donald kept signally to Leela they should take her to her room, but the discussion between the two-woman continued until he stood up and announced loudly.

"I'm going to pay the bill. It's time to call it a night. We've all had a bit too much to drink so let's not do anything or say anything which we shall regret tomorrow, okay?"

The two-woman sat silently staring at each other.

Donald picked up the bolivars that were left on the table by Jorge and walked towards the cashiers. When he had finished paying the bill, he looked and saw Leela having a problem in trying to get Marina up on to her feet. He went over put his arms underneath her, picked her up and walked upstairs to the room.

Leela had the room door ready in front of him. He placed Marina on the bed but as he went to move away, she hung on to his neck pulling him back on top of her. She continued holding on to Donald and with slurred speak she pleaded.

"Don't go Donald, I want it five times in one night. Can you really do it five times in one night without stopping? Oh God, you're my kind of man. I want sex, lots and lots of sex. Oh, love sex."

Looking up at Leela she called.

"Just leave us alone Leela. You can go and stay in Donald room for tonight. You would like to stay here with me tonight Donald, wouldn't you? We can make passionate love all night, without stopping, it will be wonderful."

All this time he'd been trying to undo her hands around his neck. He was beginning to regret his little joke, which had now backfired on him. Suddenly he was free, and Marina flopped back on to the bed. She continued the slurred muttering then she passed out.

They both stood looking at her lying on the bed then Leela turned to Donald.

"Look I know we never planned things this way, but I can't stay with her tonight. Come on let's go. I shall stay in your room tonight."

He didn't reply, he was a bit taken aback by the chain of events. He waited while she collected a few items of clothing and toiletries. Before they left, they put the top cover sheet over Marina then turned out the light. Opening the door to his room he felt a little uncomfortable and shy. He had butterflies in his stomach. Were they going to sleep together? He'd soon find out.

"So which side of the bed do you prefer Donald? Do you have a preference? If not, I shall take this side, okay? I guess if we'd know this was going to happen, we could have requested twin beds and not a double eh?"

They both smiled, her humor had broken the ice.

They both fidgeted about nervously. Leela started taking off her jewelry as Donald placed his watch on the bedside table.

"Do you want to use the bathroom first Leela?"

"Sure" she said picking up her toilet bag and an item of clothing. Walking into the bathroom she stopped and leaned her head back out of the door.

"You're sure this is okay Donald? I mean if you want, I can go back to my own room and sleep in the chair?'

"Oh no. I mean yes, everything is fine. Don't worry. I can't have you sleeping in a chair."

He sat on the bed in silence until the noise of the shower broke his concentration.

He was confused, not knowing what to do, what to say. He felt awkward like a sixteen-year-old on his first date. He'd never been in a situation like this before.

Leela seemed to be in the bathroom for an eternity. Just as he was wondering how much longer she would take, the door opened, and she appeared.

He tried hard not to stare but he couldn't take his eyes off her. She had her hair tied back with a thick ribbon. Her short nightgown had no sleeves exposing not only the full length of her arms, but also her lovely long legs. He'd secretly admired her legs for the first time he'd met her when jogging. This time however was different. She'd removed her make-up, which she wore sparingly and her face glowed. Leela had the most beautiful skin texture than any other woman he'd seen. He could smell the freshness of her body.

She turned realizing Donald was looking at her. Their gaze paused but only for a brief moment. Leela eyes twinkled and gave an innocent hint of excitement, yet they never moved. Although she liked the attention and felt flattered, the coy look on her face said it all.

Donald continued watching her as she folded her clothes into a neat pile and placed them on the chair next to the bed. He felt awkward and shy like a sixteen-year-old on a first date.

Leela sensed his embarrassment.

"Come Donald, it's your turn to use the bathroom and don't take too long."

The smile on her face was radiant.

Picking up clean underwear, he disappeared into

the bathroom. He quickly got undressed and jumped into the shower. The warm water felt good as it hit the back of his neck. After drying himself, he put on his clean shorts and looked at himself in the mirror. His eyes focused on the small love handles at each side of his waist. The texture of his skin was good for a man of his age. He took a little longer than normal in brushing his teeth. Combing his thinning hair, Donald's eyes continued checking out his body. Finally he packed up the courage, turned off the bathroom light and stepped out into the darkness of the bedroom.

He made his way towards the bed and carefully climbed in. It felt strange having her so intimately close. It was different from the times they'd held each other in an embrace. Even though they were lying apart in the bed, he could feel her next to him. A sweet, fresh, feminine odor filtered through his nostrils. His eyes got more accustomed to the dark and he could see the outline of her body under the sheet. Strange he thought, when a woman lies on her side her hips become more exaggerated making the curves of her body more prominent. It looked so sensual.

Slowly Leela turned over and looked at Donald. Before she could speak, he jumped in.

"Shall we cuddle?"

She answered with a sense of ease in her voice.

"That would be nice."

He moved closer and gently put his arm around her waist. He wasn't bold enough to press himself too close, instead with his toes he searched for her feet. Once he'd made contact, he placed his foot against hers. His toes twitched ever so slightly as a sign of approval as she responded by edging nearer to him in a little shuffling movement.

"Goodnight Donald and thank you for everything."

"Goodnight Leela and sleep tight."

Spontaneously they both leaned towards each other and after a brief gentle kiss they went to sleep.

Donald was awakened by the sound of the shower running. He sat up in bed quickly looking around as if to get his bearings. Collecting his thoughts together, he reflected on the events of the previous evening. He wondered how Marina was feeling and whether she would remember what had happened, or more to the point what hadn't happened.

He had to pinch himself when thinking of he and Leela sleeping together. He had feelings and urges like any other blue-blooded male, but he was glad things had worked out as they had. If and when the right moment arrives, he sensed neither of them would hesitate and respond instinctively.

The bathroom door opened and Leela walked out wrapped in a large bath towel. Her hair was still wet and a mass of tight black curls. The fresh gleam of her complexion made her face shine. Before they could even say good morning to each other, the telephone rang.

"I'll get it" she said picking up the phone.

"Hello. Oh hi Papa.... Yes He's here. Oh I just came to collect him to go to breakfast then we're off for our walk."

Her eyes rolled as she looked at Donald hoping her father would believe what she was saying.

"What is it Papa? What's happened? Yes.......... you need to talk to him. Hold on for one moment here he is."

She handed the phone to Donald.

"Hi Hans............Ah yes, she came and woke me up. I guess I must have overslept with having a late night, too much Chilean wine. ...... What is it Hans? What's wrong?.......My son Richard called from where.... Aruba? What number did he leave?......... He didn't? He's flying to Venezuela this morning! Did he say where he would be going or staying?............ Oh I see, you told him you would book him into the Jardin Hotel in Judibana. No that's great. Did he say what it was about or give any kind of clue? ......Oh sure Hans, I'm sure everything is okay too. Okay Hans thank you for your help............... Okay, thanks .... Oh sorry, you want to speak to Leela? Just a moment."

Leela listen to her father as he explained he didn't know all the details but there had been a family member involved in an accident in England and he'd been requested not to say anything to Donald.

As she listened, she deliberately avoided looking in Donald's direction. She knew her face could not hid her concern.

"Okay Papa, thanks for calling we will get back to you as soon as we can. Are you and Mama staying home today if we need to call back? Oh good....... that's good Papa......... I love you too and give Mama my love. Bye Papa."

Replacing the phone Leela looked at Donald and saw the worry and concern on his face.

"Something's terribly wrong Leela, something bad has happened. I knew I was too happy for it last. Mother nature has a nasty habit of creeping up and kicking you in the arse, just when you least expect it. Why didn't he call me? It's not like my son to surprise me. Something's wrong, something's bad has happened."

Donald sat down on the bed and Leela came and sat next to him. She could see the anxiety and worry in his eyes. She reached over and put her arm around his shoulder. He responded and looked up, shaking his head back and forth but never uttered a word.

Inside he felt something really terrible had happened. Why would Richard get on a plane and fly all the way over here? He'd kept in regular contact with his son and he knew how to get a hold of him if he needed too. He'd even talked to Allison on a couple of occasions but his calls to her had become less frequent of late. What had happened was bad, that's why Richard had come to see him. If it had been anything to do with his father, brothers or sisters, one of them would have called.

He knew that Richard had always been close to his mother, which was good because he had helped her and given moral supported after Donald's departure. He suddenly turned and looked at Leela who had been saying something which he hadn't heard.

"Sorry love. Oh I'm sorry I didn't catch what you said, my mind was miles away. What was it you said?"

"I said I think we'd better pack up our things and get out of here as quickly as we can. I'm not sure what you want to do but we should not waste time by going back up to Falcon Ness. We can head straight for Coro then on to Judibana. Maybe we can get there just before Richard arrives eh?"

There was a pause before he responded.

"Sure, that sound good. A good idea."

Leela went to let the group know what was going on. Marina took a long time to wake up, eventually she sat up in the bed quickly when she realized what was going on. She began to say something in the form of an apology as Leela was walking out of the room. They quickly paid their hotel bill, gassed up the Jeep and headed for Coro.

It was a four-hour drive to Judibana. This was mainly due to the poor condition of the highway and the high ratio of accidents that occurred. It did however help some drivers keep their speed down. During the journey they hardly spoke. Leela could see the troubled look on Donald's face which he was trying so hard to hide but without much success. She knew all sorts of thoughts must be going through his mind. She felt so helpless.

Donald's mind was drifting back to the morning he left, walking up the street in the rain. Apart from the calls he made back home, he hadn't given a lot of thought to the life he'd left behind. In reality not a day had gone by where he hadn't thought of Allison, after all they spent most of their life together. It wasn't that he felt guilty about enjoying his new life. It just seemed so natural to him to be living the way he'd done over the past few months. He knew he'd changed a lot. It was as if he'd a split personality, one being the person he used to be, the other being the person that Leela and her family knew. He was no longer living his life like a chameleon.

Even Julie in Aruba kept telling him he was a nice person. Leela liked his jokes and sense of humor, she thought he was funny. He'd laughed more with Leela than he had in his whole life. The feelings he'd experienced were totally new to him, but he couldn't get away from the fact that it felt good to be himself. He liked feeling good about himself. It gave him a warm glow inside. Allison had never made him ever feel the way both Julie and Leela made him feel. He now knew Allisson had tolerated him because she'd had to. She would quickly lose interest in what he was doing or saying if it didn't interest her. In fact, he realized that to her he was a complete bore and not very amusing at all. Well maybe acting the way he did, she was probably right. Even if she didn't think so, it was the impression she gave and that's how she made him feel.

Donald looked around and realized they were going through Coro. He wished he'd taken the time to come down and have a good look around. The town was steeped in history dating back to the times when Columbus traveled to South America. He wondered whether he would ever come back. Was his new adventure over?

Soon they were driving past the Medinas. It seemed so out of place seeing a strip of sand dunes stretching out to the sea. It wasn't as if they were in the middle east. A small bulldozer was pushing the sand off the road. The continuous wind in the area, the work of controlling the sand was obviously on ongoing process which continued throughout the year. Why didn't someone realize that to stabilize the movement of the sand, all that needed to be done was to spray oil on the slip face of each dune? It wasn't a secret remedy; in fact, the dozer driver probably knew this. He'd probably worked at his task for years and this was what was expected of him, he needed the job and liked it. It had become a way of life which would only change if someone consciously decided to force the change. Of course, the other aspect was the Medinas was a big tourist attraction and brought a lot of visitors to the area.

Once they got on to the peninsula, the scenery became boring with sparse vegetation sprinkled among the distance salt flats. Such a contrast from the lush and tropical vegetation of the mountains in Curimagua. Nearing the outskirts of Punto Fijo, Leela took one hand off the steering wheel and gentle squeezed Donald's arm.

"Are you going to be okay Donald? We are nearly there. I think I should drop you off at the hotel and leave you and your son to talk. I can catch up with you later. I have a girlfriend living in Judibana, she's married to a guy who works for Lagoven in the refinery. I'll leave you their telephone number so you can call me if you need me. I shall stay with them tonight so don't worry; I'll be fine. Is this okay?"

"What? Oh yes that'll be fine. You're right I think it's best to meet him on my own. I mean it's not like I don't want him to meet you. It's just that I don't really know why he has come so far unannounced. I fear the worst."

"No matter what it is, I shall be there to support you Donald and remember, you are much more than just a friend to me. I love you and if you hurt, I hurt."

"I'm so glad you are such an understanding person Leela. You're so sensitive to people's feelings and needs. You're a very special lady that's for sure."

Within a short space of time they'd entered Judibana and as the Jeep pulled up outside the hotel. Donald hesitated before getting out. Leela could sense he didn't want to go, but he needed to find out what had brought his son to Venezuela. She looked around cautiously then discreetly leaned forwards and kissed Donald on the cheek. As he turned to get out of the vehicle, he made a half attempt to smile. It wasn't very convincing.

"Good Luck. I shall be thinking about you all the time."

CHAPTER VII

Judibana, Venezuela.

Donald walked into the hotel half expected to meet Richard waiting in reception. He wasn't in the lobby, so he proceeded to the coffee shop. Richard was sitting alone at a table being served by a very petty waitress. He hadn't yet noticed his father. Donald stood frozen to the spot. He hesitated and felt a little awkward. What do I do he thought? Do go over and give him a big hug saying it's great to see you son?

Finally, the waitress left and Donald picked up the courage and walked into the coffee shop. It wasn't too crowded and Richard spotted him immediately. He stood up as his father approached.

Richard grabbed his fathers' outstretched hand.

"Hi Dad, it's good to see you. Wow! You look great. You're tanned and you've lost weight.
You look so healthy."

"Hi son, it's great to see you." Donald replied meekly.

They continued shaking hands until his fatherly instincts kicked in, he grabbed his son and wrapped his arms around his neck. They were both feeling very emotional.

"So this is where you have been hiding" Richard said lightheartedly.

"Yes, it's a nice place with nice people.

There was an embarrassing silence.

"So Dad, I bet you never imagined you'd see me out here unannounced?"

Donald didn't reply but waited for his son to continue. They just sat looking at each other locked in a vacuum of embarrassing silence until Richard again took the initiative.

"Is there somewhere a little more private where we can talk? Somewhere near the sea? The ocean gives a nice feeling of comfort and tranquility. I met someone on the flight from Aruba and they mentioned there were some lovely beaches around this area."

"Sure, let's go, we'll grab a cab. There's a nice little fishing village a few miles from here called El Pico. It's very picturesque and quiet there."

They walked outside and got into a waiting taxi. During the journey neither of them felt comfortable with the long silences in their dialogue but they persevered in trying to encourage each other to relax. The taxi driver could also sense the tension as he continuously kept glancing in the rear-view mirror. Was this the calm before the storm?

Gradually Donald began to feel a little more relax.

"So Richard, what do you think of all these old American cars you see being driven around over here? Venezuela is full of them. This taxi we're in is probably over thirty years old. I know it looks battered on the outside but as you can see it runs well."

Richard didn't reply and smiled back at his Dad. He continued gazing out of the window looking at the flat and arid landscape.

Donald was aware of Richard's attentiveness to the local scenery. Again, he tried to break the ice.

"See all those old plastic bags which are caught up on nearly every tree or bush. To the expatriates or the gringos, they symbolize he national flower of Venezuela. A plastic bag wrapped around a bush. They're everywhere, hundreds and hundreds of them. The constant winds they have here blow the garbage for miles."

This brought a faint hint of a smile to Richard's face. Soon they were passing through the village of El Pico. It was strategically placed on the point of a peninsula. A Coast Guard & National Guard Station was located on the beach. They passed through a gate manned by men dressed in military uniforms who waved as they drove by. Richard had a worried look on his face and looked quickly in the direction of his father. Through his facile expression Donald indicated everything was okay. The taxi stopped in front of a small beach cafe facing the sea. Apart from the domestic help cleaning the tables and mopping the floor, the cafe was deserted.

Donald attempted to converse with the taxi driver in Spanish. He was trying to make him understand that he wanted him to wait and would pay him for the round trip. After much deliberation and frantic waving of arms the driver finally understood and settled down for a siesta. Since his arrival Donald had picked up only a little Spanish. It had been too convenient having Leela around to translate for him. This made him realize he'd been lazy in not trying to learn the language.

While this was going on Richard had gotten out of the taxi and walked on to the beach. He took of his shoes and socks and placed them on a wall. He then walked to the water's edge. The sea felt warm. The effect of the water washing away the small particles of sand and fine gravel under his feet was comforting. He gazed along the near deserted beach.

The pale blue clear water was a perfect contrast to the white sands of the beach. For a moment his attention switched to watching great numbers of cormorants hurtling into the sea from high above. The constant splashes stretched across the whole width of the bay as the birds eagerly sort food. Closer to him he could see rows of small crudely made houses. They were so

168

basically constructed that they looked as if they had been put together with whatever material the inhabitants could find. Fishing nets hung from primitively made racks outside of many of the houses. Several fishermen were working at repairing their nets trying to get them ready in time for the evening tide. Richard speculated thinking fishing was probably their main source of food and income. They all looked so poor.

The place was so peaceful and tranquil; Richard regretted he'd not brought his camera. The scene was like picture postcard. It was beautiful. He turned his head quickly as he heard children playing and laughing. A group of small children were chasing a baby pig as it ran in and out of the open doors of houses. None of the occupants appeared to mind as the pig weaved in and out ahead of the chasing group. Many started laughing as a dog joined in the chase snapping at the children's heels as they ran.

Richard heard his father footsteps approaching. He never turned as he said.

"I never realized places like this still existed in the world. Everything is so clean and unpolluted. It's so quiet and desolate, quite breathtaking. Is it always quiet like this?"

Donald stood looking at the back of his son's head as he responded.

"Yes I believe most of the time, except on weekends when the Venezuelans come here with their families. Traditionally they arrive late in the afternoon just as the sun is going down and stay until very late at night. When I say late, I mean until well after midnight. They love to party like no other nationality in the world. They are lovely people, so full of life and they have this urge to live their life to the fullest of enjoyment. Most of them are poor yet they always seem to find a simple way to enjoy life."

Richard plucked up courage and as he turned with a tremble in his voice he asked.

"Is this what you came here to find Dad, all this peace and tranquility? Was life so bad at home you had to leave the way you did?"

Donald was taken by surprise and at first was lost for words. He walked back up the beach and moved under one of the straw umbrellas. He turned and looked toward his son who was now walking to join him under the umbrella. He sensed the emotion and tension in Richard's voice. He wondered if this was the reason why he'd come all this way? It wasn't just to ask him why he had left. Richards needed to let off steam and express his feelings of anger and frustration. Donald expected his son to go on by stating what he thought of him for leaving his mother. Was it that simple? No, it couldn't be. There had to be more.

"We're you so unhappy that you just decided to walk out on the life you had built for us? We were living in a world you'd created. What went wrong? From being a small boy, you'd always impressed upon me that our family life was above everything else. You'd continually stressed the importance of giving support to the family above anyone or anything else. I believed you Dad, I really believed you. What changed? Something changed and I need to know what. I want to try and understand what happened that made you change. It was your sincerity which made me believe in you and made me believe you were telling me the truth."

The sound of the small waves gently cresting on the loose shale along the shoreline seemed to amplify their silence. The continuous splash of the diving birds was an echo in the distance.

Talking in a quiet voice as if the whole beach were crowded with people and he didn't want anyone to hear, Donald searched for words to responded to his son's outburst.

"Listen son, it wasn't like that, truly it wasn't."

"Truly, what's true anymore? Do you know, because I don't? The truth died for me the moment you walked out of our home. When I heard you'd left I was devastated, I just couldn't believe it. I kept telling myself this only happens in the movies to other peoples Mom's and Dad's not mine. Each day for weeks afterwards I expected to hear you'd come back, but it never happened"

Richard was now becoming very emotional and distressed.

"Son, you're right I did instill those values in you when you were small and strange as it may seem I still believed in them. No one did a better job of bringing up a child as your mother did. Taking care of the family, around the home she was a perfect mother. But I want you to try and understand that she was your mother, not my mother. I wasn't looking for a mother. I needed a wife, a person to love and share my life with. When you left and went to college your Mom and I were left alone. We had to start learning to live with each other all over again. We'd never lived alone with each other for over eighteen years. When it happened, it was like we were two complete strangers. We no longer knew how to communicate. It was terrible."

Donald continued searching for the right words to say.

"I started up the consulting business not only because I'd lost my job, I needed to get way and escape from the world I loathed so much. I began to enjoy the traveling and freedom of being on my own. After each trip I made, I hated going back home. I had nothing to go back to. Your mother and I made many feeble attempts to try and communicate which always ended up in an argument. In the end I got fed up with resisting and let her have whatever she wanted just to keep the peace. Even if I knew I was absolutely right about something, I would give in. I hated all the fighting because I knew as each day went by, we disliked each other more."

Donald paused and looked up. Richard was now sitting next to him staring out to sea watching the diving birds. Even though his son appeared not to be listening, Donald knew he had to continue.

"As your Mom and I grew old we both changed. Our interests, our values and even our personalities changed. When I looked around, I realized this was exactly how many other people we knew were living. Very few of them were living their lives the way they wanted to. We all adjusted our behavior and moods to please those around us. We end up living our lives as someone else because this was what was expected of us. It's as if we are all chameleons, constantly changing our behavior and appearance so we can blend into the environment around us. It's like a kind of camouflage that prevents anyone finding out what we are really like."

Donald picked up a piece of coral and began making patterns in the sand as he continued. He didn't notice Richard was no longer watching the cormorants.

"Many married couples stay together for decades and live their life in a world of total loneliness. So many people pretend they're happily married when they're not.

They're not happy; they are content and resigned to live the rest of their life existing in the prison they've created. The painful things about living like a chameleon is that it's so very lonely. I tried hard to explain to your mother just how lonely our life together had become. I don't know whether she told you or not, but I tried to get her to understand and accept the state our marriage had reached. It took a lot for me to explain to her that I was lonelier with her than I was without her."

Richard listened intensely and looked up to see the hurt in his father's eyes. Donald continued making twirling motions in the sand with the piece of coral. Richard's attention switched looking down at the patterns his father had made. It was the shape of a heart.

"Listen Richard, we meet few people in our life that we can totally rely on. If we're lucky, in a lifetime we find one or two people who we can call a real friend. When we come across a person like this, we open up our heart to them instinctively. Part of this is because we know we shall be accepted for what we are. This is how people get close to each other. In this type of relationship everything is open and honest, there's no pretending. It's this kind of relationship or bonding which forms the basis for true and everlasting love between a man and a woman. That bond never existed between your Mom and I"

Richards responded briefly.

James Caffrey

"All those years you and Mom were married did you never love her?"

"When your Mom and I started going out with each other we were only sixteen years old and we enjoyed each other's company. We were in love, but it was a very innocent and immature type of love driven by infatuation and lust. It was young love. In the family environment we lived a nice boy and girl met, courted for a few years and then got married. Just like in a fairy story. The problem is very few stories have a happy ending. It's not necessarily anyone fault when two people fall out of love. Love cannot survive without true friendship, it's as simple as that. This is a reality many people have to face. Do they accept the situation and live the rest of their life like a chameleon or do they do consciously change the way they are living? I decided to make the change. I am not saying I've made the right decision, only time will tell. Maybe I'll end up going back and begging your Mom for forgiveness. I had to leave. I needed to find the real person who is trapped inside of me. I could no longer continue to live like a chameleon. Do you understand what I am trying to say son?"

Richard did not respond sensing his father hadn't yet finished.

"Your mother and I lived in different worlds. In the end it was like living with a stranger, a person I'd never know. I am not putting all the blame on her Richard; this was the world we both played a part in

175

creating. Your Mom always seemed to be content to live in her own little world. What went on in my life no longer appeared to be important. With three brothers and three sisters, I had been brought up in a world full of love and affection. My mother ingrained love into all of her children. Your Mom couldn't handle the visible love and affection my brothers and sisters and I had for each other. This was one of the reasons why grandma and granddad hardly ever came over to our house. Whenever I suggested to your Mom that I wanted to invite them over we ended up having a big argument. You don't really know your grandparents, do you? You don't really know your aunts and uncles either. You'd like them, really you would, they are fun people.

Donald paused as Richard moved forward placing his hand on his father's arm.

"Listen Dad there's something I have to tell you. It's about Mom."

He stopped as Donald interrupted.

"What's happened? Something happened to your Mom hasn't it? Oh my God what have I done?"

Tears were beginning to form in Donald's eyes.

"What's happened Richard? Tell me what's happened? I need to know."

"Mom was caught stealing from a shop."

Donald felt temporary relief and couldn't restrain the volume of his voice as he cried out.

"Stealing from a shop? Oh thank God, I thought it was something more serious. I mean not that stealing isn't serious."

Suddenly the thoughts in Donald's mind switched.

"Oh my God, your Mom must have been frantic with worry hoping the neighbors wouldn't find out. Is there going to be a prosecution or court hearing? Oh I can image what was going through her mind. trying to handle the shame and embarrassment. When did it happen? Where did it happen?"

Richard voice was stern as he replied.

"Please let me continue, okay Dad? It's not important where or when it happened. Just listen okay."

Richard began searching for words rolling his eyes up in heads and nervously looking away not wanting his father to see his eyes filling with tears. He tried to compose himself.

"Mom had been seeing a psychiatrist for the past three years because it wasn't the first time she'd been caught stealing. There was a similar incident three years back but after the intervention of Doctor Ross the store agreed to drop the charges. This was done only on the condition she underwent therapy, and she did. As far I know there hadn't been any further incidents until this recent occurrence."

Richard was trying to continue the best he could but was having difficulty as his emotion began to get the better of him. Donald could now see the tears starting to form in his son's eyes.

"Yes your right Dad, Mom was beside herself, living in fear of people finding out. The shame and humiliation began eating away inside of her. You see Dad you are right; you knew her more than you thought you did. She became obsessed with what the neighbors would think if they found out."

Richard was now crying with tears streaming down both his cheeks.

"She's dead Dad. She couldn't face the shame. She's dead. She's gone. Gone forever.

Donald was dumb struck. He couldn't immediately absorb what his son was telling him. It was like a nightmare from which he wanted desperately to awaken. He didn't respond as he fought to comprehend what Richard was telling him. He'd anticipated bad news but not this...not this.

James Caffrey

"Did you hear what I said Dad? She's dead."

Richard's voice seemed to be coming from a long dark tunnel like an echo repeating the words, "she's dead, she's dead."

"What happened Richard, when did it happen? "

"Over two weeks ago. We had the funeral last week."

"Why didn't someone telephone me? I would have come straight home."

"I thought about calling you but decided it was better if I came and told you face to face. I felt I needed to be with you when you found out."

After an uncomfortable pause Richard started wiping his eyes as he began to explain to his father the sequence of events which had occurred.

"No one knew anything about the shop lifting until the police turned up at the house. The fact we had police cars coming to our house meant all the neighbors were aware there was a problem. At first, they thought it was something to do with you. Then an article appeared in the local press giving details of Mom's arrest. After that she never went out the house for weeks. She said she couldn't face the neighbors. The day she received the

179

summons to appear in court she was very upset. I tried talking to her and she attempted to explain to me about the shop lifting and why she does it, but the truth was she didn't really know."

Richard took a deep swallow and then continued.

"After a couple of days, she seemed to perk up then just after breakfast one morning Arthur called around to see her. I guess he must have heard all the talk around the neighborhood and came to give her some moral support. I like Arthur and I know he's been your friend for many years. Anyway, he and Mom went in the front room and had a cup of tea. They were talking for a long time then Mom got upset and rushed upstairs crying. I think everything just got too much for her. Arthur felt bad about it and kept saying he was sorry. That's all he kept saying, how sorry he was."

Arthur was a good friend and Donald knew him for many years. The guilt must have been burning deep within him to have picked up enough courage to go and see Allison. He could only guess but Arthur must have disclosed to Allison that he'd spilled the beans and told Donald of the affair she'd been having with Kevin. If Arthur did have a fault maybe he was a little too honest at times.

No matter what happened Donald knew there was no way his son would ever find out about his mother's indiscretion. He was listening intensely as

Richard continued.

"A few days later Mom got up one morning and said she felt a lot better. She took a bath and got ready. She put on her red dress, you know the one we both liked, remember? Anyway, she got ready and said she needed to go and see Doctor Ross about a new prescription. I offered to go with her, but she refused saying she need to get out on her own as it would help her. I can still see the smile on her face as she waved pulling away in the car from the house. She looked so smart, all dressed up. That was the last time I saw her alive. I didn't realize what was happening Dad, I didn't catch on. It will haunt me for the rest of my life. I should have known. When the police came to the house to inform me of the accident one of the officers was the same one who'd called regarding the shop lifting. I think he found it difficult conveying to me what had happened. I guess he felt guilty and partially to blame."

Donald felt the lump growing in his throat as he fought to control his feelings.

"Did she have a car accident? Is that how she died?

"The officer said that when he took a statement from the truck driver all he could get out of him was that the lady drove her vehicles straight at him. It happened on the A1 Motorway close to Darlington."

Donald had a puzzled look in his eyes.

"What was she doing way down there? That's nowhere near Doctor Ross's office. Where on earth was she going?"

"That's what no one could understand. The police asked me a lot of question about why she was taking that route. When the accident occurred, her car burst into flames on impact."

"What's on the Death Certificate?"

"Accidental death. What else could they have put."

Donald's emotions began clicking like a delayed reaction as he started soliciting a response from his son.

"This is all my fault isn't it? It's my fault. If I hadn't gone away this would have never happened. Oh God what have I done to the poor women. She'd never done anything to deserve dying this way. I was thinking of myself. I never for one minute stopped to consider her thoughts or her feelings. I was a selfish bastard that's what I was. Wasn't I?"

The response he anticipated from Richard never came.

"How can you live with someone all those years

and not know they are kleptomaniac? I was her husbands I should have known. I should have spotted something. I can't believe she was having treatment and I never knew."

"Dad you're the one who has just taken a great amount of time explaining to me your theory on chameleons. Maybe there is something in what you say. I guess many people do live their life hiding behind a camouflage. Don't blame only yourself, I didn't know anything about it either. How do think I feel? None of us knew Dad. There were no signs, nothing."

They both looked at each other their eyes searching for an answer. Spontaneously the both lunged forward and wrapped their arms around one another and started crying. Their bodies twitched and jerked with emotion. They cried for a long time. Slowly they began pulling themselves together and started walking towards the taxi. The driver had been watching them from a distance. As they approached, he had a puzzled look on his face as if to ask, "I know there is something is wrong and it's not good, but I don't know what it is." They got into the taxi and headed back to Judibana.

On the journey back Richard explained to his father he was booked on the afternoon return flight to Aruba. He was planning to stay overnight in Aruba before heading back home. Donald suggested that they both stay the night in Judibana but after a brief discussion he agreed to travel to Aruba with Richard. They both needed to spend a little more time together and this was a good opportunity.

He explained to Richard he'd left his overnight bag with the hotel porter, so he had enough clothes to carry him over until tomorrow. Richard never caught on and didn't question why his father had turned up with only an overnight bag.

Donald thoughts briefly switched to Leela and how they'd spent the night together. He needed to tell Richard about Leela, but this was not the right moment. He would tell him before he left Aruba to return to Venezuela.

CHAPTER VIII

Aruba, Dutch Antilles.

It seemed strange as they landed in Aruba because Donald hadn't expected to be back so soon. On the way from the airport they'd decided they would splash out a little and stay at the Sonnesta Hotel and share a twin room. They quickly checked in and then went to get something to eat. Donald suggested a small cafe where he'd eaten before. The food was good and the beer cold and cheap.

Entering the cafe, memories of his previous visit flashed through his mind. Nice thoughts of Julie also went through his mind. Richard was looking up at all the odd items which were hanging from the ceiling. Brightly painted watering cans, pieces of old cars, tires, steering wheels and even car fenders. Donald realized he'd never noticed them during his previous visit. How could he have missed then he thought?

During their meal they made light conversation about their food. They were both reflecting on what had happened and it was coming to grips with what had happened. It hadn't really sunk in with Donald. By the time they were on to their third beer, the staff were doing a shift change with the late crew coming on to take over. One of the newly arrived waitresses made her way over to their table.

"Hi, how are you? It's been some time since I saw you here. Few months ago wasn't it? With all your friends. Boy you guy's nearing drank us out of beer."

Donald didn't want to appear to be unfriendly, so he smiled. He could see the puzzled look on Richards face. He felt a little uncomfortable and although the girl was just neighborly, he wished she would walk away. But she didn't.

"Yes, you and your friends really hung one on that night, didn't you? They still come in here you know. In fact, they were here two nights ago. Yes, it was about two nights ago."

This caught Donald by surprise. They were still here in Aruba?

"One of the them works at a restaurant over in the Harbor Village complex. It's the restaurant owned by Michael Jordan; you know the famous basketball player. Yes, that's where she works at the Waterfront. Very striking young lady. American, I think."

Just then a group of people came in and the waitress left to go over and greet them.

"You seemed to be known here Dad. How long did you stay last time?"

Caffrey

"Oh only a couple of days."

There was a pause as Richard looked at his father waiting for him to continue.

"I met up with these people, two Australian guys and two American girls. They were travelling the Caribbean on holiday scuba diving. The island of Bonaire is rated one of the top three or four areas in the world for diving. Nice people, they were very friendly."

"Yeah, well how about when we finish off here, we go over to this Waterfront restaurant and see your friend eh? What's her name? "

"Oh her name." he stuttered.

"Oh it's probably Julie or Donna. Nice girls but we weren't real big buddies I only met them once or twice. She won't even remember me. We were all drinking and then we went gambling in the Casino to get free drinks. You see, when you gamble, even on the slot machines, they serve you with free drinks. We had a good laugh. Look, I can't see the point of going over there."

"Well let's go over and find out." Richard said eagerly with the beer starting to have an effect on him.

"Come on Dad, finish off your drink. Let's go, I can't wait to meet her. So you think it's Julie or Donna eh. Which one was the better looking one?"

187

"Oh I haven't a clue. I don't really want to go but if you insist."

The Harbor Town area wasn't far, so they walked. The night air and the drinks were starting to take an effect on Donald. He was beginning to get a warm glow inside of him. He needed to feel that glow to fill up the emptiness he'd felt since learning of Allison's death. It was still difficult accepting what had happened.

When they got to the Waterfront, there were a number of people waiting to be seated. Donald suggested they forget it and go somewhere else, but Richard wasn't having any of it. He wanted to go and have a drink at the Waterfront and tell his friends back home he'd been in Michael Jordan's restaurant. Even in England everyone had heard of Michael Jordan.

After a few minutes waiting the receptionist showed them to their table. Donald's appeared nervous with his eyes constantly scanning the room. They sat down and their waitress came over and introduced herself. After ordering two draft beers Donald explained to Richard the ritual the waiters and waitresses all went through.

Hi, my name is Sally and I'm your waitress for this evening. Have a nice day!

They both laughed quietly which made them feel

a little better. They were beginning to relax. Richard was about to say something but noticed his dad's head was turned to one side looking in the direct of the kitchen door. It was as if he was frozen, like in a trance. He looked over in the direction his father was staring. He could see a waiter talking to a lady who, appeared to be one of the supervisors or managers. She was dress in a black suit, very smartly dressed.

Richard called at the same time he waved a hand in front of his father's face.

"Dad. Dad. Hello, is there anybody there?'

Suddenly Donald snapped back to reality.

"Sorry son, I was miles away thinking of something else. I'm sorry I didn't mean to be rude"

"Is that one of the girls you met up with last time you were here? Is that her, the waitress talking to the lady?"

"Err! No son. No, that's not her."

Richard didn't have to wait long before he discovered what was going on. The girl who appeared to be the manager was walking straight over in their direction, making a bee line for their table.

"Hi Don. What a lovely surprise seeing you here

tonight. I had a feeling you'd turn up again, you know just a hunch. After all you didn't even bother to say good-bye the last time you left. I knew I would see you again though, woman's intuition and all that."

"Hello Julie, how are you? It's great to see you again. You look great. Oh sorry. Julie, this is my son Richard. Richard this is Julie."

They both gave a polite hello as Richard stood up and shook her hand. Julie hardly noticed Richard as she continued staring at Donald. The silence was a little embarrassing and was only broken when their waitress came with their beers. Richard was fascinated by the whole thing.

"So Julie how long have you been working here?"

"Oh I started just after you left. I'm assistant manager now. You look good Donald, all nicely tanned, Venezuela must be doing you good. Are you on your way back home?"

"No, I've just come over here with Richard whose being visiting me. He's on his way back to the UK so I thought I'd spend a little extra time with him."

"I get off within an hour. How about we all get together for a drink and you can tell me about your adventures in Venezuela. Is that okay with you guys?"

Donald didn't have to reply as Richard eagerly jumped in and agreed. Walking away from the table Julie was happy at seeing Donald again, but couldn't help feeling something wasn't right. She couldn't not put her finger on it. Something was different. Maybe he's just shy with his son being with him she thought
Richard was drooling as his eyes lingered watching Julie walk away.

"She gorgeous. You never told me she was so beautiful. She likes you doesn't she? She couldn't take her eyes off you"

Donald smiled with a gentle and shy embarrassed look on his face.

"She does dad. She really likes you. I can tell from the way she looked at you. It's going to be very interesting tonight; I can hardly wait. What's the other girls name, Donna was it? That's right Donna. Is she as attractive as Julie? You know there's just something about these beautiful blonde tanned American girls. She's like someone out of the movies."

Donald smiled at his son's comments, he could tell the few drinks they'd had were starting to have an effect on Richard. In fact, they were both beginning to cook on gas. He called the waitress over and order another round of drinks. He fancied a change, so he switched to whiskey ordering a Black Label and Perrier water. He'd missed his Polar and wasn't used to the

German and Dutch lager beers available in Aruba.

Donald son hadn't seen him drinking hard liquor before and was watching with interest as he poured the Perrier Watering into his whisky glass. It wasn't too long before he ordered another round of drinks. He didn't want to get drunk, but the comfort he felt with each drink helped to forget just a little more. How could he ever forgive himself for what had happened?

Just under an hour and three rounds of drinks later Julie appeared. Walking over towards them they noticed she'd changed and was now dressed in jeans, a summer top and a lightweight sleeveless waistcoat, or vest as the Americans call it. She looked different but just as lovely. She had been wearing her hair tied up but now it was just flowing long over her shoulders. It had grown quite a bit since the last time Donald had saw her.

"Okay, let's get out of here. Working here isn't bad but I need to relax in less familiar surroundings. Is that okay?"

They both nodded their approval, finished off their drinks and quickly settled the bill.

Walking along the harbor front Julie began telling Donald what had been going on since he'd departed. Scott had left but Donna and Pete were still here. Donna was working as a waitress and Pete had been getting casual work crewing on the large motor launches that go out deep water fishing. She'd been living on her own but had moved in with Donna who'd managed to rent a great apartment from a friend. She shared the rent and expenses with Donna, so everything worked out well. She was very candidate about her social life indicating she'd dated one or two guys but nothing serious.

Donald then went through the process of telling her what he'd been up to in Venezuela and where he'd been living. He explained how he'd been working on the hotel extension. The only thing he left out was Leela. He wished he'd called her before he left but had misplaced the telephone number, she'd given to him. He had however managed to leave a message with the girl at the hotel reception. He'd also left a message with the waiter whose brother had taken him to Falcon Ness. He hoped Leela would at least get the message from one of them.

Richard had been listening to the conversation absolutely fascinated. He'd never seen his father like this before, so relaxed, quietly confident, yet shy. It was strange.

They stopped at a small sidewalk cafe. Richard looked up at the neon sign above the door, "Rick's Place" They looked at each other and all nodded their heads in approval and walked in. Once they were seated, they he looked around soaking up the decor. Everything was thirties and forties style with posters of Humphrey Bogart and travel posters advertising Casablanca. The background music was also from the same era.

"You like it?" Julie asked.

"Yes" they both replied together.

Richard enthusiasm continued. "This is great. I really like this kind of place"

.

They all laughed. With the waiter hovering around their table, Julie ordered a white wine and soda, Donald continued with Black Label and Richard ordered a beer.

Julie was continually staring at Donald as the waiter put their drinks in front of them. She'd never stopped looking at him since they'd arrived. With a hint of concern in her voice she asked

"I didn't know you drank whisky Donald. I thought you were a beer drinker?"

"Oh I do every now and then. I guess I got used to the Venezuelan Polar beer. It's great, it doesn't bloat you like other beers do."

There was a strange feeling in the air that Julie could sense but couldn't put her finger on. At times he seemed the same, then there would be this vacate look in his eyes which she'd never seen before. Something was upsetting him which he was trying too hard to hide. She kept glancing towards Richard searching for a clue.

James Caffrey

Donald took a large gulp from his glass and got up from his seat.

"I need to go to the bathroom. I won't be long, be back in a minute"

He turned shakily and headed towards the toilet with a hint of a sway in his walk.

Julie watched him leave and had a look of concern on her face as she turned to Richard.

"Is he okay?"

"Yes, he's fine " he replied.

He knew what she meant. He'd only seen his Dad this way once before. His father hadn't really said too much about what had happened, and he had a feeling thing were beginning to reach home. He himself felt more relaxed than he'd done for several weeks, which made him feel a little guilty. At the same time though, it gave him a feeling of relief. It wasn't that he was being disrespectful to his mother, but more to the fact he was beginning to understand and accept what had happened. He also now had someone else to help share the burden he'd been carrying.

Julie and Richard passed the time away in polite conversation. As they talked, she constantly kept looking in the direction of the toilets, waiting anxiously for

Donald to return. All sorts of thoughts were racing through her mind. Here was a guy she'd only known and talked for a matter of hours, yet she felt more relaxed with him than she'd ever felt with anyone in her life.

She paused wondering why she felt excited, yet at the same time she was concerned and afraid.

Richard interrupted her thoughts.

"He's taking too long; I hope he's okay."

"Richard I've never seen him like this before. I mean I don't know your father well but tonight he appears to be upset. What's wrong? Has something happened?"

Richard paused for a moment not knowing whether to open up and explain why he'd come to see his father. He looked at Julie and seen a genuine look of concern in her eyes. He knew he had to tell her.

"I came to Venezuela to give my father some very sad news. I came to tell him my mother had died."

It seemed so much easier letting it come straight out. What was more difficult was the long silent pause that followed.

Julie's lifted both of her hands to each side of her face and joined them together she covered her mouth.

"Oh my God, I felt there was something wrong, but I never realized it was anything as serious as this."

She wanted to say more but didn't know what. Her mind was full of questions, but she knew they were not appropriate. She felt totally helpless. They both sat in silence.

Richard stood up and walked towards the toilets. After a brief moment he appeared on his own heading back to their table. As he got near, he shrugged his shoulders.

"He's not there, he's gone."

Julie's eyes scanned the room darting from left to right. "Where could he have gone to?"

Again, Richard shrugged his shoulders and sat down. He picked up his drink as Julie looked at him with a puzzled and caring look in her eyes. She picked up her drink and started gulping it down quickly. She motioned to Richard to finish his drink off.

"We'd better finish and go and see if we can catch him. I can imagine what's going through his mind. I hope he is going to be okay Richard."

"No wait, he couldn't have gone too far. He's going to be fine, sit down and relax. I think he needs a bit of space. He needs to be alone. I've felt this building up all day. The way he's been drinking going off on his own is exactly what he did when my grandmother died. He was devastated when his mother died, as was all of his family. It happened so quick and she was so young. I was only a boy, but I remember vividly what happened. I remember not only because grandmother had died, but also because of the great argument between my parents. Mom couldn't understand or accept that people handle grief in different ways. With Dad he needs to be alone. When he came home, he'd been drinking but he'd also been crying and that's when the row began. This was the first time I'd ever seen my father cry. It was a strange experience because even though I was a small child I wanted so much to put my arms around him and console him. I never realized fathers cried. It was terrible for the next few weeks, the tension in the house and living with them both not talking to each other was awful. I don't think either of them ever forgot what happened."

Julie had been listening to Richard but at the same time she was starting to understand a lot of what Donald had been trying to explain to her regarding his relationship with his wife. She also saw a lot of Donald in his son. He'd had the same knack of explaining things. making them sound simple and honest. He was easy to talk too but just as easy to listen too. Just like his father.

"Come on let's go, we'd better go and see if we can find him. He couldn't have gotten too far could he? I mean you know this island better than I do so where do you suggest we start. What places will be open at this time of night? "

They both finished their drinks, paid the bill and left. After searching several of the hotels and bars in the area they decided to head back to the Sonnesta Hotel. They knew he would eventually head back to the room.

When they arrived, they made straight for the night club. The band were playing the closing number of the evening or morning as it was now close to 1.00 am. Julie was talking to one of the ladies who served behind the bar. Richard got the impression that they knew each other. After a short period, Julie hurried back towards Richard. She didn't bother to stop as she beckoned to him.

"Come on, what room are you guys staying in? Were you both given a key each? I mean do you have your room key?"

"Yes" he replied, pulling out the plastic key card as they walked towards the elevator.

When they entered the room, it was in darkness. They could see the figure of Donald lying on top of the bed. His head was twisted in a strange way to the side, not quite on the pillow. The maid had partially turned back the sheets. He was still fully clothed, and it was obvious from the way he was lying that he'd d passed out.

Julie reached down to move his head in an attempt to make him more comfortable. In doing so the back of her hand felt the dampness on the sheets. She turned and looked a Richard and tears started forming in her eyes. Richard reached down and felt the damp sheets.

"He's being crying." he said with a slight choking in his throat.

Julie didn't know what to say or how to respond. She was trying to understand everything Richard had explained earlier in the evening. She desperately wanted to try to understand and accept, this was the only way Donald knew how to handle the grief within in his heart. It was the only way he knew how to release it.

"Come on Richard let's go downstairs to the coffee shop. We need to talk."

The next morning Richard was awakened by the sound of the shower running. He lay in bed pretending to still be asleep. Thoughts of sitting in the coffee shop with Julie in the early hours of the morning were going through his mind. She'd sat in total silence as Richard explained what had happened back home in England. When he'd finished, she stood up and asked if he would walk her to the taxi stand downstairs. With a brief peck on the cheek they said goodnight and she was gone. Strange he thought, not one single question.

Walking back into the hotel he realized he'd had

better call the airline and delay his return home.

Donald grabbed at Richard's exposed foot at the end of the bed making him jump.

"Come lazy bones lets go to breakfast. I'm so hungry I could eat a scabby horse."

With the ice broken Richard jumped up out of bed and quickly got into the shower. In a short space of time they were seated in the coffee shop.

Donald had been waiting for Richard to say something about his behavior of the previous evening, but he didn't. With a sheepish look on his face he nonchalantly decided to take the plunge.

"Did Julie get home OK last night?"

"Yeah, I got her home at about three o'clock this morning. We were worried about you Dad."

"Well I suppose I should have been honest and let you both know that I needed to be on my own. I also should have explained how I felt but on some occasion's words don't come easy. It's my fault. I didn't mean to offend either of you, it was just the mood I was in. I hope you understand, I needed to be on my own."

After a brief silence the waitress brought their breakfast. With his head down moving his knife and fork around his plate Richard decide to say what was on his mind.

"I don't know what it is Dad, but you are so different to the person I knew before. I mean in many ways you're the same, but in other ways you're just different. It's just hard trying to fathom out which is the real you or me for that matter."

Donald didn't answer but continued listening to his son as he ate.

"Julie is a very nice person. She was really concerned about you last night."

There was no response from Donald. Not that he wanted to appear rude, but more because he was embarrassed at how things had turn out. Lifting up his head Richard saw the look in his father's eyes that said it all. They both knew no further explanation was necessary.

"I've got to go and book my flight back to Venezuela. I am going to try and get on the afternoon flight. I also need to make a call to Hans and his family at Falcon Ness. They will be worried about me. They treat me like one of the family, it is a pity you never had time to meet them. What time is your flight out?"

"Listen Dad, if it's okay I would like to come back with you. I maybe being a little selfish, but I need to have more time with you, and I think we need each other at the moment. What do you say?"

James Caffrey

Donald was taken aback and a surprised by his son's decision.

"Sure it's okay, that'll be great."

His reply was very convincing.

"Are you sure Dad? I mean I know you've found a new life and I don't want to push myself on you if you still need to be on your own."

"Listen, you are my son and I love you very dearly. I didn't leave to shut you out of my life. I tried to explain on the beach at El Pico why I'd left. It would be great to have you with me for a while but what about your career? You have your Degree, so you need to think about the future, like getting a job?"

"Yes, I know but I was going to take some time off before I decide what I'm going to do with my life. I'm still not sure whether I want to go back and get my Masters. This is why I thought maybe getting away for a while will give me time to plan for the future. What do think Dad?"

"It sounds like a great idea. You'll enjoy Venezuela and love Falcon Ness. It's so beautiful up in the mountains. It's a great place to think and get your thoughts together."

Getting up to leave they hugged each other, and

both felt a tingle of excitement. They walked out of the restaurant and as they stood waiting for the elevator Richard turned to look at his father.

"I think you need to talk to Julie before we leave Dad. She really cares about you. She's a nice lady and a good friend."

"Yes you're right son, you're absolutely right. I'll give her a call as soon as we get our room".

Sitting on the bed waiting for Julie to answer the phone he was trying to get his thoughts together as to what he was going to say. All of a sudden, he heard her voice.

"Hello"

Her voiced sounded as if he'd woken her up.

"Hello" she said again, getting ready to hang up the phone as no one had answered.

"Hi, it's me Donald, I'm sorry if I woke you."

"No " she said quickly getting her herself together.

"Are you OK Donald? We were so worried about you. We didn't know where you'd gone too."

"Yeah, I'm Okay now." he said sheepishly.

"Look I'm sorry about what happened last night. I truly am." he stopped as she interrupted.

"Donald you don't have to explain anything. No explanation is necessary. I'm not saying I understand how you feel because I don't. Richard and I talked for a long time over many cups of coffee. I think we drank so much coffee that when I got home, I couldn't get to sleep. I guess I had a caffeine buzz on ".

They both began laughing which took the tension out of the conversation.

"Richard's coming back to Venezuela with me for a holiday. We're leaving today. I'm really looking forward to having him around for a while."

"You're going back today? You only just got here, why so soon?"

"I've still got the hotel extension to complete for Hans and I promised him I would finish it before the tourist seasons started. I have to go, I'm sorry I can't spend more time here. We're catching the afternoon flight so we will have plenty of time to get back up to the mountain before it gets too dark."

There was a long pause before Julie responded trying hard to hide her disappointment.

"Well it was great seeing you again. I suppose things are at least progressing slowly in our relationship. The only problem I have is that you keep disappearing on me. It's a good job I'm not the type who suffers from insecurity. Well at least this time you're saying good-bye to me."

They both laughed but she couldn't hide the sadness in her heart.

"Well I'd better go Julie. Thank you for everything. You're a very nice lady and you will always be in my thoughts. Maybe when you get fed up with Aruba you'll make the trip to Venezuela like you've always talked about "

"Oh yeah, for sure."

"Take care Julie and God Bless. Say hi to Donna for me."

"I hope everything works out for you Donald. Take care."

They both hung up. Once she'd put down the phone, she could no longer control her emotions. Throwing her head down on the pillow she began crying and continued to do so for a long while.

Donald had to make another call to Falcon Ness. After he'd finished explaining the events to Hans he was relieved to learn that Leela was still at her friends in Judibana. He was also happy to learn the staff at the Jardin Hotel had delivered his message. He knew he should have tried to call her. He could have gotten the number from Hans, but he just didn't know what to say over the telephone. He hoped she'd understand once he sat down and explained everything. It was then he realized that he truly missed her.

Driving in the taxi to the airport Donald realized that sometime between now and arriving in Venezuela he had to explain to his son about Leela. The problem was he didn't quite know where to start. Before he knew it, they'd checked in and the ten-minute flight was over. They were now landing at Las Piedras airport and he'd missed his opportunity.

CHAPTER IX

Paraguayan Peninsula, Venezuela.

They stood waiting in line with the other passengers filtering slowly through Immigration. The airport was extremely small and crowded with everyone chattering away in Spanish. There weren't many gringos to be seen, only the odd few construction workers from the refinery returning from their vacation. Donald told Richard to hang back and let the crowd proceed with their pushing and grabbing at the luggage. Richard just followed his father's lead. When the crowd began to clear they picked up their baggage and walked towards the exit. As they came through the door into the main waiting area, they both stopped in their tracks. Richard looked towards his Dad knowing he was looking at the same person.

She was standing on her own anxiously waiting for someone. She was the most beautiful girl Richard had ever seen. It wasn't just the way she was dressed which was in a simple short summer dress. There was an aura of innocent beauty and purity which radiated from her. Even the Venezuelans were looking at her. Suddenly a big smile spread across her face and she came rushing towards them. His father dropped his luggage. As she threw her arms around his neck, she whispered an array of Spanish words in his father's ear. Richard was dumb struck. It seemed to take forever before she stopped kissing and hugging his father. He couldn't wait to find out who she

As quickly as it had all started, she suddenly turned and said in very good English.

"Hi, you must be Richard, I'm Leela."

Richard went to shake her hand, but she leaned forward and kissed him on both cheeks.

"Come on, follow me. I have the jeep outside. We need to get a quick start to reach Falcon Ness before dark"

They loaded the luggage into the rear of the jeep and Richard climbed into the back seat with Leela and his Dad up front. Before moving off Leela reached over and kissed Donald gently on the cheek.

"I missed you." she said quietly in English.

During the journey they didn't talk much. Once they'd driven beyond Judibana Richard was preoccupied with looking at the scenery along their route. The vegetation appeared to get thicker as they moved further off the peninsula. While driving through Coro the sun was starting to set in the distance. The whole horizon was a blaze of orange and gold. The tips of the small clouds reflected the setting sunlight giving them a much lighter glow. It was beautiful. Up to now everything he'd seen about Venezuela was as his father had described, beautiful.

Then looking at Leela he thought, very beautiful.

The trip up the mountain was scary. Leela drove fast but she was a very good driver. She'd obviously made the trip many times which increased their comfort level.

Dusk was fading fast as the turned off the narrow mountain road into the entrance of the hotel. Hans and Carla were waiting at the door to greet them. Richard looked at his father and saw the gleam in his eyes which indicated he was happy to be home. Once they'd completed all the formal introductions Hans herded them all into the hotel. As they walked Richard notice Hans had his arm around his father's shoulder and they were laughing and joking.

Donald stopped and gestured to his son to come forward and walk with them. It all seemed so natural and warm. It felt good.

They sat drinking freshly brewed coffee. Donald felt he needed to explain what had happened and why Richard had come to Venezuela. He didn't go into the exact details leading up to the accident but gave them of what had occurred. They all felt the emotion and sincerity in his voice. Richard sat listening and noticed the look of concern and feelings that Hans and his wife had for his father.

Then there was Leela.

Richard tried hard not to keep staring at her, but it was difficult. Every now and then, when he thought no one was looking he would steal a glance her way. Just through the movement of her eyes he could tell she really cared for his father. It all felt so strange, he'd never imagined anyone else except his mother could possibly be a part of his father life in this way. He was also seeing his father in a different light. He'd changed so much from the person he'd know. He felt he was now beginning to get to know Donald as a person and not just as his father. Why had events taken this turn he thought? We never really know what life has in store for us.

During the course of dinner there was lots of lighthearted conversation. Hans mention to Donald that they needed to talk about another construction project but would discuss the details in the morning. Everyone was getting ready to retire for the evening when they suddenly realized no one had thought about where Richard would be sleeping. Fortunately, the hotel wasn't full so they agreed for now Richard would use the room next to Donald.

Hans and Carla said goodnight. Donald also got up and said he was tired and was going to bed. Leela was a little surprised and Richard spotted a hint of disappointment. As Richard got up, he turned and leaned towards Leela to whisper.

"My father has gone through a lot these past few days and will need a little time to get over what has

211

happened, please be patient with him. He may need a little space. He's still trying to come to grips with what has happened."

Leela smiled as she responded to his friendly gesture.

"Of course, it's understandable. He has hurt and sorrow in his eyes. I feel so helpless. What can I do to help him? He cares so much about people and he has so much kindness in his heart. He is a very special person to my family we all love him."

Richard smiled and said goodnight. Maybe it was part of sleeping in a strange bed, but Richard was up real early the next morning. He showered and got ready. He was walking through the dining room of the hotel when he heard movement in the area of the kitchen. He popped his head through the kitchen door.

"Good morning"

Carla looked up a little surprised to see Richard up so early.

"Bounios Dias Richard"

Going through the motion of lifting a cup to her mouth she pointed out towards the dining room.

"Coffee? Fresca."

James Caffrey

"Thank you " he replied walking out of the
kitchen in the dining room where he found the freshly
brewed coffee.

Once he'd filled his mug, he walked outside gently
sipping the hot drink. The sun was shining brightly even
though it was early in the morning. He stood on the patio
looking out across the valley and realized why his father
loved the place so much. The view was quite breathtaking,
and the air was so fresh and cool. He looked down the
driveway leading to the main road. Within the confines of
the hotel grounds the garden was like a colored carpet of
many different flowers. The orange and lemon trees laden
with fruit gave the whole scene a picture book effect. He
walked down in the direction of the main gate and sat
under a tree soaking up the atmosphere. Every now and
then an old car passed. Then an old man with three
donkeys walked by smiling and nodding his head,
obviously aware of the fact that Richard was not local and
therefore didn't speak Spanish.

It is strange, he thought to himself, being British I
assume everyone speaks English. When we find ourselves
in an environment where no one speaks our language we
feel totally inadequate and insecure. His concentration
was broken as he looked up through a gap in the trees. In
the distance, down the road which led to the village he
spotted a lone figure jogging up the hill. The person got
nearer then he realized it was Leela. He sat hidden
watching her as she approached. When she'd reached the

213

main gate, she stopped and sat on the wall and started untying her running shoes. Even with her hair tied back with a sweat band and her body covered in perspiration, she looked beautiful. He'd been watching her for a short period and felt to embarrassed to make her aware of his presence. It was as if by some animal instinct she quickly turned and looked in his direction.

"Oh for a moment you scared me."

"I'm sorry, I didn't mean to scare you. I was sitting here soaking up the splendor and beauty of the place. It's so peaceful here."

A broad smile filled her face.

"Yes, it is. Maybe it's because I have lived here most of my life that I don't really appreciate the beauty of Falcon Ness."

She got up and began walking towards the hotel. Richard got up and walked alongside her.

"So Richard, how long are you going to stay here?"

"Oh I am not too sure at the moment. Probably for two or three weeks, that is if we can work something out on the accommodation. I don't want to leave Dad on his own after what has happened. I thought a few weeks

214

together will help him get over things a little better. He suddenly realized what he'd said. Oh don't get me wrong I don't mean that you and your parents will not support him. In fact, I know he's in good hands when he's here with you all. I just had this feeling in Aruba of wanting to be with him. Maybe I feel we can both help each other to get over what has happened. I have an urge to get to know him as the person he is now and not just my father. It's a strange but exciting feeling."

Leela didn't reply but smiled at Richard acknowledging she understood how he felt. As they neared the main house she looked up and saw her mother hanging out the washing. She waved and greeted her. There was a hint of concern on Carla's face which puzzled Leela. Maybe Mama and Papa had a disagreement she thought.

"Good morning."

Donald's voice surprised them both.

"Buenos dias." Leela replied, kissing Donald on the cheek as she passed him and continued walking into the house to take her shower.

"Dad it's so beautiful here. Now I know your secret."

Alerted by the voices outside Hans came out of the hotel on to the patio area.

"Good morning. I hope you both slept well? Listen Donald we need to talk about an item of business. If it's okay can we do it now or do you want to wait until later?"

"No, now is fine. Let's talk."

"Well I 've been thinking, we need to sort something out more permanent with your accommodation. What came to my mind was the cottage down near the gate. If we can get it fixed up maybe you and Richard could stay there for a while. At least as long as he's here?"

Both Donald and Richard looked in the direction of the gate.

"I know it will need some work to fix it up, but it is not too bad. I used to lease it out as a holiday cottage to the Americans working at the refinery. Then there was an incident a few years back that wasn't good. Someone broke in during the night and tried to steal some of the guest's belongings. Anyway, the intruder had a gun and so did one of the Americans. There was gun fire, but no one was killed. We knew who the intruder was but as he is the nephew of one of the most powerful judges in Coro no one could touch him. I'm telling you this because I want you to know the background of the place before you decided."

Donald paused for a moment then walked over to Hans and put his arms around his shoulder.

"That's great Hans, great and I am so grateful to you and your family."

Grinning like a Cheshire cat he turned to Richard.

"Well it looks like you have got yourself a job, painting and decorating?"

They all laughed and as the joking subsided Hans motioned for them to sit down at one of the tables.

"There is something else that I want to talk to you about. On the Coro side of the mountain overlooking the Lake there are many beautiful villas. Many of the wealthy Venezuelan's use these villas as holiday homes. Well, I have a good friend, a business associate, who came to visit me while you were in Aruba. He was impressed with the quality of the hotel extension. When I mentioned the part you have played in the project he asked to meet you. He needs to know if you would be prepared to build a new villa for him? I told him I would talk to you when you got back. He has the architectural drawing already drawn up and the land has been graded ready for construction. If you are interested and feel comfortable with taking on the project, he wants you to cost out the program and name your fee. What do you think?"

Donald was taken by surprise, but it didn't take

him long to agree to the meeting.

"Good." said Hans, rubbing his hands together.

"He has invited us all to his restaurant in Coro for dinner on Saturday night. It will be a great evening of good food, dancing and great music. This will give us all a chance to enjoy the night life of Coro. It will also give us a chance to welcome Richard to Venezuela eh? You'd better be careful Richard the Venezuelan girls are the most beautiful in the world."

They got up shaking hands pleased with the outcome of their discussion then all went in to breakfast.

During breakfast, Hans told Carla and Leela of the plans for Donald to move into the cottage. They agreed that after a quick coat of paint they could probably move in within the next few days. The rest of the upgrading could be done as needed. Carla was watching Leela and saw the happiness in her eyes. When Hans went on to explain the villa project, the gleam in Leela eyes got even brighter.

When they'd finished breakfast, Donald asked Hans if he could go and have a look around the cottage and get a feel for what needed to be done. Once he had the keys in his hand he headed off down the drive. Richard thought he would follow but saw a look on Leela's face which told him she needed to be alone with his father. He then turned and headed back to his room.

Donald looked around the place. It wasn't half as bad as it looked from the outside. He like the large stone fireplace; it gave the place a rustic look. It was bare of furniture, so he wondered whether he was meant to purchase some items.

"The furniture is stored in the barn at the back of the hotel."

He turned and saw Leela standing. She must have read his mind.

"We can get this place fixed up in no time at all."

He started walking over towards her and she reacted by holding out her hand towards him.

"Listen Donald I need to say something. I can't say that I know how you feel because I don't. All I want you to know is that I'm here for you. I shall be close by to help you in any way I can to get over the tragedy which has occurred. I'm not going to say all the things other people would say like it's not your fault so don't feel guilty. You feel anything you need, and I shall understand. Grief is a very personal experience which leaves many scars. It can take time but eventually they do heal."

"Oh Leela." Donald cried putting his arms around her and squeezing her close to him.

"She was a good woman. She didn't deserve to die, not that way. I never knew about the shop lifting and the police. Why was I so blind? I Was so wrapped up in my own dreams that I failed to see she needed help! Is this the price I have to pay for my happiness? Why was I so arrogant to think only I had been living the life of a chameleon."?

Leela was baffled. Chameleon? In her mind she was trying to put the pieces of the jigsaw together. They stood embracing and she felt warm teardrops falling on to her bare shoulder.

Richard had stopped at the front door of the cottage when he'd heard voices. He stood listening and wanted desperately to reach out and help his father. He felt the anguish and torture which was twisting his father's heart. He also realized Leela was in love with his father. What was difficult to judge was how his father felt about her.

In a strange way he was jealous. She was extraordinarily beautiful and voluptuous. The natural movement of her body aroused his manly instincts. He tried to rationalize his thoughts. How had this beautiful young girl fallen so deeply in love with his father? He didn't intend any form of disrespect but Leela was not only beautiful she was twenty years younger than his father. She was nothing like his mother. He pulled himself together. He had to stop thinking this way.

James Caffrey

Walking into the cottage Richard deliberately called out loudly.

"Hello. Anybody here? Dad are you here?"

"Yes through here son"

"Hi, oh sorry did I disturb you?"

Richard sounded apologetic, Leela and Donald responded by moving slightly apart.

"No not at all son. We're just talking about what we can do to fix this place up"

Leela didn't move away from Donald but kept her arm around his waist, like a friendly gesture of territorial rights.

"Come on Richard lets go. Leela said there is a barn full of furniture for us to sort through at the back of the hotel. We have to get to work. Do you feel in the mood?"

"Sure, I'm ready to go. I have to earn my bread and butter, so let's go."

Walking to the barn Leela felt the close bond of friendship which existed between Donald and his son. She was happy for him. She was a little concerned because she had noticed Richard looking at her in a

221

strange way.

Over the next few days the transformation of the cottage took place. Donald worked on the inside while Richard concentrated on the outside. While they worked, Leela kept showing up adding little woman's touches which turns a house into a home. Eventually when they'd finished, they invited Hans and Carla down to review their efforts. They could hardly believe their eyes. Carla toured the cottage inspecting each room from top to bottom. Walking around the cottage she occasionally touched items and constantly nodded her head as a gesture of approval. They all agreed a miracle had taken place. They decided to celebrate with a bottle of champagne. When they'd finished the bottle, Hans reminded everyone that they all needed to go and get ready for their dinner engagement. They agreed and decided they would leave at seven.

During the trip to Coro Hans explained to Donald that their host's name was Alphonso. He'd started off as a small contractor working with the larger American construction companies in the refinery. His interested then diversified into many other activities including, property development, transportation, catering and a restaurant business. It was also rumored he was a major shareholder in the Bank of Maracibo. At the end of the conversation, he casually mentioned that Alphonso was also the Commander of the local DISIP police unit. He went on to explain that this was a special police force unit similar to a SWAT team. Donald and Richard looked at each other not knowing what to think. Hans saw the look of concern on their faces and laughed telling them not to worry. Alphonso was a great guy and they would like him.

They arrived at the Jardin Familar just before 8:00pm. Upon entering the restaurant, they were immediately spotted by the head waiter who'd anticipated their arrival. Suddenly a loud and cheerful voice was greeting them.

"Hans. Senor Hans, Hola."

They all turned and walking towards them was a distinguished looking gentleman in his early forties. After all the kissing and hugging, Donald and Richard were formally introduced to Alphonso. They quickly realized the ability to speak English was very limited. His greeting sounded as if he had been rehearsing all day, but his beaming smile spoke a language all of its own.

"Welcome to the Jardin Familiar"

Donald and Richard both smiled and nodded their heads.

Once they'd sat down the waiter immediately took their order for drinks. Donald and Richard sat in silence as the conversation around them continued in Spanish. Their eyes scanned the room around them. The decor was very rural with bare stone and red brick walls. Large dark beams stretched the whole length of the ceiling. In one corner was a small grotto with rocks and plants and a waterfall with running water. Multicolored lights hidden among the shrubs high-lighted the effects. Although everything had a touch of simplicity, it had been tastefully blended into the atmosphere of the restaurant.

The conversation was still continuing in Spanish with the rest of the group occasionally breaking out in load laughter as Alphonso or Hans cracked a joke. Alphonso had a contagious laugh which was close to being a loud giggle. Donald and Richard listened trying to get a feel for the subject under discussion but without success. They were talking so fast. Their attention strayed to other activities going on around them. The restaurant was full. Most tables consisted of large family groups. Everyone seemed to be talking at a fast pace and very loud. It was as if there were in competition with the group on the next table.

The band was getting ready to play. Richard counted the number of musicians in the band. It was fourteen and they were all girls! He couldn't believe it. Back home most bands had four or five musicians or six at the most. He checked out the girls in the band one by one. Now he realized what Hans had meant about the Venezuelan girls. Some were more attractive than others, but they were all very appealing to the eye, especially in the tight hot pants they wore. His eyes discreetly continued scanning the room. There were lot of very attractive woman in the restaurant. Most of them wore extremely tight fitted clothes. The height of the hemline of their skirt best described as being dressed in a wide waist belt. He had never seen a woman dressed in such a short mini. It was very difficult not to stare especially as he didn't want to offend any of the groups around him.

Every now and then Alphonso would look at Donald or Richard and smile. It was a warm and happy smile that made them both feel comfortable. The waiters hovered around their group eagerly to please their boss and his guests. No sooner had someone finished their drink when another one would immediately appear. They also served a continuous stream of food. One of the dishes was scallops coated with grilled cream cheese, served on large seashells. It was fantastic. Leela smiled over at Donald trying to attract his attention. Eventually she managed to quietly inform both he and Richard they should leave room in their stomach for the main meal, but it was too late, they'd eaten their fill.

When the band struck up their first number Hans and Alphonso stood up and beckoned to the group to move over to the dinner table. No sooner had they sat down, when the waiters started placing large platters of food in the center of the table. There was a mixture of chicken, beef and seafood. They all looked great, but Richard and Donald were already bloated with the snacks. During the meal Leela explained the different traditional dishes of the area so Donald and Richard had to make an effort to at least taste them. They were amazed at the appetites of the other members of the group. They'd eaten as many snacks but still found the room to devour huge plates of food. The drinks just kept flowing to wash the food down. Two large bottles of Johnny Walker Black Label were placed on the table with a bucket of ice. The feeling of a fiesta began to take over the place.

The dance floor was now crowded with couples dancing to extremely loud and fast Latin music. The rhythm was having a hypnotic effect on the dancers. Even Richard could not prevent himself from tapping his hands and feet.

As the evening wore on, the atmosphere in the restaurant developed into a carnival. Hans, Carla and Alphonso were now constantly laughing and drinking the Black Label. Donald, Leela and Richard were also beginning to warm up with the combination of a few drinks, great food and loud music. Without saying a word, Leela stood up and reached out for Donald's hand. At first, he just shook his head in a reluctant and shy manner but eventually responded to Leela's perseverance. When he stood up and began walking towards the dance floor Richard's mouth dropped open in sheer disbelief. This in turn changed to amazement as he watched Leela and his father start to dance.

The band were in full swing playing a fast meringue number. Donald and Leela were totally emerged into the frenzy of the Latin music along with the rest of the crowd on the floor. Richard looked down the table and caught a glimpse of Alphonso looking at Hans and his wife slowly nodding his head in approval at the dancing performance of Leela and his father. The song and the music seemed to go on forever. Richard continued to stare in disbelief. Where? How? When? he thought, had his father learned to dance this way? Even taking into consideration that Leela was a great dancer the hip movements of his father was as good as the indigenous people on the dance floor. Eventually the music finished, and everyone cheered and clapped. When Donald and Leela started walking back to their table the people at the tables around them clapped and complimented them. Everyone was happy.

Alphonso reached over and shook Donald's hand placing his other hand on his shoulder.

"Buenos, Senor Donald." Alphonso said loudly with a large grin on his face.

Donald sat down feeling hot and sticky. He looked over towards Richard who smiled back and winked. When Leela returned to the table she sat next to Donald. Putting her arm around his neck, she leaned over and kissed him. Her sign of affection was spontaneous done very openly and although it was done with instant feelings, the wine had made her a lot bolder.

During the rest of the evening Hans and Alphonso remained locked together in deep conversation and although they periodically smiled at each other and shook hands several times, it was obvious that they were discussing business. Eventually Hans stood up signaling to everyone that it was time to call it a night. They completed the formal farewells and they all climbed into the jeep and headed off for home. Within a short period Leela and Carla were both asleep. Richard sat dozing but listening to Hans talking to his father about the building project he had been discussing with Alphonso. Strangely though, Richard wasn't uncomfortable about the fact that Hans had been drinking at the restaurant. He would have been very concerned if it had been back in England. It was also comforting to know that Hans knew the road up the mountain like the back of his hand.

As they pulled into the driveway of the hotel Leela and her mother awoke. Richard got out of the jeep at the gate and made his way into the cottage. Donald remained in the vehicle and after a brief silence Hans continued towards the hotel. They all got out of the vehicle with Leela saying she was going to make some coffee. Hans and Carla both said they were going straight to bed. Hans shook Donald's hand saying they would discuss the villa project the next morning. He smiled as he looked at the clock on the wall realizing it was now morning. Carla walked over to Leela and kissed her goodnight. She then walked towards Donald and as she gave him a peck on the cheek she whispered in English.

"You are a good dance for a gringo. You dance well with Leela"

Donald's mouth fell open in amazement. He'd never heard Carla speaking English before and never realized that she could.

Leela and Donald sat drinking their coffee.

"Leela I really enjoyed myself tonight. In fact, I always enjoy being with you."

She didn't reply but smiled waiting for him to continue.

"I don't know what it is Leela, but I just feel so good when we are together. It's a feeling I have never experienced before. It feels like going on a roller coaster at the fairground. The thrill of knowing it's going to be a dangerous but craving the pleasure of being scared out of your wits."

Leela still never spoke but continued looking at Donald. Slowly she leaned forward inviting him to kiss her. Donald responded tenderly kissing her on the lips. He felt her react as he began kissing her on her neck. Slowly his kisses moved over to her ears then gently he kissed each of her closed eye lids. Although the emotion they were both responding to was exciting, they both felt that their true feelings of passion were being controlled deep down inside.

Donald moved away whispering soft in her ear.

"We'd better go. It's getting late"

Leela responded moving closer to him and taking

a firm grip of him with her arms.

"No, not yet. I need to talk to Donald, if it's okay with you?"

Donald placed his arms around her waist signifying his concurrence.

"I want you to know how I feel, so I'm going to, how do you say, jump in with both feet. I've fallen in love with you Donald. You're such a nice kind person and a good man. I've never felt about any man the way I do about you. It's because I love you that I know it's right for us to be together this night. My heart tells me it is right for us to make love. I feel you also love me and that our love for each other is pure."

She paused and waited for a reaction which never came. His silence and lack of response gave concern indicating she'd picked the wrong time and the wrong place.

"Leela I truly feel the love and the affection you give to me. I want so desperately to respond and show you what I feel in my heart. Have I fallen in love with you? My heart is too heavy at the moment to truly know what I feel. It's just too soon after everything that's happened. I need a more time to let those scars you talked about heal. I'm sorry but it's just too soon."

He gently moved away, turned and walked back

down the hill towards the cottage. Leela remained there
watching him as he walked away.

Richard was on the verge of drifting into a deep
sleep when he heard the door of the cottage open. He
heard the sound of his father's bedroom door closing. He
began thinking over what his father had told him about
people being chameleons. The more he thought of it the
more he began to realize there was a lot of truth in what
he'd said. As he fell asleep, his thought then drifted to his
mother.

The following morning Donald awoke with the
sun streaming in through the gap in the curtains. He
jumped out of bed and put a fresh brew of coffee on,
then jumped into the shower. He dressed quickly as if he
was late for work. In reality he wanted to walk down
towards the village and meet up with Leela returning
from jogging. With as fresh mug of coffee in his hand he
started walking down the hill. Getting nearer to the village
he was surprised that he'd not yet met up with her.
Approaching the bridge over the river he looked down
and saw her. She was sitting on the riverbank with a piece
of a twig in her hand swishing it around in the water. He
waited a while watching her. Quickly she turned startled
by the sound she'd heard behind her.

"Buenos Dias" she called at the same time patting
the grass next in a motion for him to join her.

"Good morning"

He felt shy and a little uncomfortable, not knowing how she was going to react after last night. Sitting down he took hold of her hand.

"Listen. I am sorry if I disappointed you last night. But let me clarify one thing about how I feel. There's not a day that goes by where I don't think about what it would be like making love to you."

She started to reply but he gently put his finger to her lips.

"No, wait I haven't finished. I need to explain how I really feel."

After taking a deep breath he resumed.

Leela when I look at you, I see a beautiful young lady full of warmth, affection and vitality. I then look at myself in the mirror and wonder just what can you possibly see in someone like me? I also try to rationalize and wonder what I can offer you?"

She squeezed his hand as he continued.

"I want so much to return the love and affection I truly feel you are giving, but in an old-fashioned way, I am shy and not used to the attention and affection I am getting."

He paused finding it difficult to continue but he
wanted to clear what was on his mind.

"I need to talk to you about Allison and why I left.
It's important you know exactly what took place and why.
Allison was not a bad person, in fact she was a great
mother to Richard, the best. The problem was that we'd
forgotten how to communicate with each other. Don't get
me wrong, we talked but when we did neither of us
listened. There was no interest. Over a period of years, we
slowly drifted apart. In the process, the feelings we had
for each other died. It was all such a waste of time. I
suppose Allison was prepared to continue the charade
forever, but I wasn't. I had to get away. Before I left, I
tried hard to explain to her how I felt in my heart. She
just didn't understand what I was talking about. It was if I
was talking to her in Spanish. When I left, I didn't really
know where I was going or what I hoped to find. Now I
realize that once we turn our back on a part of our life, it
can never be the same. There's no turning back the clock.
I feel responsible for what has occurred, yet I wonder
what would have happened if I'd stayed. From the
moment I met you I came alive. I felt for the first time in
my life I'm not living like a chameleon. What you and
everyone else sees is the real me and I feel great about it. I
know I'm a good person and I can feel it. The people I've
met, even total strangers, have made me feel good about
myself. I've never felt like this before. The difficulty I'm
having is that I feel so remorseful about how my actions
has effect other people's lives. This remorse or guilt I am
experiencing is because I feel happier than I have ever felt

in my whole life and I am afraid."

He moved closer to Leela.

"I love you Leela and I feel I always will. The thought of spending the rest of my life with you not only excites me, it also scares me. I never dreamed I'd be so lucky to find someone like you."

"Oh Donald," She wrapped her arms around him as her body began shaking with emotion.

"Don't cry, please don't cry Leela"

"I can't help it; I too am so happy. So very happy. I love you."

They walked the rest of the distance back arm in arm. Nearing the hotel Carla called to Leela that her brother was on the telephone from Caracas. Leela walked straight through to her room and picked up the phone.

During the process of their greetings, Leela sensed something wasn't right. Alberto was his usually friendly self, but she could tell there was something hidden in the tone of his voice which wasn't right.

During their conversation Alberto asked about Donald.

"How is Donald getting along? Mama told me

about the new construction project. I guess this means he will be staying on longer eh? I know this makes you happy Leela and I am happy for you. How's everything else going? Is Donald's son having a good time? How does he like Venezuela?"

"Oh things are fine. Yes I'm happy and I'm not saying anything else on this subject okay! Richard really likes the place and he is helping Donald out with a number of things".

There was a silent pause then Alberto continued.

"Mama told me what happened to Donald's wife. I'm so sorry. I don't know what else to say. Is Donald there or has he left already?"

"No he's here. Do you want to talk to him?"

"Yeah. Why not after all he might be my future brother in law." he said teasing Leela but trying to be casual and nonchalant about it.

"Hold on, I'll get him for you."

She put down the phone on the small table next to her bed. She called to Donald.

"Donald, Alberto wants to talk to you."

Donald entered the room with a puzzled look on

his face. Leela responded by shrugging her shoulders.

"Hi Alberto. How is Caracas?" Leela stared at Donald watching for a hint or a clue as he listened to Alberto.

"Well how is college? When are your finals?......Whow.. that's not too far away. Oh so you're coming here this weekend, great. What was that?.... getting here Saturday morning? All right we look forward to seeing you. Take care of yourself and keep studying hard okay."

Donald hung up the phone.

"What was that all about?" Leela asked.
"I'm not quite sure but he wants me to meet him next Friday evening in Coro"

"But I thought he said he wasn't coming here until Saturday?" she responded.

"Yes I know. He said not to mention to your mother and father about wanting to meet me on Friday night. He's told your mother he's arriving on Saturday"

"I shall go with you " Leela replied very firmly.

"He said he wanted to talk to me, alone."

"He's my brother Donald and something is wrong

and know there is. I need to go. I need to be with him if he's in trouble".

" Listen Leela, I know Alberto is you brother and I know you love him. This is all the more reason you should realize that if there is something on his mind and he wants to handle it this way, you should respect his wishes. If he felt he could talk to you or your mother and father don't you think he would."

Leela didn't reply. She knew Donald was right. Her mind was spinning wondering what it could be. Alberto had always been a very shy person. Even during their school days he was one of those guys who just drifted on the outside of the main pack. Everyone liked him but he didn't want to be bothered. Serval of Leela's girlfriends, although a few years older than Alberto, were attracted to him. He'd never really had a steady girlfriend she thought. He would rather spend his free time studying or playing the piano. He loved his music.

They walked out of the bedroom and Donald put his forefinger to his lips gesturing not to say anything. Carla was giving direction to one of the hotel staff. When she heard them approach, she asked Leela in Spanish?

"Como?"

"Oh he just wanted to let us know he is coming here next Saturday morning. He hopes to go fishing in Lake Coro with Donald and wanted to make the arrangements"

Carla nodded her head and walked away. They both headed for the coffee pot and as they sat down Hans walked in bellowing.

"Good morning. Isn't it a lovely day? I am glad you are both here I need some help. Leela I need you to go down to Las Peidras today and meet the Aruba flight. We have four guests arriving, two Dutch and two Americans. They're booked for a week, but the Americans may stay on a little longer. Can you do that for me?"

She hugged her father.

"Yeah sure Papa. Give me the keys to the jeep".

As Leela walked away Hans turned to Donald.

"What about you Donald? What's your program today are you going down to the Villa?"

"Yes, I think I shall ride with Leela. I only need to call in and check on the workmen then I have to call in at Coro to purchase more materials. After that I can go with Leela to the airport and help her with the new guest. If that's okay?

"Sure, there's plenty room in the jeep."

Hans called out to Leela.

"Donald going with you".

She walked back into the room with a big smile showing on her face. Twirling the keys around one of her fingers, she twisted her head provocatively back over her shoulders looking at Donald. With a quick motion of her neck she swished back her long hair and signaled to Donald they were ready to leave.

"Come on let's go, I'll drive"

He followed her out to the jeep laughing at her antics. He really loved Leela's sense of humor. When he'd climbed into the jeep, Leela turned and looked back at the hotel. When she was sure that no one was watching she leaned over and kissed Donald.

The call in to the villa to check progress was brief. The workmen had developed a good understanding with Donald, and they were working well. After being satisfied that everything was okay they proceeded on their way. After a stopping and loading a few small supplies they left Coro.

During the rest of the journey Donald could tell that Leela was thinking of her brother. He could see the puzzled and searching look in her eyes. The radio was playing romantic music and occasional she would look over in his direction and her beautiful big smile would beam out. His response would be a quick wink of the eye which just made her smile more.

His mind drifted thinking of how he really loved the affection Leela gave to him. She was so open with her feels. At any given moment she would hug him, kiss him, or even just give a look that told him she loved and cared about him. He couldn't help but compare her to Allison. He realized what he'd missed during all those years he and Allison were together. Even when he was young and courting, he never experienced the feelings he had now. The more he continued to think about it the bigger the tingle grew deep inside. Where was this all going to lead, he thought. He needed to sit down in a quiet place and have a serious talk with her. Although he loved her there are so many other factors to consider in making a long-term commitment. It's wasn't only the age difference which concerned him. He felt fear that if he loved her too much and ever lost her, he wouldn't be able stand the pain and anguish. Maybe it was the fear of being unhappy and hurt that was holding him back. The opportunity to discuss how he really felt had just never been there. They arrived at the airport just as the plane from Aruba was landing. Good timing.

They stood together waiting for the passengers to come through Immigration and Customs. The porters were already unloading the luggage. Slowly the passengers began to drift out. The newly arriving gringos walked out with a bewildered look on their faces. They spotted the Dutch couple very quickly, both tall and fair.

The crazy rush following the flights arrival began to clear and they were still waiting for the two Americans to appear. They were at the stage where they began to think maybe they'd missed the flight or maybe they were having a problem with their visas. Suddenly they appeared.

"My God " he said quietly, but not quietly enough so that Leela couldn't hear him.

"What is it? What's wrong? Who is it, do you know them?"

He didn't have to answer.

"Donald. Oh my god it's Donald."

Leela stood her ground as the two American girls ran over and both wrapped their arms around Donald hugging and kissing him. Leela felt a twinge of jealousy.

"Hi ladies, how are you both. Oh I am sorry let me introduce you. Julie, Donna this is Leela."

Leela greeted them both politely but with a little sarcasm in her voice.

"Hello. How are you? Donald has told me so much about you both. Shall we go? The transport is outside."

Once a Chameleon

Leela turned and walked away towards the exit. She could hear Donald and the two girls chatting away as they collected the bags and began following her.

Once they'd loaded the luggage they were soon on their way. The Dutch couple sat in the front talking with Leela, mainly asking tourist type questions. It's seemed odd that they were Dutch, Leela was Venezuelan, yet they conversed to each other in English. As they were talking, she occasionally looked back through the rear-view mirror checking on Donald and the girls. It was very difficult for her to concentrate on the question the Dutch couple were asking because she was trying to listen to the conversation going on in the back of the vehicle.

By the time they'd left the peninsula and reached the road leading up the mountain, Leela had listened to the two girls explaining to Donald about their jobs in Aruba and about two other friends he obviously knew. Well the other two were guys. In a funny sort of way this made Leela feel better.

As they got farther up the mountain everyone's attention switched to the beautiful scenery. It never ceased to amaze Leela just how beautiful it was even though she had lived there most of her life.

They soon reached the hotel and turned in to the driveway. When they were passing the cottage Leela slowed down as Richard was sitting on the patio drinking a cold beer. Leela pulled down the window and called out to Richard.

"Come on up to the house. We need help with the luggage, okay."

They continued to drive as Richard got up and began following them. Donna and Julie looked at each other as Donna asked.

"Wow, and just who is that hunk? He's gorgeous. Is he here on holiday as well?'

Donald didn't answer neither did Julie, but as Leela looked in the mirror she smiled. Somehow, she now felt a little better. While they were getting out of the vehicle Richard approached walked up to Leela a pecked her cheek then putting his arm on Donald shoulder.

"Well what a welcome. Don't we all get one of them?" Donna asked.

Before Richard could respond Donald jumped in.

"Julie you've met Richard. Donna I would like to introduce you to Richard.... my son."

Donna and Julie looked at each other and started giggling. Everyone else picked up pieces of luggage and walked into the hotel to be greeted by Hans and Carla. Leaving the guest to register, Donald walked into the bar area and Richard followed.

"Oh I could kill for a Polar." Donald gestured placing his hands around his sons' neck. He reached into the refrigerator and popped open a cold beer then stuck twenty bolivars in the cash register then sat down.

"So Richard did the sand and blocks get delivered to the Villa?

"Yes. Hans has a friend in the village who has a small truck which I rented for the day. We now have enough material for the rest of the week."

Richard stopped talking as the new guest walked into the bar area.

Julie picked up Donald's beer

"So Donald this is the famous Polar you've talked so much about."

She turned to Richard.

"Hi Richard, it great to see you again. Are you enjoying yourself up here in this little piece of paradise your father has found? It's absolutely beautiful. How on earth did he ever find it."

She walked over to the window facing out on to the patio and continued to soak up the gorgeous view. Hans walked in and immediately took up station behind the bar.

"So, what would everyone like as a welcome drink?
I see you've taken care of yourself Donald. The journey
must have been dusty and dry."

"Two Polars for the ladies." Donald replied.

"Do you have any Dutch or German beer?" The
Dutchman enquired with his wife nodding her head as a
sign of approval.

"Oh course we do. Yes sir coming up."

After a while Leela walked into the bar. There
were now several empty beer bottles on the bar and tables.
Only Donald, Richard and the two American girls were
remaining. The Dutch couple had gone off to their room.
Leela walked towards the group. Donna spotted her
approaching.

"So Leela do you work and live here in the hotel?
What a beautiful place. It's much nicer than Aruba."

Leela didn't reply, she turned and looked towards
Donald, he saw the signs in her eyes that she was not
amused. He responded quickly.

"Leela's parents own the hotel. It's run by the
family with hired help from the local villages."

"I work on the accounts and the administration.

Handling the bookings, paying the bills." Leela added proudly.

Donna nodded her head in approval. Although she'd not sensed anything Julie had. She'd seen it two or three times since they'd arrived. It was the way Leela had looked at Donald. She was sure she wasn't imagining it, there was definitely something there. She finished her drink and nudged Donna.

"Come on let's go to our rooms, we need to get unpacked."

Julie turned to Leela and with a friendly smile asked.

"Do you have an iron?"

"Sure. I'll get one dropped off to your room. If you want, I can get one of the maids to do the ironing for you?"

Donna jumped in taking up her offer.

"Oh that would be great. I've a bunch of clothes which need doing. Come on lets go."

When they left Leela followed leaving Richard and Donald sitting looking at each other. Donald broke the silence with a mimicking gesture.

James Caffrey

"That's another fine mess you got me into Stanley. Come on let's go."

Donald and Richard ate dinner together in the cottage that evening. When the hotel was full, they found it was better to do it this way. They could have waited until all the guests had eaten dinner then dined with Leela and her family but decided not to. They'd arranged to meet Leela after dinner had been served. Anyway, it felt good for just the two of them to spend some time together.

While clearing up the dishes Richard cracked open another two beers. Donald was washing with Richard drying. They were both miles away in their thoughts. Donald was thinking about when he would get the chance to talk to Leela which he knew he had to do soon. Richard's mind was on the two beautiful American girls would just arrived. He sensed Julie was carrying a torch for his father. He was interested to see what was going to happen. Donna appeared to have similar mannerism as Julie, however she appeared to have a bit of a devil in her. This was going to be a fun evening.

Strolling up the path towards the hotel Donald and Richard could hear the music playing and the laughter of the guest. It sounded as if they were all Cooking on gas. The party had started early.

They walked in and sat at the end of the bar. It was the same corner where Donald always sat. Several of

247

the guest were dancing. Through the doorway into the dining room he could see Donna and Julie finishing dinner. Each of them had a large Brandy glass in their hand. They noticed him looking and raised their glass in his direction. Donald responded, as did Richard.

"Donna was the other girl you met when you were with Julie wasn't, she?"

"Yes, she was."

Donald replied, but wasn't really listening and paying attention.

" She's a really good looker as well isn't she Dad?"

"Yeah, I suppose they're both very good-looking girls "

They stopped talking as the girls approached them.

"Good evening ladies, would you like to join us?"

Richard motioned with his hands and pointing to his now vacant stool. His father followed his lead and also stood up. Both girls sat down giggling away at some private joke they'd shared.
Donald followed on from where his son had left off.

"Good evening ladies, you both look so lovely and fresh. Doesn't it feel good to get cleaned up and rid of the dust from your trip. Now you have taken care of your outer cleanliness, we need to concentrate on cooling down your inner needs. What would you like to drink?"

They all burst out laughing.

Suddenly Donald notice a change in Julie face She was looking over his shoulder. Quickly he turned and saw Leela standing in the doorway. He moved forward to greet and heard Julie quietly remark to Donna under her breath.

"Now I know why he had to come back. She's so stunningly beautiful. I don't think I've ever seen anyone so attractive. She's perfect."

Leela was dressed in a very simple light cream dress. It was short but that was normal for the average Venezuelan girl. Her jet black tightly curled hair shone reflecting the lights above the bar. Even though the dress hung straight, the curves and shapes of Leela's body could be seen as she walked towards them.

Donald and Leela joined the group. Donna hadn't taken her eyes of Leela since she'd arrived, as she joined them Donna commented.

"Leela honey you look beautiful. Tell me is that hair of yours natural, I mean all those lovely black curls and all?"

249

Leela smiled politely and sat down. Donald quickly got her a drink. Richard came and stood next to her. Putting his arm around her shoulder he gave a reassuring squeeze. At that moment all of Leela's fears and feelings of jealousy disappeared. She knew right then she had the floor. Tonight, would be her night.

The drinks continued to flow and so did the party with all of them beginning to let their hair down a little further with each drink. Donna and Julie had been dancing with Richard and Donald. Leela leaned over a said something in Spanish to the barman. He reacted by going over to the music center behind the bar and changed the cassette. He turned and smiled at Leela.

The music started with and Indian type chant accompanied by drums in the background. Just as it was about to become monotonous, the beat suddenly changed bursting into a very fast Latin beat.

"This is great music, who is it? It's terrific." yelled Donna.

Leela replied with a friendly gesture.

"It's called El Costa De La Vida by Juan Luis Guerra and a band called Quatro Quarenta. In English it means Four Hundred and Forty. The music is Meringue which is now very popular in South America."

Leela reached out her hand in the direction of

250

Donald.

"Come on let's dance, I feel good tonight"

"This is great music but it's too fast, I am not sure that an old man like me can keep up with you."

"Of course you can! It's just the same as what we are used to dancing but a little faster. Come on let's go I'll show you."

Everyone began urging Donald to dance. Leela patiently waited with her outstretched hands and started moving her body to the music. She didn't speak but gradually began increasing the motion of her body, swaying her hips from side to side. With the crowd egging him on Donald had no option but to dance. Walking over towards the dance area Donald leaned over and whispered to Leela,

"You are going to have to carry me through this one love. This is fast."

All eyes were on them as slowly they began to work out their dance movements. In what seemed and eternity to Donald but was actually only less than a minute, they were dancing. His confidence grew and with quiet coaching hints from Leela they started to move together as one. The first number finished which was quickly followed by another. They got better with each song played. With all eyes on them, they both rose to the occasion. Richard had seen them dance before at the Jardin Familiar, but this was different they were great together. Donna and Julie sat amazed watching them twist and turn to the fast Latin beat. Eventually after the four songs Donald called it a day. Leela felt ten feet tall and could have danced all night, she felt like a million dollars. When the music finished, they walked hand in hand back to the bar with everyone applauding. Donald was about to sit down when Leela wrapped her arms around his neck and kissed him very passionately on the lips. This was the first time Leela had openly shown her affection for him. It was something she felt she wanted and needed to do. She sat next to him and linked her arm into his.

Richard knew Leela was in love with his father, but he was a bit surprised the open show of affection. He looked towards Julie. Reaching out with his outstretched hand he motioned as an invitation to dance.

"Come on Julie let's change the tempo and slow it down a bit ".

The barman overheard their conversation and responded by changing the music.

Moving around the floor for the first few minutes Julie was very quiet and apart from smiling at on the odd occasion, she never said much. Richard knew her mind was pre-occupied. Eventually she broke her silence.

"Your father and Leela look very good together. She obviously is in love with him. Does he feel the same way about her?"

Before answering Richard paused collecting his thoughts.

"I am not too sure how my father truly feels about Leela. He has a lot of feeling and affection for her but too what extent I am not sure. I am just not sure."

As they made their way back towards the bar Donald and Leela were conspicuous by their absence. Donald had taken Leela to one side and indicated they needed to talk.

Outside in the night heat the place sounded alive with the creatures. At times the sound of the crickets was deafening. Leela and Donald walked arm in arm through the moonlight orange groves until they stopped and sat on a roughly made bench crudely wrapped around a large tree.

"Listen Leela I need to explain something to you. I know and feel the affection you have for me and I am very flattered. I mean which guy would not be. Dozens of men would only be too pleased and proud to have someone like you to call their own. You're also a very nice person who is gentle, kind and caring in your nature. I could never do anything that would hurt or harm you."

"What is it Donald, what is wrong? I don't understand what you are trying to say to me?"

"Leela what I am trying to say is that you deserve someone better than me, someone from your own country, someone who is closer to your own age."

Leela's response was quick.

"Donald, I don't care. Age is just numbers. How someone really feels is reflected in their heart. People are only as old or as young as their heart wants them to be. You appear to everyone as a person who is a lot younger than your actual age because you have a young heart. Don't tell me you don't care for me and you don't have any feelings for me. This would be a lie. Donald you cannot hid your feels forever. I remember the day we first went out to lunch together and the stories you told me about your life. As we sat across the table........"

She stopped in mid sentence frustrated and desperately searching for words to express how she felt.
"Quando te miro a los ojos, puedo ver tu corazon. When I looked into your eyes, I saw your heart.
This was when I fell in love with you. I've never met anyone like you in my life. You're such a good and sensitive person who cares about everything and everyone. You told me that you'd lived your life like a chameleon and wanted to find the real person trapped inside of you. Well look who's now being a chameleon? You are Donald. You're not following your heart; you're not following

your instincts. What is it Donald? There's something else, I know there is, I can feel it. You're not fully expressing yourself. Tell me Donald, tell me. Do you not love me or are you afraid to love me? Is the thought of possibly being happier than you've ever been in your life so frightening? If you want to know the truth, I'm afraid. Yes, I am afraid of what the future may hold for us, but I will not run away. I want to give us a chance, both of us. If the future doesn't turn out as we've planned it shall be no ones' fault."

Leela turned and walked away with tears streaming down her cheeks. Donald's immediate reaction was to respond but in the second he took to hesitate she was gone.

The next few days went by quickly. Both Donald and Richard were up before dawn and were working at the villa before the sun broke across the valley. They were now in the final stages of the project and it felt good that they were going to finish it well ahead of schedule. Alphonso was pleased with the progress and visited every day now. Donald liked him a lot, he always had a big smile on his face. Even though he was a very wealthy person, he was very ordinary in his living habits. He would sit with the workers drinking coffee and joking with them. They responded by working harder and being very honest in their efforts.

Julie and Donna had gone off for a three-day trek and would be back at the weekend.

By the time they reached home each evening, Donald and Richard would clean up and eat in at the cottage. Richard sensed something wasn't right but kept his thoughts to himself. They hadn't seen Leela for over three days, which was unusual. He was looking forward to the weekend when the girls got back from their trip, the place seemed quiet without them around.

Friday arrived very quickly. The workers got paid on a Friday which gave them a good reason to finish earlier. Donald and Richard walked through the villa inspecting the work which had been completed that day. It looked good.

On the drive back home Donald advised Richard that as soon as they got back, he had to get ready quickly and go to Coro. He had a business meeting and would not be back until later in the evening. Donald showered quickly and as he went out of the door, he shouted good-bye to Richard.

As the Jeep turned left up the hill heading towards Coro, Donald didn't see the lonely figure of Leela jogging up the hill.

James Caffrey

CHAPTER X

Coro, Venezuela.

Upon reaching Coro, Donald needed to ask directions several times before he found the Cafe where he and Alberto had arranged to meet. Walking in Alberto spotted him straight away, which was not too difficult as he was the only Gringo in the place. Donald sat down and Alberto ordered him a drink.

"So Donald how are things at home? Is everyone well? How is Leela?'

"Everyone is fine. The question is, how are you? On the telephone you sounded worried. Is there something wrong Alberto? Are you in some sort of trouble?"

The waiter brought their drinks and put them on the table, they both paused waiting for him to leave. Donald went to pay but Alberto spoke to the waiter who left without taking any money.
Donald looked puzzled.

"I opened a tab; I hope that's okay?"

"Yes, sure"

Donald wiped the top of his bottle with a napkin

257

then lifted it in the air.

"Cheers. God this taste good. I don't know why, but Polar tastes better every time I drink it. It really is a great beer."

Alberto smiled and sipped his Black Label.

Donald had been surprised to learn from Alphonso a statistic regarding the amount of Black Label Whisky consumed in Venezuela. Apparently, in spite of the widespread poverty that existed in the country, Venezuela was the third highest consumer country of Black Label in the world. Only the USA and Japan consumed more. Even in the small cafe's it is common to see a group of men with a bottle of Black Label on the table which they shared amongst themselves.

"Listen Donald, I am very sorry to have called you away from your son and Leela tonight, but you were the only person I felt that I could talk to. I cannot explain it Donald but in a short period of time I feel that you've became like a brother to me. I feel so comfortable and relaxed with you."

Alberto paused searching his mind in an effort to choosing the right words to say. He wanted to express himself from his heart but somehow when he translated his feels into English, it just did not seem to come out the same.

"When I was a young boy and I was in trouble, I always had Leela to take care of me. Even now when we are much older and we see some things differently, we still remember the fear we felt when Papa was angry. Papa is a very proud man and a good man at heart but at times he can be very stern, and he has violent temper. He used to drink a lot in those days but had to slow down because of his health. The doctor told him if he continued the way he was going he would die."

Alberto paused and ran his fingers through his hair. As he lifted his head, Donald saw the pain in his eyes. He knew he was hurting.

"What is it Alberto? What is it that you cannot tell your family?"

" I've been living in Caracas attending College for nearly three years now. You've not been to Caracas have you Donald? The city is like many other big cities. During the day there is the hustle and bustle of people and traffic, but at night it is different. Caracas is vibrant at night, alive with music and dancing. Oh and the girls, the beautiful Venezuelan girls. They have this arrogance which makes them believe that one day they are going to be a beauty queen or movie star. This is part of their culture and what they've been brought up to believe. They're so many beautiful women in Venezuela but sometimes the competition is fierce to attract the attention of men.

Once a Chameleon

Donald let him continue.

"Anyway, I guess Mama and Papa had great expectations that when I was in Caracas I would meet some nice girl, fall in love, bring her home to meet them all, get married and we would live happily for the rest of our lives. It never happened. Apart from all the beautiful girls in Caracas there is also a lot of crime. Each weekend there is over thirty murders in city. There are armed robberies, prostitution, pickpockets and yes, oh yes there is drugs, lots and lots of drugs. Why shouldn't there be eh? We are right next door to Columbia. Over 60% of the drugs that come out of Columbia past through Venezuela, mainly through Caracas then on to Margarita Island then USA. The other main route is via Aruba. They are both very busy tourist spots, so it is difficult to check and catch all the couriers. A lot of the couriers who transport drugs are ordinary everyday people, husband and wives traveling with the kids. They are like the chameleons you talk about. No one really knows who they are and what they are up to."

"You're not in trouble with drugs are you Alberto?"

" Oh how I wish it was that easy Donald. No I am not into drugs. Apart from smoking the odd joint a couple of years ago I've never touched them. Apart from our beautiful women, do you know what else Venezuela is famous for? We have the highest waterfall in the world. Angel Falls its located in the southern part of Venezuela.

James Caffrey

Last summer a group of my friends and I went camping
down to the Angel Falls area. It was a mixed bunch of
young guys and girls just looking to have some fun, and
we did. We got drunk every night and we used to dance
until the early hours of the morning, it was a great. The
night before we left, we all put together the remaining
money we had left and went out for a meal and drinks at
one of the local villages. By the time we got
        back to our Camping Area we were all very drunk.
It's strange how things just seemed to happen without
being planned or pre-arranged. I went back to my tent
and collapsed in a drunken state. I was in a deep sleep
when I was being aroused. Someone was touching me,
touching my body. At first, I struggled in a loose sort of
way but then I thought it was Angelica one of the girls in
the group. She'd shown signs of affection to me
previously but I 'd not been too responsive. All I knew
now was that it felt good and the feeling was getting
better. I'd never bothered too much with members of the
opposite sex. Not even when I was at high school, so the
feelings I was experiencing were new to me. Oh it felt so
good. Even when I realized it wasn't Angelica but my
close friend Roberto who was making me feel this way, I
did not want it to stop. It all happened so quickly, and it
was over before I realized what had actually happened.
The strange thing is the next morning when I was getting
my thoughts together, I felt that what had happen seemed
so natural. I'd no feeling of guilt or remorse. We just
packed up the camping equipment and headed back to
Caracas. Several months later Roberto left college and
moved to Brazil. We remained good friends but never

261

talked about what happened that night."

Donald had been sitting listening intently to Alberto's story. When they'd finished each drink, the waiter would appear with another. Donald broke the silence.

"So now you think being a homosexual is going to be totally unacceptable to your father? Is that the problem? Well maybe you are not a homosexual, things like that can happen and never happen again. This occurs in many of the public schools in England but very few of the children grow up to be gay. I've often wonder why they call homosexuals "Gays". I remember when gay used to mean happy or merry."

Alberto smiled and took a large gulp from his whisky glass. The waiter was quick to refill it.

"I am sorry if I appear to be a bit flippant Alberto but you know sometimes when we have a big load on our minds and we feel there is no tomorrow, when tomorrow comes the problem always seems so much smaller than it was the day before. You have a family who loves you no matter what you may do with your life. The strange thing about love is that it cannot be controlled, we cannot turn it off and on like a water tap. It does not change with the weather. It makes no difference whether it is family or friends, if we love someone, we love them warts and all. We love them in spite of what they are and this is what true love means."

Alberto reached across the table and took
Donald's hand in his.

"Donald if only it was that simple, life would be
so much easier. My problem is not going to look better
tomorrow or the next day or the next. In fact, things will
just get worse as each day goes by."

Alberto was now speaking with a harsh tone in his
voice and he'd a strange look of pity and anger in his eyes.
He gathered up the courage inside of him and opened his
heart to Donald.

"I had a medical examination last week Donald
and the doctor confirmed I've got Aids."

A vacuum of total silence hovered over them as
they sat at the small table. Donald was frozen to his seat,
his mind totally blank of all thoughts. All he could do was
stare into Alberto tear filled eyes. Here he was the guy
with all the answers he thought, until now.

"Do you think they will still love me now?"

"Do you think my father will welcome me home
like the prodigal son? Do you?"

"Do you think Mama and Leela are going to enjoy
watching me slowly die?"

Donald sat back in his chair in a state of shock. Never in his wildest dreams did he imagine anything like this.

"I guess now you could classify me as one or your star chameleons eh? This is one chameleon who will start losing the ability to change color but no problem, I shall be changing from a chameleon to a leper. Do you think Papa will enjoy sitting around the bar after dinner proudly listening to my music as I slowly waste away and die?"

There was silence.

Alberto continued speaking in a softer tone of voice realizing he'd been shouting and the people in the cafe were looking at them.

"What about you Donald, how do you feel sitting in a bar with a homosexual who is dying from aids? Do you still love me, warts and all?"

Donald remained speechless not knowing what to do or say. It was as if they were playing a scene from a movie and at any moment the director would shout cut. He was lost for words.

Alberto stood up and gulped his drink back.

"Come on drink up and let's get out of here."

As he turned to leave Donald followed enquiring.

James Caffrey

"Where are we going?"

"Oh let's go to the Jardin Familiar. I like the place its always warm and happy in there. I need cheering up, what about you?"

The Jardin Familiar was only a short distance, but the walk seemed long and silent. Donald was thinking over in his mind what had transpired in the Cafe. He wondered just how Hans and Carla would accept Alberto's sickness. In the real world, most people looked on aids as some form of stigma. His mind began racing thinking how on earth is Alberto going to tell them. The suddenly another thought hit him. Surely Alberto wasn't expecting Donald to break the news?

It was as if Alberto knew what was going through Donald mind as he turned to him.

"Donald you are my friend and you are like a brother to me. I need you to help me. How am I going to tell Mama and Papa? How do I begin? Where do I begin?"

Donald put his arm around Alberto shoulder as they walked.

"Don't worry Alberto I will help; I will be with you all the way."

265

Once a Chameleon

When they enter the restaurant the head waiter recognized them as friends of Alphonso and quickly got them seated at a very good table near to the dance floor. Alberto order whisky for himself and went to order a beer but Donald advised the waiter to bring him a soda water. He'd had a few beers and needed to stay sober for the drive back to Falcon Ness.

It wasn't too long before Alberto passed out, with his head slumped across the table. Donald got one of the waiters to help him carry Alberto to the car. Within a short space of time they were on their way up the mountain. The good thing about driving in the dark is that the oncoming vehicles can be seen, headlights gave warning even before turning a bend in the road. Donald still had to keep his wits about him because many of the farmers and local village people drove their trucks and cars without lights. Donkeys and bicycle riders were another problem.

Driving into the hotel driveway everything was in darkness. He decided to park the Jeep at the cottage and let Alberto sleep it off there. He would sort something out in the morning. He went into the cottage to awaken Richard to help him carry Alberto. Richard was not in his room and wasn't to be found anywhere in the cottage. Donald was not too concerned; his main priority was to get Alberto into the house and get him to bed.

After spending some time trying to wake Alberto, he eventually got him on to his feet but could not get him to walk. He weighed like a sack of potatoes. Suddenly as if by magic the load lightened, and Alberto was moving. He soon realized why when he looked over and saw Leela with her arms under Alberto. She smiled at Donald then got on with the task of helping to get him inside. Once they'd gotten him onto the bed, they placed a blanket over him and closed the bedroom door.

After a brief and slightly embarrassing silence Leela broke the ice.

"Do you want Coffee?"

"Yeah, sure if you'll have one with me?"

"Okay"

He could hear her in the kitchen running the water and filling the coffee pot. He felt a little ashamed about what had happened between them earlier in the week. Leela was a lovely person and didn't deserve to be hurt. When she entered the room, he went over and hugged her.

"Come let's sit over here" he said, walking across the room and sitting on the couch by the fireplace.

"What happened to Alberto?" Leela asked.

"Oh it's a long story. He just drank too much Black Label and went to sleep. I thought it was better he

267

stayed here tonight than wake up your Mama and Papa and the rest of the hotel."

"What's wrong Donald? Something isn't right, I can feel it. When Alberto called last week and asked to meet with you, I knew then something was terribly wrong. It's not like Alberto to act this way, all secretive. It has to be serious. Tell me, please tell me" Leela pleaded.

Donald took his arm from around Leela and leaned forward putting his head into both of his hands. Slowly he opened his hands and lifted up his head and looked at Leela. I have to tell her he thought, Alberto will need her strength to help him through the months ahead.

"Alberto is sick Leela, very sick."

Donald paused try to search for words then came straight out with the truth.

"He has Aids Leela. Alberto has aids........."

"Oh my God no, please don't tell me. Not that, not Aids. There must be some terrible mistake"

Leela began to gently sob. Donald took a tight hold of her and as her feelings began to swell, she began crying her heart out. Her body jerked with emotion.

"Oh Donald I love him and I don't want him to die" she cried.

They both held each other and the more Leela cried the closer he hugged her.

After a while she began to quieten down. When he felt the time was right, Donald started to explain to her what Alberto had told him. He noted a slight reaction when he got to the part about the homosexual relationship or experience Alberto had gone through. Then it was as if things were now a little clearer in her mind. He wandered whether she'd suspected anything previously.

Leela wiped her eyes.

"When is he going to tell Mama and Papa?"

"I don't know we never got around to talking about how or when he intends telling them. What do you think? I mean they're your parents as well. I know he's frightened to tell your father. There was real fear in his emotions when he talked about your father finding out.

Leela did not answer but Donald couldn't help feeling there was a raw nerve somewhere within the relationship between Alberto and Hans. They both sat in silence, but their minds were whirling like the sails of a windmill caught in a hurricane. Nothing seemed to be real. Leela shuffled and lifted her feet on to the couch and curled her body closer to Donald. It was as if the closer she could get, the more protected she felt from her fears.

Eventually they both slipped into a shallow sleep.

The cottage was now dark and quiet. Occasionally Leela body would jerk slightly and although it was disturbing, it wasn't enough to bring them out of the sleep they'd lapsed into.

Donald was woke suddenly by the sound of the cottage door closing. He got up carefully trying not to disturb Leela and walked towards Richard's bedroom. When he looked in Richard was in bed buried under the sheets. As he was about to turn and walk away Richard appeared from under the sheets and half sat up ruffling his pillow in an attempt to make himself more comfortable. Donald then realized Richard had only just got back home. He looked at his watch, it was ten minutes to six, dawn was just about to break across the mountain.

Once he'd put on a fresh pot of coffee, he decided to take a shower. He closed the bathroom door so as not make too much noise. The warm water hit his back and shoulders and it felt so good. He turned up the temperature of the water trying to balance it to the point where he could just barely stand the heat. His mind drifted back to the events of the night before. Although he'd seen documentaries on the television about people dying from Aids, he'd been insulated from the brutal reality of the illness. Up to now all the aids victims he'd seen either on television or in the newspapers had been totally strangers to him. Now it was different. He not only knew Alberto, but he was Leela's brother, he'd started to think of him as a friend. He felt that no matter what happened he'd stand by Alberto. He had to help and support him.

He wondered if what he felt inside was the same feelings which Princess Diana experienced when he'd seen her on the television visiting Aids victims in hospitals? Diana appeared to be a very caring person who always wanted to help the sick and people in need. Even though she had a gigantic personal burden on her shoulders she found the time to try and help others in need. Here was the classic case of a Chameleon. A beautiful young girl so full of life and vitality forced into a marriage with a strange and serious man who had been born to be king. She had sad eyes, the look of loneliness. He knew the feeling. No one can imagine what it feels like unless they've actually experience real loneliness. Words can't be found to describe the empty feeling of loneliness which starts right down in your feet and slowly creeps up through your body destroying the heart before it reaches the soul.

He jumped as the shower curtain moved.

"Donald is that you?" Leela called softly.

"Yes, I won't be long, I'm nearly finished. Can you get me a towel please, they're in the cabinet in the corner, on the top shelf."

Leela passed Donald the towel but didn't leave the bathroom. He heard her close down the toilet lid realizing she sat down to wait for him. He wrapped the towel around his waist a drew back the shower curtain. Leela sat crying with her head down on her knees.

Donald quickly finished off drying himself. Stepping out of the shower stall he reached down to Leela.

"Come on love, let's go into the kitchen. I've got some fresh coffee on. If we are to help Alberto the first thing we need to do is to be strong, he's relying on us to support him through this terrible thing."

They walked into the kitchen and Leela sat at the table trying to compose herself. Donald poured the coffee into two large earthenware mugs.

"Here get this in you, get the old caffeine trip working. That'll make you feel better."

A slight sign of a smile showed on her face. They had a long long day ahead of them.

They agreed they would awaken Alberto and after he'd cleaned up, they would go up to the hotel. They would have Alberto explain he'd traveled from Caracas by car with a friend and they'd dropped off in Coro last night. He and Donald had met up at the Jardin Familiar and had dinner together. It didn't sound great, but it was the best they could do under the circumstances. While Alberto was cleaning up and having a cup of coffee, they explained to him what they'd decided. He nodded his head in agreement not really knowing whether Donald had told Leela the full story or not. He suspected he had because of the extra attention she was showing him.

Hans and Carla were pleasantly surprised. They hadn't expected to see Alberto, but it was great he was back home. After formal greetings and another cup of coffee everyone began to disburse and go about their regular work. The hotel was full, so everyone had a busy schedule ahead of them. Alberto had offered to help his father with the cleaning of the rear yard. Hans willingly accepted. Although the labor crew didn't work on a Saturday Donald had decided to spend a few hours at the villa checking the past weeks progress and starting the final punch list that had to be done.

On the drive to the villa suddenly Donald remembered that Richard hadn't spent the night in his own bed. He began to wonder where he'd slept speculating that it might have been with one of the girls. For some unexplainable reason he secretly hoped it was Donna. It wasn't that he was in love or had any kind of feelings for Julie but more that he cared about her. Maybe there was a little hint of jealousy.

A few hours later Donald had finalized his punch list ready for the crew on Monday morning. As he put down his clipboard, he heard someone approaching.

"Hello. Hello. Donald where are you?" it was
Leela.

As he walked out of the villa she saw him and
hurried to greet him. She had a wicker picnic basket over
her arm which she placed on a garden seat. It was as if by
telepathy they both threw their arms around each other
into a very passionate embrace. The embracing continued
for several minutes with neither of them speaking. At last
Donald moved away.

"What are you doing here? How did you get here?"

"Well to answer your first question I thought we
could have a picnic lunch together. I know a great place
not far from here which is very quiet and secluded. How
did I get here? I managed to get a lift from the baker who
delivers the bread to the hotel."

They both started laughing. Donald was pleased
to see her, and it showed.

"Come on" she said picking up the basket.

"We can't take the jeep to where we are going but
it is not too far to walk".

The area was thick with vegetation. Many wild
banana trees and vine like plants twisted up high
engulfing the larger trees, sometimes appearing to

completely choke them. Everything was deep green and lush. Although it was hot and humid, they did get a high amount of rain up in the mountains. Leela led the way occasionally turning and looking back towards Donald. There was no track or path which made their footing a little unsure at times with the odd stumble.

"What's that noise?" Donald called to Leela.

Apart from turning to smile she never replied but just pressed on. The noise was now getting a lot closer and Donald realized it was running water. Sudden they entered a clearing.

"Isn't it beautiful Donald? This is my most favorite place on the earth."

Donald couldn't answer as he stood looking around him. It was as if he'd suddenly walked on to the set of Tarzan movie. It was absolutely spectacular.

The clearing was not very large. It had a waterfall on their right gushing out clear water into a small pool. Although the power of the falls pushed the water away from the foot of the falls, it very quickly settled to create a mirror surface which reflected the tall vegetation around them. The banks of the pool were covered in thick spongy green moss which from a distance, could had been mistaken for astro turf. They walked around the edge of the clearing with their feet sinking through the moss.

"Come on, let sit over there". Leela called.

Donald followed her lagging behind only because of his efforts to absorb everything around him. Eventually when they'd settled down he asked.

"How on earth did you find this place? It's beautiful, just like the Garden of Eden. It is so natural and unspoiled. It's like paradise."

Leela felt good and was glad she'd decided to have lunch with Donald. They sat eating lunch and drinking wine. Donald's mind drifted, he couldn't believe where he was, what he was doing. It all seemed so far away from the life he'd left behind. He thought about Allison and how she'd died. He took another sip from his wine glass and lay back putting his hands under his head. He stared up at the large trees towering over them. Suddenly Leela's head appeared in view. She stooped over him kissing him gently on the lips. He responded as he wrapped his arms around her in a passionate embrace. For several moments their passion grew until suddenly Leela broke away and jumped to her feet.

"Come on " she teased, slipping down her shorts and undoing her blouse exposing her swimsuit.

Before he could get up, she'd vanished diving into the water. He walked over to where she'd disappeared waiting for her to surface. Suddenly to his right there was a loud splash and gasp as she appeared.

"Come on Donald. What's keeping you?"

"I don't have any bathing trunks" he answered her.

"I didn't know we were going swimming. Why didn't you tell me?"

She swished around in the water screaming with laughter and began fidgeting about. Suddenly she was swinging and whirling something around her head.

"You don't have swimming trunks? I don't have a swimsuit " she called, throwing her swimsuit on to the edge of the bank.

"Come on. Now you don't have an excuse. The water is beautiful".

He quickly undressed and dived into the pool. As he surfaced Leela was swimming towards him. When she got close to him, she put her arms around his neck moving her body to and fro in a paddling motion with her legs. Every now and then their legs touched. Donald gazed at her, she looked so beautiful. The water had turned her hair into a mass of tight black curls. He reached out and placed his arm around her waist and slowly moved her towards him.

He started kissing her very tenderly with a hint of shyness. First her eyes, one at a time. His kisses were soft and quick as he moved down around her neck and ears. He felt her body react as she moved closer to him. It all seemed to happen so naturally as her mouth sought out his, making small whimpering sounds of pleasure. He drew her closer to him. She responded by curling her legs around his waist lifting her body higher out of the water. His kisses covered her breasts and she felt her nipples reacting to his wet lips. All of sudden they both sank beneath the surface of the water. Wrapped up in the intensity of their emotions they had disregarded any need to remain buoyant. They floated underwater continuing with their embrace and passion, it was only their pure survival instincts and their need for air which forced them to surface.

They remained in their embrace as they silently moved their bodies in sync slowly swimming to the side of the lake. Donald's feet touched the bottom and he felt something like liquid powder. They were now only lying in only a few feet of water. Donald reached out and caught hold of a large exposed tree trunk which was jutting out of the bank into the water.

Leela's legs were still around him as she continued to cover his body with kisses breaking only to move her tongue in circling motions on his stomach. He moved his body trying get into a more comfortable position, yet not wanting to disrupt their passion. They remained locked together. He wanted her so much and as she began rubbing her body against his, the need to make love to her grew greater.

He reached out with one free hand and caught hold of the tree trunk. He eased himself a little closer to the shore and his body relaxed. Leela responded by moving her body higher and with her arms outstretched she reached out to clasp Donald's wrists. His mouth sought her breasts. She slowly glided down his body stopping only for a moment as she felt him enter her.

The movement of Leela thrusting body made Donald feel as if he was immediately going to explode. Oh it felt so good he never wanted it to stop. He wanted to touch her, touch her all over. It was all too much. He let go of the tree trunk and as he did, he landed on his back into the deep mud. The ritual of their love making never broke pace as they gently fell backwards. He brought his hands out of the mud and reaching up he grabbed at Leela's hair. In a frenzy of sexual abandonment, he lost control smoothing her with kisses. Breaking away for a brief moment, he saw the mud running from her hair, slipping down her neck then dripping of the end of each of her nipples on to his chest. It was as if the feeling of the warm mud had some kind of aphrodisiac effect on Leela as she began speeding up the motions of her body. Donald responded to her movements and the intensity of their passion began to build. Oh God he thought, I'm going to explode, I can't hold on any longer. I must, I must. I don't want it to ever end. He didn't have to hold back too long. As their love making reached a climax Leela threw her head back, arching her body as her arms beat the surface of the water.

Donald lay back in the mud gazing at Leela in amazement. He'd never experienced love making with such intensity and passion. As she lifted her head the mud on her face highlighted the whites of her teeth. Lying in each other's arms their bodies gave an occasional small shudder as a reaction indicating
that equal fulfillment had been reached.

Oblivious to the fact that they were both caked in mud they enjoyed the moments of silence. Donald had never known anything like it in his life. The passion and energy in their love making was a new experience to him. It seemed so perfect the way it had happened and where it had happened.

Leela lifted her head off Donald's chest and looked into his eyes.

" Deep down inside I always felt you loved me, but now I know you do"

They kissed and hugged each other tightly.

"You know Leela, although the act of making love and reaching a sexual climax is one of the most wonderful experiences of life, the holding and hugging afterwards is the like the icing on the cake"

Without warning he suddenly plunged his hand under the shallow water scooping up a large handful of mud and started rubbing it all over Leela's body. Within minutes they were both wrestling and covering each other in mud. Their laughter could have been heard for miles. They stopped only out of sheer exhaustion They spent a few moments just floating on their back getting their breath back. They then began swimming towards the bank plunging their bodies into the clear deeper water to remove all the mud.

Donald was the first out of the water. He sat watching Leela splashing around, every now and he'd catch a glimpse her beautiful body. He felt like pinching himself not really believing what had just happened. How could someone so lovely as Leela fall in love with him. It gave him a tingle from his head to his toes just to think about it.

As she got out of the water and lay on the soft moss, she closed her eyes. Donald looked down at her. The water was dripping from her hair and running off her glistening body like pearled droplets gliding across silk. It wasn't just the golden color of her skin but the silky texture, it was smooth like a newborn baby. He leaned over and kissed her. She popped open her eyes and a big smile made her face shine like a beacon.

" I've never experienced anything like that in my life Leela and never knew love making could feel so good. It's also the first time I've ever made love where I

climaxed at the same time as my lover. Not being very
experienced with woman, in fact Allison is the only
female I've ever made love to, I'm a little old fashioned
when it comes to fidelity and things like that. I've wanted
you for a long time Leela and fantasized many times
trying to imagen what it would be like making love to you.
Never in my wildest dreams did I think it would be as
good as it was. I guess I held back showing you how I felt
possibly because of what happened to Allison and also it
seemed strange and a little uncomfortable with Richard
around."

Leela lay staring up into Donald's eyes listening to
him as he expressed his feels.

" I love you Leela more than you could ever
possibly realize. I've just been afraid to admit it, not only
to you, but also to myself. I love you."

"Oh Donald, I have waited so long to hear you
say that. I felt in my heart you loved me, but I was afraid
you would never accept or admit it."

Their embrace soon began to develop into
passion as Donald rolled over closer to her moving one
leg in between Leela's legs. Her reaction was immediate as
she arched her body wanting him again. She reacted to
the fondling of his hands as they began searching and
exploring the responsive areas of her body. This time
their love making was much more tender, both reacted
and responded to each other's touch as they sought out

newfound feelings of pleasure.

On the journey back to the hotel they didn't talk much. The look on their faces and the constant grinning and smiling told the story. Donald wondered whether anyone back at the hotel would notice. The same thought was also passing through Leela's mind. She didn't care too much but was sensitive to how Donald felt knowing how shy and reserved he was. She would have to control her feelings for Donald when they were around other people, but now it was going to be little more difficult.

As they reached the driveway of the hotel, Donald's mind switched to Alberto. He speculated on what had transpired during the day wondering if he'd talked to his parents. I guess they'd both find out quick enough.

Donald parked the Jeep's and switched off the ignition. The noise of the argument going on could be heard even outside of the hotel. It was Alberto and Hans.

Leela and Donald hurried into the hotel heading for the restaurant area.

Hans and his son were really getting into it.

"But you always help Mama in the kitchen when you are here Alberto. What's so different this time? Why do you feel like this, not wanting to help with the cooking? You're a good cook. I don't understand. Do you feel that now you're going to University that helping to run the hotel is above you? What we've built here over the years, the business, the hotel, everything is for you and Leela."

Hans stood staring at Alberto waiting for his response.

Alberto couldn't find the word to reply. He turned and looked towards Donald and Leela. The message in his eyes said it all with a look of total despair. Leela tried desperately to hold back her tears and responded by grabbing the apron that Hans's was holding in his hand.

"Don't worry Papa, I will help you." she said tying the apron around herself.

"Anyway I 'm a better cook than he is. Isn't that right Alberto?

Alberto didn't answer but they all began to respond to the injection of humor that Leela had added to the conversation.

As Leela began moving around the kitchen she turned her back away from her father and mouthed words to Donald.

" It's okay, you go, everything is now fine. I'll see you later. I love you."

284

Donald quietly slipped away. As he reached the cottage Richard was sitting on the patio with a cold beer waiting for his father.

"Hi Dad. How's things? I looked for you earlier on but couldn't find you."

"Oh I went off to the villa and checked a few things out. Then Leela turned up with a picnic basket so we had lunch there."

"Oh that was nice" continued Richard.

"Listen Dad about this morning I am sorry I sort of sneaked in and slipped into bed. I wasn't quite sure about what was going on and didn't really want to walk into the middle of anything. Is everything okay? I mean what's going on or is it none of my business?"

"No it's not that son it's just that I met up with Alberto last night in Coro and he got pretty drunk, so I brought him home and he crashed out in my bed."

Donald didn't want to lie to his son but felt that only telling him half the truth was acceptable in the circumstances. He decided not to ask Richard too many questions and knew his son would tell him what he'd been up to last night in his own time. Maybe Richard sensed this in the silent pause in their conversation. This was the queue to get things off his chest.

"Listen Dad, about last night. When the girls got back from their trip, we sort of had a celebration and had a few drinks. Well one thing led to another and we ended up in Donna's room with a large bucket of ice and a couple of bottles of vodka. We were playing music and dancing and we all got pretty drunk. I passed out on Donna's bed. I don't know what time Julie left or whether she helped Donna undress me before she left. Anyway, that's where I woke up this morning, not really remembering what happened. I hope I didn't do anything to embarrass myself or you. I just don't remember anything."

Richard waited for Donald's response.

"Richard you are a grown man and you are responsible and accountable to yourself and for your actions. You're a good guy and I love you as no other father could ever love a son. I am sure that you acted just as any man would in the circumstance. Yeah come on... remember your old Dad was young once. I know what it's like to wake up the next morning trying to remember what happened the night before. I've been there and done it... So don't worry. Okay"

They both hugged each other with Donald patting his son's shoulder as they broke apart.

"The girls are going back to Aruba tomorrow." Richard said with air of question to follow.

\

Donald waited for him to continue.

"They've asked me if I would like to go and visit with them for awhile. They reckon I can get a job pretty easy this time of year. The basic pay is not much but the tips make it really worthwhile. It sounds fun to me. What do you think Dad?"

"Yes, why not if that's what you want to do. I suppose it's okay taking a few more months before you decide what you're going to do with your life then settle down to a steady job"

Donald hoped he hadn't gone too far in mentioning Richard future plans.

" I know you love me Dad and that you care about me and my future. I had said all along that I wanted to take about a year off after I finished college. I got so fed up with all the exams and the midnight hours spent doing homework. It burnt my batteries out and this is my way of recharging them. I hope you understand Dad?"

"Listen Richard you've always been a levelheaded person, so I have every confidence in the decisions you make. So how about deciding whether you want me to have another beer eh?"

Richard smiled at Donald's humor and quickly returned with a cold beer. Handing it to his father he casually enquired.

"So what's your program for tonight. We're all meeting in the bar then going down to the village to a cafe Alberto knows. Do you want to join us?"

"No thanks son." replied Donald.

"Leela is coming here and we are going to cook a little something and have a few drinks. You go ahead and enjoy yourself".

"Do you love Leela Dad? She's absolutely crazy about you. She hasn't said so, but you can tell by the way she looks at you. Leela is a very nice person and everyone who meets her sees her the same. Now there is one person who doesn't qualify as one of your chameleons."

Donald didn't reply as he was thinking about what his son had said. It was true, Leela was the same person no matter who she was around. She just acts very natural.

"Did I embarrass you Dad? If I did I am sorry, I don't want to get in to your personal life".

" What. Oh sorry I was miles away. I was thinking about what you said about Leela. I guess you're right she is very natural and treats everyone the same. Everyone loves or likes her because she is so natural and sensitive to people's feelings. Do I love her? Yes, I suppose do. No disrespect to your mother Richard but I've never experienced feelings like I have for Leela. I never knew that someone could feel about another person they I feel about her. The odd thing is that I can sense her feelings about how she cares for me. I'm like a new person and it's a strange situation to be in. I can't believe I could be so lucky to have some like Leela love me the way she does. It's as if I want to run and show her off to every person in my life I have ever met shouting...

" Hey, isn't she beautiful, isn't she gorgeous and she's a wonderful person who's in love with me."

"I cannot truly find the right words to say Richard."

Richard responded, touching his father's hand.

"It's okay Dad, it really is okay."

"Go on go and have your shower and get ready son, you'll be late meeting your friends. Thanks for listening to me. It means a lot to me."
Richard smiled at his father and walked into the cottage.

Donald finished off his beer and went inside for another. It was still early and Leela would not be coming down until they'd started serving dinner. By then all the chores of preparing the guest dinner were well under control.

Donald walked out back on to the patio and sat

on the chair. He didn't notice the shadow of someone standing on the edge of the trees. He took a drink out of his bottle turning quickly as he heard a movement.

"Hi Donald, how are you? Been a bit of a stranger, lately haven't you?

"Oh it's you Julie. You gave me a bit of a scare. I never saw you or heard you coming. How long have you been there?"

"Long enough. I didn't mean to eavesdrop on you and your son but when I heard you talking it was so beautiful the way you were describing about how you feel. She really is a lucky girl. I guess you know the real reason I agreed to come to Venezuela with Donna was that I hoped I would find you. Although we'd only spent a few days together in Aruba, those days were very special to me. You're the first guy I've ever met who wasn't looking for anything other than my company. You liked me as a person. You had the opportunity for sex if that's what you'd been looking for, but it wasn't. I knew then you respected me and that's something I've never experienced before."

Julie sat down next to Donald.

" Most guys are only after one thing but your different. You're special. I feel as if I've left it too late and may have missed my chance. I should never have let you go when I met you in Aruba. My instincts told me not to. That little man inside my head kept telling me this is the guys for you, but I never listened. I've been disappointed and hurt in the past and thought it was too good to be true."

Donald was surprised by Julie comments.

"Listen Julie I'm sorry, I never knew you felt this way. You're a friend, a dear friend and I care about you very much. I just never imaged you and I being together that way"

'Well not to worry Donald, tomorrow we are leaving and going back to Aruba. Richard and Alberto are coming with us."

Julie turned to walk back up to the hotel.

" I'll try and catch you in the morning before we leave. If I miss you good luck. She's a beautiful girl Donald. I hope you find the happiness you've been searching for. Don't forget if all else fails you know where to find me. I'll be waiting. Bye..."

"Oh sorry, bye. Yes, I'll see you in the morning Julie before you leave"

Donald's answer faded as his thoughts were elsewhere. Alberto is' going to Aruba? Richard's going to Aruba.?

Donald couldn't help but think in his mind about

Alberto, the girls, sex, Richard. He didn't want to think this way, but he was a father and he cared about his son. He was afraid. He reassured himself it was a natural instinct to care about his son. Donald then tried to start thinking reasonable and logic about the situation. The fact they were all going to Aruba together didn't mean they were all going to have sex with each other. He pondered, should he say something to Richard or not?

His thought was interrupted by Richard getting ready to go out.

"Okay Dad, I'm off up to the bar. Are you sure you don't want to join us? Maybe you guys can come up later on. It's the girls last night before they leave to go back to Aruba".

Richard paused.

"It is okay me going with them isn't Dad? I mean you don't mind do you?'

"Yes it's okay but be careful son."

Richard smiled as he turned and walked away up towards the hotel.

Donald sat on the patio deep in thought as he drank his beer. It wasn't long before Leela arrived. Although they chatted together while preparing dinner, Leela couldn't help but feel that Donald had something

James Caffrey

on his mind. She was a little concerned but decided to wait feeling if he wanted to, he would tell her. She didn't have to wait too long.

As they were finishing their supper Donald picked up his glass, he began twirling the wine around. He continued his twirling motion just enough to bring the wine up to the inside edge of the glass. Being ware that Leela was watching him, he leaned over and kissed her.

"I'm sorry love I haven't been very good company, tonight have I?"

Before she could answer he continued.

"I'm worried about Richard. I guess I'm also worried about Alberto as well. They're going to Aruba with the two girls tomorrow. Did you know?"

"Yes I'd heard them talking. I've been thinking about it as well. Don't you want Richard to go?"

"I don't mind him going it's just that". Donald stopped in the middle of his sentence.

Leela waited for him to go on. He lifted his head and looked into to her eyes.

"I'm sorry Leela, I can't help it. I know you love Alberto and I love Richard, but I am afraid."
" It's all right Donald." Leela said reaching over

293

and touching his hand.

"You're only human and it is natural for a father to love and care about his son. Alberto and Richard are very sensible and levelheaded. Everything will be okay, I am sure. So don't worry, everything is going to be fine, honest it is."

Donald wanted to believe Leela but he'd a terrible feeling that something really bad was going to happen. He searched his thoughts trying to focus the image or picture he felt was buried deep in the back of his mind.

Leela sat very quiet watching the movement of Donald's eyes. He appeared to be disturbed and she wanted to reach out and help him.

"Come on love" Donald said taking Leela's hand.

"I'll walk you back to the house. I'm sorry if I am not sociable tonight. I thought it best we have an early night."

As they began walking up the path Leela turned her head and smiled at Donald. It was as if she'd a special kind of magic power as he began to feel the warmth of her smile spreading throughout his body. It was these kinds of small signals which reinforced his believes they were very much in love. She was his soul mate.

After they'd said goodnight and Donald turned to

walk back to the cottage, he heard music and laughter
coming from the area of the bar. He didn't want to go in
but could not resist walking over to the window. Looking
in, he watched the group as they enjoyed themselves.
Richard was dancing with Julie twirling her around and
around. She was throwing her head back laughing loudly.
Occasionally Richard would pull Julie close to him and
she would respond by flirting and teasing him. In a very
unoffensive manner she cleverly moved her body away
from him just as she thought he was getting to close for
comfort. Donald chuckled to himself.

Alberto and Donna were sitting on the large sofa
near the fireplace, he had his arms around her shoulder.
Donald switch his attention back to Richard and Julie.
The music had changed to a much faster number and as
they danced Donald's eyes were fixed on Julie. She was
twisting her body and hips, rubbing her thighs with each
hand. She looked very beautiful moving her hand up
around the back of her neck lifting her long flowing hair
at the same time turning her head provocatively to one
side. Donald looked at Richard and saw the look in his
eyes as he watched her. For some unexplainable reason
he felt a little twinge of jealousy. He tried to control it and
shake it off, but it puzzled him why he felt this way after
all he loved Leela very dearly. Walking down the path
back to the cottage he could still hear the music.

The sound of Richard moving around the cottage
made Donald stir. He looked at the clock, it was just after
six, the sun was rising. Donald got up and poured a cup

of coffee stopping as he walked past Richards room.

"Morning son. How do you feel? Did you enjoy yourself last night?

"Oh hi Dad. Yes it was great we had a really good time."

Richard followed his father into the living room.

"Listen Dad I really appreciate what you've done for me since I arrived here. I know you and Leela love each other very much and I am very happy for you both. I hope everything works out. I can truly say hand on my heart that I've never seen you so happy. You're a different person."

Donald smiled at his son. The sound of a car horn alarmed him.

"That's them. Gotta dash, I'll call you from Aruba and don't worry about me I am going to be okay. Oh and I'll be back even if it is only for the wedding. Who else could you have for your best man eh? Take care Dad, I love you, bye".

With the noise of the car disappearing Donald poured himself another cup of coffee. Sitting on the balcony with a steaming hot coffee in his hand he watched and listened to the dawn as it broke. He loved the early morning, even better than the splendor of dusk with the blazing golden sky. Mornings always sounded and felt fresh. It's as if the night dew washes everything sparkling clean ready for a new day.

Donald heard a sound and looked up towards the hotel. He saw Leela starting her stretching exercises before she started jogging. He thought about their lovemaking at the waterfall. He still couldn't get used to the idea that of all the people Leela could have chosen she'd fallen in love with him. He continued watching her as she twisted her body, reaching forward touching her toes. Even from a distance she looked terrific.

She started jogging down the path towards the gate and was surprised to see Donald.

"Good morning Donald. Isn't it a beautiful morning? Do you want to come with me? I won't go to quick."

"No love, I'm just soaking up the fresh smell of early morning. It's really nice just sitting here listening to the sounds of the birds. You go ahead and enjoy your run. I am going to shower and get ready. I need to go down to the villa this morning to check out a few of the finishing touches we're working on."

"Okay but be back by noon, then we can go and have lunch, if that's okay with you?"

"Yes that's fine. I'll see you later."

Donald sat finishing his coffee as Leela disappeared down the road.

CHAPTER XI

For their lunch date Leela arrived on time and within minutes they were on their way. She'd decided she would take him to a restaurant called the Araguil which was located at the foot of mount Santa Anna. The dining tables were outside within a courtyard which had large trees giving plenty of shade. As they sat sipping their first drink Leela signaled to Donald to follow her as she got up and walked down to the far end of the restaurant. As he approached, he saw what the attraction was. There was a large open roast pit which threw off tremendous heat. Across the top of the pit lay long poles with beef and chicken strung down them. The aroma of the cooking meat smelled great. During lunch he found out that it also tasted great. When he'd finished, he lay back in his chair patting his stomach.

"That was great. I've not tasted meat as fresh and as tasty as that for some time. In fact, is was so good I think I need another Polar to wash it down. How about you love, do you want another glass of wine?"

Leela didn't respond. Donald was about to say something, but she held up her hand as a sign that she was trying to listen to someone talking. She got up and started walking away from the table.

She got up and as she walked away from the table with concern in her voice, she advised Donald.

"Stay here, I won't be a moment."

Donald watched as Leela went over to a group of people talking. She turned quickly hurrying back towards Donald.

"Come on. Let's go, quickly, we need to go."

"What's going on Leela? What is it? What's happened?"

"There has been a plane crash Donald. The Aruba flight from Las Piedras has crashed"

As they drove towards Judibana the tears were streaming down Leela's face.

Donald's mind was confused and in a whirl.

"I don't understand, the flight to Aruba was this morning. What time did this happen? I mean how do we know is was the flight which Richard, Alberto and the girls were on. Something doesn't make sense Leela. What did the people in the restaurant say?"

Leela wiped her eyes.

"There is a lot of confusion Donald, but it appears the plane was very late arriving from Caracas. This is not unusual in Venezuela. Anyway, as the plane

300

was taking off from Las Piedras there was an explosion and it disintegrated in mid-air"

Leela started crying again.

"Oh my god, they can't be dead, they can't." Donald cried.

As they neared the airport the concentration of traffic began to build up. Soon they were at a standstill. There were vehicles and people everywhere, hundreds of them. Getting nearer to the airport was going to be a problem. The crowd began to clear a path as the sound of police sirens approached. Three police vehicles drew up alongside Donald and Leela. The tinted windows of the middle vehicle slid down as a voice called to them.

"Come, quickly." It was Alphonso.

The police convoy vehicle slowly moved forward weaving a path through the crowd. Leela and Alphonso were deep in conversation. Donald sat waiting to hear what had happened, it seemed an eternity. His inability to speak Spanish made him feel totally inadequate. Why hadn't he taken the time to try and learn the language. He kept nudge Leela's arm wanting to know what was going on. Donald couldn't stand it any longer.

"Leela, what's going on? What happened, is it the morning flight? tell me please?"

"Yes Donald it was the morning flight but there is
a lot of confusion and even Alphonso doesn't yet know
all the details."

They'd now reached the entrance to the small
airport terminal. The place was swarming with police and
the military. Alphonso got out of the vehicle as two police
officers walked over and saluted him, soon they were
deep in conversation. Donald assumed they were giving
him an update on the situation. One of the police officers
handed Alphonso a piece of paper. A puzzled looked
came across his face. He turned to Leela and began
talking in Spanish. Donald watched Leela face waiting for
some sign of hope. This can't be true he thought. This
happens to other people in the movies or on television.
His son can't be dead, it can't be true. Leela turned
towards Donald taking a hold of both of his hands.
Under the circumstance she was acting very calm.

"Alphonso has the passenger manifest. Now
listen carefully, before you jump to any conclusions and
get upset let me finish. Richard, Alberto and the girl's
names are on the passenger list but this doesn't mean they
were on the flight."

"What do you mean? I don't understand."

"Please Donald let me finish. Remember this is
Venezuela and not Europe or America. There's a lot of
confusion as to whether the list is accurate. Six people
who had confirmed seats were bumped off the flight at

the last moment. Apparently, a group of Colombians bribed the ticket clerks to get seats, so they just canceled the other people's seats. This happens all the time here. The ticket clerks have fled, and no one knows what's happened to the passengers they dropped from the flight. There is an unconfirmed report that they took a chartered flight with Avia, which is a small charter firm too operate from this airport. The latest reports indicate that Avia took six passengers, but again the passenger manifest has gone missing. They are trying to find it. There's an unconfirmed report that among the six people taken off the flight three of them were Gringos who took the Avia flight."

"Oh please God let it be them, please let it be them. Are they checking with Aruba to find out from immigration which passengers were on the Avia flight? That's what they should be doing."

"Yes Donald they are trying to check but because the plane blew up in mid air there is a complete security blackout both here in Venezuela and in Aruba. They suspect a bomb blew the plane out of the sky."

Eventually the calm control Leela was applying to the situation got the better of her as she began sobbing. Donald reached over and put his arms around her.

"Oh I'm sorry love, I'm so sorry. All I was thinking about was myself. I'm sorry, come on let's sit down over there. I never stopped to think of how you felt.

Please forgive me. Everything is going to be okay just wait and see."

Leela sat next to Donald with her head buried in between his neck and shoulder. Donald patted her head consoling her at the same time watching the mass confusion going on around him. He couldn't help reflecting on the events of the past few months. If he hadn't decided to leave, none of this would have occurred. Allison would be alive. Richard would never have come to Venezuela. It was all because he'd wanted to change his life. Did he really consider the feelings of the people around him or did he just make a very selfish decision? His mind was whirling with thoughts of guilt and blame.

He looked around the small airport terminal. People were sitting and lying around everywhere. There were several groups of families with small children. Many of them were crying continuously but as they gazed about their eyes searched for some small sign of hope. Occasionally gazing eyes locked on to Donald with a mutual look of despair. Gradually as the hours went by the sobbing around him receded.

Occasional a jerking spasm followed by a bout of prolonged crying broke the silence which had fallen on the terminal building. He knew how they felt, he was experiencing the same pain, the same anguish they were going through.

Leela lifted her head up quickly as she felt Donald's body stiffen. Alphonso was walking towards them with a sheet of paper in his hand. As he neared them, he motioned with the paper holding his outstretched arm towards them.

"Manifesto Avia." he said.

Leela went to take it from Alphonso but he hesitated and quickly handed the paper towards Donald.

They all stood there. Donald needed to know but didn't want to take the paper from Alphonso Why had he given it to him and not Leela? Did this mean his son was dead. Alphonso pushed the paper again towards Donald. Slowly he reached up and took hold of the crumpled paper. His heart skipped a beat as his eyes scanned the small list of names.

"He's alive. Richard is alive." he called out loud.

Quickly he turned his attention again to the list. Leela stood in silence. The only other name the list Donald recognized was Julie's. His eyes moved quickly up and down the list searching for Alberto's name, it wasn't there neither was Donna's.

He didn't have to say anything to Leela as she began sobbing. As her crying got louder, he was unable to lift his head from the paper. His eyes kept searching for names which were not there.

"Oh no, not Alberto, why? why?" she cried out

loud.

Donald didn't know what to do or to say. The joy he originally felt had now turned to grief and the feelings of helplessness. Leela moved forward and clung to Donald, her body convulsing as she cried and cried. Suddenly she moved away trying to control her crying.

"Mama and Papa. Oh Donald they must have heard what happened. We need to get back quickly"

Donald put his arms around her shoulder.

"Let's go love, come on. I'll drive if I can get us back to our car."

Leela turned to Alphonso and began talking very fast. When she finished all he said was "Si" and started shouting at two police standing close to them. Donald hadn't understood what had been said but knew they were their escort out through the crowd.

The drive back seemed to take hours. Leela had her legs up on the seat with her body curled up in a ball. She never stopped crying. Donald tried comforting her by reaching over and touching her arm. What could he do? What could he say? His son was alive, but Alberto was dead. Hans and Carla will be devastated. He knew it was going to be bad when they got back to Falcon Ness.

The car was now turning into the hotel drive and

even before they reached the car park Hans and Carla were out on the patio, both of them were crying. Leela got out of the car and they all threw their arms around each other hugging, sobbing and trying to console each other.

Donald just stood not knowing what to do or say. For the first time since his arrival he felt on the outside looking in. He felt alone. He wanted so much just to join in a wrap his arms around them. Through the sobbing and crying Leela was talking very quickly in Spanish to her mother and father. He knew she was explaining to them what had happened. During the conversation both Hans and Carla would occasional glance in the direction of Donald. He couldn't put his finger on it but as the conversation went on the look in Hans and Carla eyes began to change. His instincts could sense there was now anger in their thoughts and feelings. Donald took a few steps forward towards them but stopped as Carla turned and started screaming at him in Spanish. Although he couldn't understand a word she was saying, he felt the anger and hatred in her voice and actions as she waved her arms around. The tone and volume of her voice did all the translation needed.

Leela broke away from her father's arms.

"No Mama, no. It is not Donald's fault. What happened was God's will. It is not anyone's fault."

She had conversed in English so Donald could

understand. Donald held up his arms outstretched in front of him as if defending himself from an imaginary foe.

"I'm sorry, so very sorry. Truly I am. I should never have come here. I came here to change my life, but I never meant to change your lives. It's all my fault. You've all been so good to me since I arrived, and this is how I have repaid you by destroying your lives."

Donald turned and walked quickly away. Leela ran after him

"No Donald. No. please don't go, it's not like that really, it's not. What happened is not your fault. How could it be?"

Donald continued to hurry away. Leela wanted to go after him but her instincts told her that at this moment her mother and father needed her more. She felt as if a knife had been driven through her heart.

Donald kept walking and didn't look back. He didn't want them to see the tears that were now rolling down his cheeks. He knew he' had to leave immediately so when he got back to the cottage, he started throwing some of his clothes in to a holdall. He packed a number of essential items and hurried out of the cottage heading for the village. He searched for a taxi, anything in which he could get a ride to Coro. He searched in vain. There was no other hotel so he thought he may be able to pay one of the local village people to take him down the mountain. By the time he got to the village square dusk was falling and it was getting dark quickly. The whole place was quiet with hardly a sole around. He stopped and went into a couple of stores and tried to make the shopkeepers understand he needed a taxi. The result was a combination of them not being able to understand English and he not being able to understand Spanish. He found himself sitting on a stone bench under a tree in front of the church. He put his bag down on the ground in front of him and placed both his elbows on his knees. His head sagged into the palm of his hands as he began to cry. His body jerked violently as his sobbing increased. Suddenly he felt a comforting hand on his shoulder and as he looked up he saw a priest stand next to him. He was muttering something in Spanish.

"I am sorry I don't understand Spanish father." he said trying to pull himself together.

"Yes I know, now that I can see your face. After all, do you think you look like a Venezuelan? I mean you 've caught the sun a lot but not that much"

The priest's English was perfect as he tried to cheer up Donald.

The priest sat down on the bench next to him and reached over, he placed his hand on to his back, giving him gentle pats.

"You know my son sometimes terrible things happened to us and when they do, we think it is the end of the world. It would be easy for me to say that this is God's will, his way of testing us but I won't, that would be too easy. Whatever it is that disturbs and upsets you is a sign you are a good person and that you care. The only way we can truly express our sincerity is through our emotions."

Donald didn't reply.

"What is it you're looking for or where do you want to go to? I saw you going into a number of stores and it was obvious that you were trying to obtain information or searching for someone."

"I am looking for a taxi to take me to Coro." Donald replied, still trying to control the quivering in his voice.

"Come with me. I know someone who can take you there, let me call him."

They both stood up and walked into the Church. The priest disappeared only for a few minutes before he returned.

"Okay, I've found you a driver, Manual is his name. You give him one hundred and fifty bolivars, no more okay. If you don't have anywhere to stay and you are looking for a hotel in Corco I've told him where to take you. It is a small hotel but very clean and owned by a good family, they will take care of you tonight. Go now, the car is outside. God be with you my son. I hope your prayers help you find peace of mind. Go quickly, it's getting dark and the trip down the mountain can be dangerous."

"Thank you father. Thank you."

Within minutes Donald was in the car and on his way. The car twisted around each bend in the road and Donald could see the lights from Coro way down in the distances. He'd not even had time to try and contact Richard in Aruba. He would try tracking him down when he got to the hotel. He hoped that he doesn't call Falcon Ness.

In his mind he kept seeing the look on Carla's face. He remembered that Hans couldn't look him in the eyes and oh his beautiful Leela, had he lost her forever? Maybe none of this would have happened if he hadn't come to Venezuela. It all seemed like a bad dream. He couldn't bear to think what he would have done if Richard had died in the air crash. Poor Donna. In all the confusion he'd completely forgot about Donna. He thought of her family. What will they be going through, how will they find out? Things where bad enough when there was this kind of disaster in Europe or the USA but here in Venezuela, they didn't have the same infrastructure and resources to respond to situations of this nature. Suddenly the car stopped, they had arrived at the hotel.

After checking in and getting to his room he began searching through his wallet, eventually he found the telephone number of Donna and Julie's apartment in Aruba. It took nearly half an hour to get his call through. The phone rang several times and then the answer machine came on. Although he left a message asking them to call him, he felt agitated and frustrated because he wanted to hear his sons voice. He felt the need to actually talk to his son to make him believe he really was still alive.

He finished his shower and lay on the bed; his thoughts were racing in so many directions. What had happened at the airport? How did they end being split up with only two of them being on the ill-fated flight? There were so many things he didn't understand. He eventually fell asleep through sheer exhaustion. He must have really been worn out because when he awoke it was after 9.00am which was unusually late for him. He showered then went for breakfast. He dined alone not knowing whether it was because he was late in getting up or whether it was because the hotel wasn't full. After his breakfast he decided to go for a walk. He needed to get his thoughts together. When he got back to the hotel there was a message from Richard.

"Sorry I missed you Dad. Julie and I are fine. We've got to go back to the airport this morning to finish off our statements etc for the official's investigation regarding the accident. We are both fine but very upset over what happened. Why are you in Coro? Try to catch you later. Love you.

Oh thank God he is safe, Donald thought. He sat in the lounge and order a coffee. Now he knew that his son was okay he had a strong impulse to get away. He didn't know where he wanted to go but he knew he needed to spend some time on his own. He needed somewhere peaceful where he could relax. He stood up and went to the desk clerk and ordered a hire car. Within a matter of a few hours he was traveling east on the Caracas road heading for Chi Chi Rivichi. Although the last time he'd been there he'd with Leela it had only been for one night. He liked the feel of the place. It had a very strong local flavor with very few gringos which was just what he sought right now.

Checking into the La Garza hotel he felt comfortable and familiar with the surroundings. Several of the staff nodded politely as a sign, a recognition. That evening he ate early and after dinner sat outside by the pool having a few drinks. He tried to relax.

When he got back to his room, he decided he needed to call Richard. He waited patiently as the call went through. Suddenly he heard Richard's voice and his heart skipped a beat.

"Hello"

"Richard, how are you son"

"Hi Dad. Oh it's great to hear from you I've been trying to get through to you for the past few days. Trying to dial into Venezuela is very difficult from here. What are you doing in Coro? I was surprised when I got your number that you were not at Falcon Ness. Is everything okay?"

Richard's voice faded as he asked the question.

"Yes son, things are fine but never mind about me. You and Julie have been through a terrible time. It's awful, the whole thing is a tragedy. I just can't believe what's happened. Is Julie okay?

Richard assured his father Julie was upset but she was fine.

"What happened Richard? How come the four of you got split up?"

Richard then began to tell his father the whole story.

"When we arrived at the airport the place was so crowded. I know it is a small departure terminal but this time the place was packed with people all trying to get on the Aruba flight. Seemingly the previous evenings' flight had been canceled and they had many people double booked. Anyway, we were standing in line to check in and

314

people kept making deals with the airline staff. The ticketing clerks would suddenly disappear into the back room with a passenger who would then come out with boarding card in their hand. It was obvious they'd bribed the airline staff. Alberto eventually got to the counter with all of our tickets. They'd checked two of the tickets through when this group of tough looking guys appeared. Right in the middle of our checking in process the clerk stopped to talk to these guys. I began to object but surprisingly no one else did, I soon found out why. Alberto quickly told me they were Colombian businessmen. I realized straight away what he meant. Sudden they'd done a deal with the Colombians giving them all the remaining seats and then they announced that the flight was full. The two tickets which had been checked in were Alberto's and Donna's. There was nothing we could do about it. The whole place was like a zoo, it was awful."

After taking a quick pause Richard continued.

"Alberto suggested that we go over to the Avia desk to see if they would be operating a small charter flight. They usually do this when a scheduled flight is so overbooked. Well, we were lucky they had two seats left and Julie and I managed to get them after a lot of assistance from Alberto. We talked before we departed and agreed we should all just make for the apartment when we got to Aruba. Our flight left before theirs and when we arrived Julie and I went straight to the girl's place. When we arrived, there was a message on the machine, she had to go and meet a friend. I went with her. We never heard about the crash until later on in the day. We were devastated, we couldn't believe it. Julie cried and cried; it was terrible."

Donald quickly responded.

"I know how you feel son. Leela and I were out at a restaurant when we heard the news. We took off and headed straight for Las Peidras airport. We couldn't get near the airport from all the crowds of people and cars. The place was crazy. Fortunately, we met up with Alphonso who helped us a lot. There was a lot of confusion on the passenger list. There was a moment when I thought that I'd lost you. Thank God that your safe. Oh I don't know what I would have done if anything had happened to you Richard."

"I know Dad. I am safe. How has Leela and her parents taken all this? I mean they idolized Alberto, they must be devastated. I know they are a very close family."

"It was bad Richard, very bad that's why I decided to get away for a few days. You know I think it's better for them to grieve as a family than have me hanging around. I felt so helpless. I didn't know what to do or what to say. They were very upset."

When Donald finished talking there was a distinct silence.

"Is everything okay Dad? Richard asked with concern in his voice.

"Sure everything is fine, just fine son. Oh by the way I am now at the La Garza Hotel in Chi Chi Rivichi "

Just as Richard was about to answer the line went dead This was not unusual for Venezuela. Donald thought about trying to get back through but decided not to, he would call in the next few days after things had settled down a bit. He was just happy that Richard was okay.

Richard was disturbed by the fact that his father was not at Falcon Ness. He couldn't put his finger on it, but he knew something wasn't right. He thought about ringing him back but felt his father wasn't telling him everything. He considered waiting until tomorrow but then decided he would call Leela. The telephone rang several times before someone answered

Richard jumped in straight away.

"Leela, is that you?'

"Yes Richard." she said in a very soft voice.

"I'm sorry to disturb you and your family Leela but I just called to tell you how terribly sorry I am about Alberto. I know you all loved him very dearly. I'm so sorry about what has happened, truly I am."

317

Once a Chameleon

Leela felt the emotion in Richard's voice.

"I know you are Richard and I shall tell Mama and Papa you called. It was very thoughtful of you to take the time."

"Listen Leela I know you and your family are very upset and grieving the loss of Alberto but has something else happened? I mean why is Dad not there with you all. He's been like family with your parents. Why is he in Chi Chi Rivichi.?"

Richard waited for Leela to responded. He heard her give an emotional sniffing sound as if she was trying to control her crying.

"He left Richard. There was a bad scene when we got back here from the airport. Mama and Papa were very upset, and a lot of things were said in the heat of the moment. It was their reaction in trying to handle the death of Alberto. Oh Richard it was bad, very bad. I know your father was so hurt by it all. I wanted to go after him when he left but I felt at that moment Mama and Papa needed me more. I love your father so much and I'm so worried about him."

"He's at the La Garza hotel" Richard responded.

"Do you have the telephone number Leela, he's there now in his room. I just talked to him in the past half

318

hour. He needs you Leela and he loves you. When I see you and him together, I can feel that there is something special about what you have for each other. I never ever saw that between my mother and father."

After catching his breath Richard continued.

"When I see how happy my father is with you, I realized just how unhappy he was with my mother. I know she is dead, and I don't mean to speak badly of her. She was my mother and I loved her, but I can see that Dad lived all those years with all his feelings bottled up inside him. I know he only stayed because of me. Once I 'd grown up and he felt I was getting my own life together, that's when he decided to start living the life of the person, he knew he really was. It's amazing how he's changed. I can hardly recognize him to the person he was. The great thing is I truly feel he's no longer just my father but a really good friend, a buddy."

Leela didn't respond but waited for him to continue.

"Please Leela help him, he needs you. I know he feels so bad about what happened and wants to be there with you and your Mama and Papa. Go and bring him back to his home, that's how he feels about Falcon Ness and all of you."

"I can't Richard, I can't." Leela replied with a quiver in her voice as she started to cry.

"Papa's very sick Richard. The doctor has just left. Up to a few years ago he used to drink heavily until the doctor told him if he continued his heart would give out and he would kill himself. Well he always managed to control his drinking to moderation until now. When he realized he'd lost Alberto he was overcome with not only grieve but guilt. He and Alberto hadn't been seeing eye to eye over the past few years. He's been drinking very heavy over the past few days. This was the only way he could handle his sorrow. Today while he and Mama were having a big fight about his drinking sessions, he collapsed. It was his heart; he's had a stroke."

"Oh Leela I am sorry. I apologize for bothering you about my father with all the troubles you have there. Now I feel really bad, I'm sorry."

"No Richard, it's okay, really it is. I love your father very very much, but he can't continue to run away from things he does not want to face up to. He's said many times that he doesn't like being a chameleon, well he has to start showing his true colors. If he loves me enough to want to spend the rest of his life with me then he has to show strength and commitment. Yes I know his feelings are hurt, well sometimes we just have to put other people's feelings before our own. I know he's a good person and has a very kind heart. Don't worry about him Richard and don't worry about us, if our love is strong enough it will bring us back together."

"I know what you mean Leela and I believe what you say. Well I'd better let you go; you need to take care of your family. I'm sorry to have disturbed you but I was worried. I hope you understand?"

"Of course, I do, you take care of yourself. We've all been through a lot these past few days. Oh Richard, if you talk to your father please don't tell him about Papa being ill. If he is going to come back, I want him to do so because he wants to and not because of Papa's condition or guilt, if you know what I mean."

"Sure Leela, I know what you mean. Goodnight and thanks for listening."

"Goodnight Richard."

They both hung up the phone.
The next few days Donald got into a regular routine. After a light breakfast he would walk down Main Street to the sea front. There he found he could take a boat taxi to a number of very small island scattered around that area of the coast. After trying one or two he had settled for Sombrero.

The island was like something from a Bounty Bar commercial off the television. It had white sanded beaches with overhanging palms trees and a large number of bushes that grew straight out of the sea. He later found out that these plants had a special root system that filtered the saltwater from the sea just like a desalination water treatment plant would do. There was one small restaurant on the island that served ice cool Polar and the specialty of the day at lunch was always freshly caught fish. If he could have stayed overnight, he would but as the islands area is deemed a Nationa Park everyone has to leave by sundown unless they'd a permit issued by the Ministry of Tourism. Donald felt as if he was in the Garden of Eden.

He used the same boatman each day to take and bring him back from Sombrero and as time went by they became amigos. This was odd due to the fact that Donald couldn't communicate with the boatman. He was however a lot bolder in trying to learn Spanish more so on the return journey from the island. Maybe this was due to the number of cold Polars he had consumed during the heat of the day. His boatman's name was Edwin, an extremely friendly and likable guy who never tried to overcharge him on the costs of the boat hire. Some days when they'd cleared the shelter of the bay, the waves would be quite high. Donald never ceased to be amazed in watching Edwin steering his craft. He always stood on the rear seat of the boat with the rudder from the motor between his knees. From this position he never faltered from steering the boat on a straight course not matter how large the waves were.

Even through their limited ability to communicate, each evening as they approached the shore Edwin would repeatedly proposition Donald telling him that Chi Chi Rivichi had Bonita Senorita. Donald would wave his hands smiling saying, No, gracias. It became a little game which they both saw the funny side of.

Lying on the beach on Sombraro, Donald had noticed each morning an old man in a small fishing boat would appear around the point and anchor at the jetty in front of the restaurant. He was obviously the provider of the "catch of the day". The old man had a fair complexion for a Venezuelan and his face was so weather beaten it looked like a piece of parchment with a map etched on to it. He wore a battered old straw hat and had sun bleached lily-white long hair protruding from under the hat. Right from the very first day as he walked past, the old man would greet Donald with Buenos Dias. Donald would smile and acknowledge his greeting.

Donald had finished his lunch and was about to order a coffee. Looking around for the waitress the old man caught his attention.

"Good afternoon Senor. How are you today? Good?"

Donald was surprised the old man spoke such good English.

"I'm fine thank you. How are you? I never realized you spoke English. Not many people do around here."

"Oh yes I learned English many years ago when I

studied in America at the University of Florida. Many years ago."

The old man's voice faded as if sleeping memories had been gently awoken.

"Well you've not forgotten, you speak good English"

Donald's reply was friendly.

"May I buy you a drink? How about a Polar? I love the Venezuelan beer"

"No thank you, but I will try a Rum if that's okay?"

"Sure that's fine."

Holding out his hand Donald introduced himself.

"My name's Donald. And yours?

"Everyone calls me Pedro but my real name is Peter Thompson"

Over the next few hours Donald discovered that Pedro, or Pete as he said he wanted to be called, was a retired businessman. Apparently, he'd started off as an engineer but later on expanded into the plastics industry where he built up an operation of three factories. He'd no sons and neither of his two daughters had shown the inclination to follow him into the industry so he sold out. Although there appeared to be a hint of sadness in his eyes, Pete indicated he was now enjoying his leisurely life. Donald enjoyed talking with him and time seemed to fly. In no time at all Edwin had arrived to take him back to the mainland. Over the next few days Donald and Pete got to know each other more and more. Donald found it so easy to talk to him. He'd been very open about his feelings and opinions especially on the issue of politics within Venezuela. He'd not directly enquired whether Donald was on holiday or lived in Venezuela. This was typical of the character of the old man, very laid-back taking life as it was being served up. With the sun beginning to sink fast they were getting ready to leave when Pete turned to Donald and asked.

"How would you like to go fishing with me tomorrow morning? You can help catch your lunch or your supper?"

"Sure that would be great. What time do you start and where do we meet up?

Donald sounded eager.

"I shall pick you up at 6.00 am at the jetty where you pick up your boat each day. Is that okay with you or is it too early?"

"No that's fine, thanks. I'm really looking forward

to it. What do I need to bring?"

"Nothing, just yourself, but be punctual we need to be at the fishing grounds very early to catch the tide turning. That's when the fish are plentiful. Okay Donald, I shall see you tomorrow."

"Sure." Donald said shaking Pete's hand.

He turned and walked towards Edwin who'd been waiting for him. As their boat pulled away Donald sat looking back towards the shore. The sun was setting behind the island and the palm trees were beginning to turn into black shaded shapes against an orange and golden blaze of sky. It was moments like this which made Venezuela one of the most beautiful places on earth.

Donald retired early that night. He'd not been sleeping too well since his arrival. It had been two weeks now and he couldn't forget the hurt he still felt in his heart. Each night as he fell asleep his thought was always of Leela. He'd wanted to call her on several occasions but as time went by each day it felt more difficult. He just didn't know what to say to express his sorrow and regrets.

He thought about how they'd first met in Miami. Then the coincidence of how he'd gone to Falcon Ness and Leela arriving there. Do coincidence really happen or are our lives planned and mapped out for us. Maybe it's just the roll of the dice. He thought about the meeting in Coro with Alberto and the sadness he saw in his eyes.

This brought back the memories of the air crash. He was
still puzzled how the four of them had been split up. The
thoughts that the split could have gone the other way sent
a shudder down his spine. His thoughts returned to Leela
as he fell asleep.

The following morning, he was up bright and
early. Pete was waiting for him at the jetty even though he
got there ten minutes early. Soon they were on their way.
On the table in the small cabin of the boat Pete had laid
on breakfast of Coffee, fresh bread and cheese. Pete was
going through the schedule for when they reach the
fishing grounds and what role Donald could play in
helping him. Donald was very excited by it all. The old
man was right, the fish were plentiful. In a matter of a
few hours the ice chests on the boat were full. Donald
had really enjoyed it but now they could relax.

Donald expected them to head back for the island
but instead Pete headed due east heading further up the
coast. As they hugged the coastline Donald sat soaking up
the beautiful scenery of miles and miles of white beaches.
Everywhere was totally unspoiled and quite deserted. He
then became aware that Pete was now heading for a small
cove ahead of them. During the docking of the boat Pete
remained silent eventually he put his arm over Donald's
shoulder as they walked along the small jetty.

Pointing to his right Pete called.

"There, over there."

Donald held his hand over his eyes to shield them from the glare of the sun.

"That is my home. This is where I live. Today we both cook lunch and guess what we are having?"

"Fish" replied Donald laughing.

"Yes, but not only fish, we are having fish and chips, that's what you English love isn't it. I have often wondered why the English call French fries, chips?"

They both laughed heartily.

Pete's home was a small cottage located right on the edge of the beach. The main part of the house was built with stone blocks which had been painted over and over again with white emulsion paint. The porch was made of a dark wood and looked as if it had been built as an extension at some later date. The bleached red tiled roof completed the perfect picture of an Andalusian styled cottage. It was simple but very clean and comfortable. Donald looked around and his eye caught on to an old picture in a worn silver frame. He moved closer to examine the picture. It was a British soldier. The style of the uniform and the handlebar mustache indicated it had been taken a long time ago.

Pete noticed Donald looking at the photograph.

James Caffrey

"My Great Grandfather."

"Your Great Grandfather?" Donald exclaimed in a surprised tone of voice.

"Yes. He came from England. His name was George Alfred Thompson. He was a sergeant in the British army for many years. I guess when he retired from the army, he realized he'd spent most of his life as a professional soldier and this was the only life he knew."

Donald looked at Pete with an interested look on his face waiting for him to continue.

"He was a member of the British Regiment of mercenaries which Simon Bolivar recruited from England to help fight for the liberation of Greater Columbia, as most of the northern part of South America was know at the time. In 1811 Greater Columbia consisted of Venezuela, Peru and the country now know as Columbia. There was a great battle and a historical victory at the Battle of Carabobo. This was when Venezuela obtained her liberty and independence. In honor of the British soldiers of fortune that helped them to gain their freedom, the people of Valencia gave them the freedom of the city and named many streets after them. We have Jones, Thompson, Smith and there are many others."

"God I never realized that Pete, that's great. They should make a movie; it would be a smash hit."

'Come on let's get on with our lunch, I'm hungry I hope you are". said Pete walking into the kitchen.

As they prepared and cooked lunch they laughed and joked. The wine tasted good washing down the fish and chips. Donald hadn't tasted fresh fish as good as this since he had left home. The leaves of white soft fish just peeled away using only a fork. After lunch as they sat on the porch. There always seemed to be a strong breeze blowing in Venezuela. This was just as well because of the intense heat.

Pete's face had a more serious look on it.

"So Donald your eyes tell me there is a lot of sadness in your heart. Paradise is a place for enjoyment not sorrow."

Pete rolled his eyes indicating the beauty that surrounded them.

"Yes Pete you are right. I came to Venezuela to escape from the life I'd been living. The life of a chameleon. I thought I could change everything and start to live my life as the person I knew I really was. I wanted to find the other person who'd been trapped inside of me for many years. What I didn't anticipate was the effect the changes in my life would have on those around me. I certainly didn't realize the hurt and sadness I would inflict on the people close to me."

Pete had a puzzled look on his face.

"A chameleon? I don't understand?"

Donald then began to open up his heart. Pete sat silent and motionless completely absorbed by what he was hearing. When Donald finished there was a long silent pause. Pete just rubbed his chin with his hand, drink in his other hand. Donald had expected an immediate response, but it never came.

Suddenly Pete stood up and swallowed his drink quickly.

"The chameleon is a very timid creature who spends most of its life being afraid. It changes its color to try and disguise it's self by use of camouflage This allows it to meld into the surrounding vegetation so it cannot be seen or caught. It is capable of changing its color many times but what it can't do is change it's shape. Nor can it change itself into a frog. a fish or any other animal. At the end of the day a chameleon will always be a chameleon"

Donald did not reply as he soaked up Pete's words of wisdom.

"It is not wrong to dream Donald. Many people live out each day of their life living on dreams. Have you ever had a dream where something really bad is about to happen when suddenly you wake up? Have you ever had a dream where something beautiful is about to happen and you still wake up?"

Donald sat listening as Pete continued.

"Not many people are fortunate enough to find real love, true love? How many couples you know are really deeply in love with each other? True love is so unique that when it occurs it shines like a beacon. When we see it in a man and woman who love each other our instincts tell us that this couple will spend the rest of their lives together. When we look at them, we feel envy. The envy is because we know they are the lucky ones who've found their true love. In this world there is only one person who is made for us, our soul mate. If you are lucky enough to find that person never let go, there is no second chance"

Donald didn't know what to say to Pete. He sat playing with his drink making the ice chink on the side of his glass.

Pete got up from his seat and gulped his rum back then started crunching the chunks of ice in his mouth.

"Come on let's go. We need to get back. I shall drop you off first."

The whole journey back was in silence. It was strange. The boat docked and after a friendly good-bye Pete cast off and headed back in the direction of Sombrero. Donald stood on the shore watching the fishing boat getting smaller and smaller in the distance. He didn't know what to make of what Pete had said. He knew he felt much better after being able to talk to someone about the hurt he felt in his heart and the trouble on his mind.

That night after dinner he headed for the pool bar and after ordering a large Remmy Martin he walked over to the far side of the pool and sat down under a cabana. His thoughts were reflecting on what Pete had said that he did not notice the rain as it began to fall. A few people sitting around the pool made a dash to get out of the rain. It started falling more heavily and loud rumblings of thunder began bellowing out. A really big storm was coming, and the temperature was beginning to drop quickly. Donald remained under the cabana fascinated by the ferocity of the rain droplets bouncing of the ground. His thoughts drifted back to the Sunday in the garden shed when he'd decided to leave. It had rained all that weekend. It always appeared to rain most weekends in England, especially in Newcastle. It's strange how the weather effects our moods. Would he have left if it had been a glorious sunny weekend? Who can tell?

He wondered what people had thought when they looked at him and Allison together. Did they look at them and think, God they look unhappy, they'll never make it together into their old age? Allison was a good person and deserved better than what happened to her. He was still totally amazed when he thought about the shoplifting. How had he missed it? Maybe he'd never really known

Once a Chameleon

her just as she'd never know him. Was it true about her infidelity? The thoughts of her death filled his eyes with tears.

The storm intensified and the rain came down like sheets of water. Huge fork lightening seemed to stretch across the heavens illuminating the sky spectacularly.

"Senor. Senor. You must come inside the storm can be very dangerous. Please come with me."

Donald looked up. It was one of the hotel staff with a very large umbrella. He got up and slowly walked into the hotel.

Usually after a few drinks Donald slept well, but tonight was different. He lay in his bed drifting in and out of his sleep, tossing and turning. He was dreaming, about Allison, Richard, about Leela, Alberto and the crash.

He was sitting on the aircraft next to Alberto who was laughing as he turned and called.

"It's okay Donald don't look so worried. I know the plane is going to crash but why should I care, I'm going to die anyway, I have aids, don't you remember. I have aids"

He twisted and turned in his bed. His body jerked violently as he experienced the impact of the plane hitting the ground.

Suddenly he was in the emergency room of the hospital. There was blood and bodies everywhere. He was being attended to by a group of doctors and nursing staff. What are they doing to me, he thought? I'm not hurt, I don't feel any pain. The medical staff seemed to be speaking in muffled tones and it was hard to catch what they were saying. Suddenly he realized they were speaking in Spanish. He felt a prick in his arm and turning his head he watched as the nurse prepared him for a blood transfusion. I don't need any blood he shouted in English, but no one understood him. His eyes followed the length of tube which was protruding from his arm. It went up and over to a man laying on the next bed who had his back to him. Who is he thought Donald? Why is he giving me blood? Suddenly the man rolled over and looked at Donald and waved.

"Hi, nice to see you Donald. How are you? Fancy meeting you here".

It was Alberto.

"No! No! Please no, you can't give me his blood he's got aids."

No one was taking any notice as panic set in. Donald wanted to struggle but couldn't move. He turned looking again towards Alberto who was now laughing loudly. Donald eyes moved focusing on the tube stretching out from Alberto's arm to his. Suddenly there was blood beginning to flow through the tube but traveling agonizingly slow.

"No, please, no. Please stop you don't understand he's sick. He can't give blood. Not too me!."

He tried to kick his legs. They wouldn't move. Slowly, very slowly the blood in the tube got closer and closer to entering his veins.

"Noooooo......."

Donald awoke with his own screaming. He lay dripping in sweat, trembling. His bed sheets were soaking wet. He got up and went into the shower. The rest of the night he spent on the chair with his dressing gown wrapped around him.

The next morning while having breakfast Donald decided he would go back to the island once more to say good-bye to Pete. He knew he needed to leave but was not sure about where he wanted to go. He thought about Leela and her family.

During the boat trip to Sobraro Donald hardly spoke a word. Edwin wasn't sure what was going on and as they couldn't converse in either English or Spanish, he had no way of knowing. He was smart enough to sense and feel all was not well and something was bothering Donald. When they reached Sombrero, Donald indicated he needed Edwin to wait. Edwin nodded his head indicating he understood and tied up the boat. Donald didn't have to wait too long before Pete arrived.

"Hi Pete, did you have a good day fishing?"

"It was okay but not that great, I think we caught them all yesterday. What are you up to?"

"I came to say good-bye, I'm leaving. I'm not too sure where I am going to, but I need to move on. Maybe I shall go back to Aruba to see my son Richard before he leaves to go back to England. I'm not sure. I'm just not sure."

"What about Leela? Are you just going to walk away and shut her out of your life? From what you have told me you love her very much. It appears to me you may be walking away from the only true love of your life. If you go now without seeing her you will regret it for the rest of your life. You'll never find another person like her and you'll return to living your life like a chameleon again. Is that what you want to do? What happened to her brother in the air crash wasn't your fault. These kinds of things happen every day all over the world. Life can be cruel, very cruel at times. You need to think hard about going back to Falcon Ness. You've spent most of your life running in search of happiness. Leela can end your journey. I realize her family is in a lot of pain and grieving the loss of their son but time heals those kinds of wounds."

Donald didn't reply, he didn't know what to say. Maybe Pete was right. A long silence followed.

Pete eventually advised Donald in a reluctant tone of voice.

"If you are thinking of going to Aruba you can go by boat. There's a ferry from Maracoy three days a week, it leaves tonight at 7:00 PM and arrives there early morning, depending on the weather."

"There is? I never realized. Listen Pete at the moment I think this is the best thing to do. If I go back to Falcon Ness I wouldn't know how to begin never mind what to say. You've been a great help and a good friend. I shall miss you. I won't say good-bye because I know in my heart, I shall see you again."

They both wrapped their arms around each other, hugging one another in friendship. Donald turned quickly and walked away, he never looked back.

On his return to the hotel Donald quickly packed his belongs and checked out. Within no time he was in a taxi heading for Maracoy. He hoped Richard and Julie were still in Aruba. His life was in such a turmoil l at the moment he needed to be with friends. He needed to be with his son.

CHAPTER XII

Upon reaching Maracoy he still had three hours to wait before sailing time. He idled the time away looking around the town. He decided to have a small snack and found a small cafe. The time went by a little quicker than he thought it would. Soon he was on board looking over the rail as the ferry cast off and set sail for Aruba. He'd booked a sleeping berth but remained on deck looking back at the shoreline as it slowly got smaller and smaller. The sun was setting very fast and the whole sky began to take on the color of an orange blaze. The edges of the small puffy clouds glowed bright golden yellow. The dark shadow of the retreating shoreline showed up as a black silhouette against the fiery red sky. Looking at the sun Donald realized for the first time he could actually see the sun dropping on the horizon. This was because twilight in this part of the world is so very brief.

After a few hours Donald decided to retire to his room to see if he could get a few hours sleep. He had a restless night, tossing and turning as the dream about Alberto kept coming back. He was glad when the ferry eventually arrived in Aruba. He found a taxi and shown the driver a piece of paper with Julie's address on it. Soon they were heading for her apartment. In the taxi he sat wondering how surprised both Richard and Julie would be at seeing him. The taxi came to a halt and Donald paid the driver. Donald looked up at the apartment building in front of him. It looked new compared to the other buildings around in the area. It was also a lot more elegant than he'd imagined. Walking up to the front entrance he looked down at the list of apartment numbers and names. He was surprised to see that the Colombian Consulate was in the same building.

After ringing the doorbell several times an old lady appeared from one of the other apartments.

"There's nobody home. They left last night with the police. They took them away. I listened up during the night, but they never returned. I think they are still at the police station. Funny going's on, really strange. I wonder what they've been up to"?

"Who did the police take away? Was it an American lady?"

"Yes, an American lady, not the one who usually lives here but her friend who stays with her on occasions. They also took the young man as well. He had a strange accent, not American that's for sure."

Donald did not reply but made a dash for the stairs. Outside he quickly waved down a cab and headed for the police station. The taxi driver kept glancing at him in a strange way through the rear-view mirror.

Upon arrival at the police station he talked with the duty officer explaining his purpose. He was politely advised to take seat and wait. After an hour had gone by, he was just about to approach the duty officer again when the door opened.

"Hi, my names Inspector Van Clerc, I believe you are looking for your son Richard?"

"Yes I am, is he okay? I've been worried about him. Is he in some sort of trouble? What's he done? I'm sure there is some mistake that's been made."

"No it's okay he's fine. He's been helping us with our inquiries and answering some questions which we now seemed to have cleared up. He'll be with you in a little while, he's just finishing off his statement. Would you like a cup of coffee?"

"Statement, I don't understand, what's it all about?"

"It's about the air crash sir, in Venezuela. I'm sure you've heard about it. In fact, your son is a very lucky young man, he could have easily been on board. It was a bomb which caused the explosion."

The officer had just finished talking when the door opened, and Richard walked in. They both looked at each other for one brief moment then hurried towards one another wrapped their arms around each other hugging very tightly. As if by telepathy they both broke away at the same instant. The inspector felt a little uncomfortable by his presence, so he decided to leave them alone for a while, he knew they had a lot to talk about. When the office door closed behind the inspector Donald jumped straight in.

"What the hell is going on here? Why have they brought you in for questioning about a bunch of Colombians who decided to blow each other up? I don't understand. What about Julie, is she here with you? Have you seen her since you were both brought here last night?"

"Calm down Dad, calm down, everything is going to be fine. The police are just doing their job. A lot of people died in the air explosion. They're just trying to find out what happened, that's all. Julie's here somewhere. I've not seen her, but the inspector said she's fine. She's in good hands Alphonso's here. He's working with the Aruba police on the investigation he's really been great. I can tell you when I saw him my heart skipped a beat. I've never felt so relieved in my life"

"Alphonso's here? Yeah I guess he would be. Were the Colombians drug barons? Does anyone know why this happened? All those poor innocent people why did they all have to die that way?"

"I don't have the answers Dad. It's a very violent world we live in where the value of life means so little to some people."

They both stopped talking as the door opened

and Julie walked in with Inspector Van Clerc. When she saw Donald, she rushed to him wrapping her arms around his neck with tears running down her cheeks. He wasn't sure whether she was happy to see him or just glad the ordeal was coming to an end. She was still crying as the inspector coughed as a sign he needed their attention. They all turned in response.

"Okay Madam. Sir. Thank you for your help, we're very grateful for the information you have given to us. You can both go home now."

No one spoke as they hustled their way out of the building. Even in the taxi on the way back to the apartment the journey was in silence. Donald quickly paid off the taxi driver and followed Richard and Julie into the apartment. Walking through the door he was very surprised by the decor and elegance of the place. It didn't quite look like the apartment of two young ladies making their living as waitresses. It was an odd feeling he felt. He sat down on the large couch in the living room area. Richard and Julie were in the kitchen mixing drinks. He heard the sound of ice clinking as it was being put into the glasses. They both walked out together.

"Can someone please explain to me just what is going on? Now I know what a mushroom feels like. What's this all about, what am I missing?"

Julie looked at Richard with a funny look on her face she responded.

"When the police started checking into the background of all the passengers on the aircraft, they discovered some very detailed information especially regarding Donna. They thought we were a part of the operation, but we were obviously not. At first, they wouldn't believe us then Alphonso convinced them he knew us personally. In the end they backed off. That's it."

"That's it. That's it. What the hell are you talking about Julie? People died on that aircraft, innocent people, wives, husbands, children and friends. All of the people who died were loved by someone and will be missed. What operation are you talking about? I don't know what you mean. Am I missing something?"

Julie and Richard were both surprised by the angry tone of Donald's voice. Julie continued.

"Look around you. Does this apartment look as if it's inhabited by two working class waitresses? I've been paying Donna half of the rent for months. I never dreamed she owned the place. She took rent from me each month even though there were times when I had to struggle to make the payment. I always thought she rented the place for a steal. She told me it belonged to a friend who'd had gone abroad to work. Never in my wildest dreams did I think she owned the place. I was shocked when the police told me. The police also found out she'd over two hundred and fifty thousand dollars in her local bank account here in Aruba. Can you believe that. This place is worth at least another two hundred thousand."

Donald sensed the anger and rage building up inside Julie.

"She was my best friend. We've known each other since our high school days, and she deceived me. I can't believe it. I thought she was my friend. All those trips she persuaded me to go with her. She used me that's what she did. How could she do that to her best friend? How? Do you know how many times I went through so many different airports with her and thought nothing of it when she asked me to help her with her baggage? I could have ended up being locked away in some dark dingy prison for the rest of my life. She used me to peddle all that filthy shit that kills people. Those guys who blew up the plane
were her partners, her partners that's who they were. It's so ironic they all died together. When we left Falcon Ness to go on that three-day trek it was all arranged to meet her contacts. I feel so stupid but most of all I feel deeply hurt. What she's done to me still doesn't stop me from loving her, that's the crazy thing. I am going to miss her so much."

Julie had tears in her eyes but didn't cry. She'd a staunch determined look on her face as she wiped her eyes with a Kleenex. Richard and Donald sat gazing at each other. Donald was shell shocked. Julie started walking towards the bathroom and half turning she called.

"I'm going in the shower. Then I'm going to crash for a few hours. I feel awful. It's as if I've not showered for a week. I must smell terrible; how can you guys stand it. Listen I'm sorry for blowing up as I did. It's not your fault. It's my own stupidity. Anyway, how about we all get dressed up and go out to dinner tonight. I need cheering up. Is that okay?"

They both nodded their head in approval.

Donald and Richard were now alone. Donald got up to go into the kitchen.

"Not for me Dad, I don't think I can finish this one off. I'm not used to drinking so early."

"Oh neither can I, in fact what I have left is going down the drain. How about a nice cup of coffee, do you fancy that son?"

"Sounds great to me Dad."

Richard got up and walked towards the kitchen.

"Listen Dad I'm am just as shocked as everyone else about this whole thing with Donna. I never had a clue what she was up to. Apparently, the police think Donna was not only a courier but an important player in some large drug organization. The police out of Holland have been working for months with the FBI and the

James Caffrey

DEA in America. It's amazing, the whole thing is quite amazing. Who would have thought? Anyway, enough about that let's talk about you, what the hell are you doing here? I never expected you to turn up. Have you been back to Falcon Ness? Have you seen Leela yet?"

Donald poured the hot water into the coffee cups and stared down at the coffee granules as they fizzled away melting with the heat of the boiling water. He picked up the two cups and handed one to his son. They both walked back into the living room and sat down. Donald began to explain what had happened. and Richard sat silently listening to his father's story. He wasn't the only one listening. Julie had finished her shower and was now curled in a ball on the bed. The bedroom door had been left open only a few inches, but it was enough for her to overhear what was being said. She eventually dropped off to
sleep with sheer exhaustion.

Within the next hour Richard had started nodding off as his father's voice became a faint hum in the background. At first Donald didn't notice just how exhausted and tired his son was. Reaching over he adjusted the cushion under his head and moved him into a more comfortable position. He leaned over and kissed Richard on the forehead.

Once he had finished clearing up the coffee cups, he felt he needed to get out so decided to go for a walk. This was the third time he had been to Aruba, but he hadn't really seen much of the island. It didn't occur to him to get a taxi as he began walking along the broad walk. Only occasionally did the sound of the waves distract him from his thoughts. He started thinking about how this had all began. He wanted to change his life and he certainly did. He wondered whether there would be anything good, anything worthwhile that would come out of it all. Then as always, his thought turned to Leela.

The sounds of the shower running first woke up Julie who sprung up in her bed then relaxed as she got her thoughts together. She'd slept well and felt as if a load had been lifted off her mind.

Richard stirred two or three times before he eventually sat up. When Julie walked into the room, he was rotating his neck round and round to take out the stiffness he felt from the way he had been lying. He watched Julie as she walked across the room into the kitchen.

"Do you want anything to drink Richard? I'm gagging for a drink."

"Errr yes, I'll have a beer please. Boy I slept good what about you, did you sleep well?"

"Yeah, like a log and I needed it. I absolutely crashed out. I guess all that stress really wears you down. What did your father do all day as we slept? Did he go out? It must have been a great day for him with both of us just crashing out."

At that moment Donald walked out of the bathroom.

"I had a lovely day I walked and walked for miles. There is not any part of this island I don't know about. Ask me, go ahead ask me?"

This seemed to break the ice as they all started laughing together. Donald continued drying his hair. He turned and asked in a mocking Oxford English tone of voice as if he had a plumb in his mouth.

"Okay young lady, tonight is your night, where would you like to go? Pick somewhere really nice where you only go to on special occasions. I'm sure you have a special place here in Aruba. Oh we're not going to the Waterfront, the staff and service there leaves a lot to be desired. I mean you wait an hour for a drink, it's bloody awful."

Now he really had them all laughing. It was just what they all needed to get the night started off on the right foot. Julie walked over to Donald and kissing him gently on the cheek she whispered.

"You're a beautiful person Donald and I love you."

Just as he was starting to blush, she suddenly

tugged at the bath towel around his waist.

"Yeah, you naughty woman, not now, not in front of the children. Come on you two let's get ready and hit the town. Tonight, we forget all our worries and troubles."

The restaurant Julie had selected was "Chez Pauline" which was located near the rear of the Sonesta Hotel. It was situated on the corner of small square and had a number of tables with umbrellas which were scattered around the pavement outside the entrance. They'd decided to eat inside as it was air-conditioned and also the atmosphere inside suited their mood.

The menu was French Cuisine but not too sophisticated. They all order the same dish which one of the specialties of the house. A fillet steak and several large shrimp served on a scorching hot skillet. Around the outside edges of the skillet was onion, tomato, green and red bell peppers and raw chopped garlic Before the hot skillet arrived the waitress tied a bib like napkin around each of their necks to protect their clothing from the fat and juices of the hot sizzling food as it splashed out. The skillet was placed on the table and all the items in turn were the dropped on to the hot skillet with a loud sizzling sound giving off a cloud of steam. The idea was that each diner could turn and cook the steak and shrimp to suit. Their appetites were good, so the food went down well. The beer and the wine also helped to wash everything down.

James Caffrey

They were now drinking their cappuccino and cognac and listening to the gentle music of the small combo who were playing. During the whole course of the meal nobody had spoken much. Maybe it was because they were hungry but now they were beginning to relax and soak up the ambiance of the occasion. Donald was staring at Richard who now appeared to be so grown up. He'd matured an awful lot during the past few months. Richard smiled at his father as if he knew what was going through his mind. Julie's head was slightly turned in the direction of the small stage in the corner where the band was playing. The features of her beautiful face stood out against the candlelight from the surrounding tables. Donald had always felt she was attractive but tonight she looked gorgeous. Julie turned her head quickly as if she'd sensed he was looking at her. The smile on her face and the look in her eyes said it all. She was happy.

The effects of the beer, wine and cognac was beginning to give them a warm glow inside. Donald broke the spell as he asked.

"Well then, how does everyone feel? Are you all starting to cook on gas? I feel great. What shall   we do? Shall we have another drink here then go on to somewhere else? I fancy another one of those cognacs, how about you two?"

They both agreed and in no time at all the waitress had brought another round of drinks. The service had been excellent all evening, so Donald had made note to tip well. While enjoying their cognac they talked and agreed that when they'd finished at Chez Pauline they would then go to the night club at the Sonesta Hotel which was close by.

Making their way to the hotel Julie walked between Donald and Richard with her arms linking each of them. Donald was on form with his joking which had the other two in stitches from laughter. Richard had never realized that his father could be so funny.

When they arrived at the night club is was just beginning to get busy. They were lucky and got a good table against the back wall away from the dance floor and stage. He remembered the story Leela had told him about the Venezuelan boy who when asked by his schoolteacher, "What kind of music do you like" he replied, "Loud". That's the way it was is this part of the world no matter where you went the music was always played very loud. It was part of their culture. At least where they were sitting they could hear themselves talking. The festivities quickly livened up and the place was in full swing. The band played a mixture of old standards and a few current top ten hits. When they switched into a melody of Latin music the floor immediately filled up with couples eager to dance to the Latin beat. Donald thoughts drifted back to Leela and the way they'd danced together. He was deep in thought and at first didn't hear Julie calling to him above the din of the music. Suddenly he turned his head quickly as he heard her ask.

James Caffrey

"Come on Donald, show me how to dance the Latin way, which you and Leela dance so well to".

Before he could respond she'd reached out her hand taking a hold of his gentle pulling him on to the dance floor. He didn't really want to dance but didn't have the heart to turn her down. In fact, he was not too sure he could remember the movements. Leela had always been the one that had led him through their dancing. Donald and Julie were dancing together and giving it their best shot, but it wasn't the same.

In fact, even when he put his arm around Julie's waist it didn't feel the same. Leela's body felt so soft and her skin silky smooth. Even through the fabric of her dress Leela's skin and muscle tone that felt soft.

Richard had been watching them as they danced, and he sensed what was going through his fathers' mind. Although he knew that his father was enjoying himself with Julie, he felt Leela was always on his father's mind. When they returned to their seats Julie ordered another round of drinks. She was knocking them back pretty fast now and starting to get a little drunk. Neither of them had seen her like this before but they both accepted if this was how she wanted to get everything out of her system then it was fine by them. The evening wore on, but Julie's drinking slowed down. Apart from the fact she wasn't a really al drinker, she had sensed their concern. Richard was now beginning to yawn and decided to call it a night letting his father and Julie know he was going home. They both still had about three quarters of a glass of drink to finished but indicated they wouldn't be very far behind.

Opening the door of the apartment Julie dropped the keys with a loud clatter as they hit the floor.

"Shush Julie. Richard is asleep, you don't want to waken him do you?"

"No, no we don't Donald." Julie replied trying to whisper but without much effect as she kicked off her shoes with a thud.

"Sit down over here and I will make you a nice cup of coffee." Donald continued, still trying to be as quiet as he could.

Julie staggered towards the couch. As she fell on to the cushions, she bounced causing her legs to fly into the air. Her eyes were already closed as her head hit the cushion. She was too far gone to realize her dress was now around her waist exposing her thighs.

After a few minutes Donald walked in from the kitchen with two steaming hot cups of coffee. He nearly spilled the coffee as he attempted to place the cups on the small table. He was distracted by the sight of Julie's legs. Slowly his eyes moved up the length of her legs to her exposed thighs. He felt a little embarrassed knowing she'd had a little too much to drink. Reaching over he attempted to cover her legs when suddenly she woke up.

Donald attempted to move away but Julie caught hold of his hand. She moved her hand on to the back of Donald hand placing his open palm onto her thigh. With her eyes only half open, she begin prompting his actions by moving his hand up and down her inner thigh.

Julie's body began responding as she arched her back and reached up wrapping her arms around Donald's neck. The movement of Donald's hand on her thigh continued without her coaching. Her lips gently nibbled at his neck.

"Do you want me Donald? Do you? I've wanted to make love to you from the first night we met. Sometimes I'd lie in bed at night fantasizing, imagining yours hands on my body."

Julie continued nibbling at Donald's neck and ears. She shifted her position on the couch slowly but deliberately parting her legs ever so slightly, leaving very little to the imagination. Donald never moved as she continued talking to him.

"I know you want me Donald, I've always known. I can feel it when you look at me. I know you're a shy person and always act the perfect gentleman, but I feel there's a fire burning deep inside of you. Remember what you told me about the right time and the right opportunity. Well your time's up."

Once a Chameleon

Donald was dumb struck.

"I love you Donald, I guess I fell in love with you the day we spent together on the beach. You're the first man I've met who never tried to hit on me. You continually made me feel that you respected me, and you always treated me like a lady. That's a real nice feeling. A woman needs to feel like this way because it gives her a warm glow deep down inside. I know you've never admitted it, but I feel you love me if only a little. I'm sure your love will grow stronger and stronger the more time we spend together."

Julie moved her body into a horizontal lying position. Donald ended up a half kneeling on the edge of the couch. She looked up staring into his face moving her hands around his neck and arching her back she reached up to kiss him passionately. Just for a brief second she felt a response from him but in a moment is was gone.

He quickly moved back into an upright sitting position.

"No Julie, I can't, I just can't. It doesn't feel right."

Julie hesitated then sat up. After straightening her clothes, she didn't lift up her head but continued to stare at the carpet. She felt bad, really bad and was trying desperately not to cry. She felt she'd made a complete fool of herself and now she didn't know what to say. She felt cheap. Slowly she lifted her head and turned to look at Donald.

"Don't you like me Donald? Even if you don't love me just a little, you must like me?

Donald never responded

The tears were gathering in Julies eyes.

"Oh God, I've made such a fool of myself and I've embarrassed you as well. You must think I am an awful person throwing myself at you like I did. I am so sorry"

Donald moved towards her and took both her hands in his.

"Listen Julie of course I like you, in fact I like you very much. You're a beautiful girl and nothing would be easier than for me to tell you that I loved you, except for the fact that I love someone else. You are very desirable, and some men would die to be able to make love to you, but I can't deceive you. What's the difference between liking you a lot and loving you a little? Julie there is no such thing as a little bit of love, either you love someone, or you don't it's as simple as that. I don't want to hurt your feelings but it's impossible for me to fall in love with you. I've already given all the love I have in my heart to someone else. There's no more left."

Julie stared into Donald's eyes as he continued.

"When I first met you and the rest of your group at Friday's Cafe in Aruba, you were all so friendly. Without knowing who I was, where I'd come from you invited me to join your party. That initial contact was the booster I needed. You made me feel good about myself. At the time it was alone, in search of the real person I knew existed within me. I'd taken a bold step in search of my new identity not knowing whether everything would blow up in my face and send me packing back home. Those first few days we spent together will always live in my heart. This was when I discovered my real character and identity. I shall never forget the beautiful day we spent together at the beach. For the first time in my life I experience a sense of freedom which will forever live in my memory."

Donald paused not knowing how to continue. Eventually he slowly let go of her hands. She saw a look of shy embarrassment in his eyes and it was at that moment she realized there was no hope for her.

As she stood up Julie forced a hint of a smile.

"I guess we had better to go bed. Well what I mean is you and I sleep separately."

Before she could continue they both smiled and gave each other a hug.

As Julie turned to walk into her bedroom Donald

quietly called out.

"Good night Julie."

Julie did not respond but continued to walk into her bedroom.

CHAPTER XIII

Return to Falcon Ness

As the taxi driver turned off the main Coro road to start the journey up the mountain, Donald hadn't any idea on how he was going to handle things. Fortunately, during a telephone call with Alphonso, he had offered Donald the use of one of his cottages which was located about two miles from Falcon Ness. He decided to accept Alphonso's offer to spend some time alone to reflect on what had happened. He didn't feel the time was right to suddenly turn up at the hotel when Leela and her family were still grieving.

Near the top of the mountain the driver stopped and asked for directions to the cottage. Eventually the taxi came to a halt. As Donald got out of the taxi, he could see that the entrance was overgrown with vegetation. Well he thought, I know what my first task will be. The taxi driver took the money from Donald and smiled as if he had read Donald's thoughts.

When he walked through the door, he was pleasantly

surprised by the décor and cleanliness of the cottage. He took his suitcase to the bedroom which was located at the rear of the cottage. The front of the house was on the main road, but he knew the traffic would be light. He walked into the kitchen and found a note from Alphonso advising him that the cleaning lady provided once a week service. She'd also picked up a few basic food supplies. Donald turned and opened the refrigerator door. The shelves inside were well stocked with milk, cheese, butter, eggs and plenty of salad and fruit. There was also a good supply of polar beer. As he turned, he saw three bottles of Johnnie Walker Black Label on the table. He reached back in the fridge and took out a cold Polar. Oh…. after the long journey its tasted good.

Over the next few days Donald worked at clearing up the outside areas of the cottage. He chopped back a large amount of vegetation. He paid a couple to local workmen to take the garden waste away. Things were beginning to look ship shape. He'd found some old tins of paint and set about trying to brighten up the outside of the cottage. When he was painting one of the window frames he turned when he heard someone approaching. It was the priest from the village church.

As he placed his bicycle against a wall, he greeted Donald.

"Good morning senor. Isn't it a beautiful day?"

"Good morning father. Yes, it is but then again every

day is a lovely day."

The priest smiled and walked over to Donald to shake his hand. Donald placed the paint brush on the lid of the can and wiped his hands. They shook hands.

"My name is father Gomez."

"It's nice to meet you Father Gomez. My Name is Donald"

Father Gomez looked at the front of the cottage and the small garden and continued his conversation.

"Well Donald you really have done a good job cleaning this place up. It now looks like it used too, several years ago when it was occupied. An old couple lived here; it was many years but when the husband died his wife sold the place to a businessman from Coro."

Donald nodded his head as he responded.

"The owner is a friend of mine and he offered me a place to live for a while. I'd previously done work for him supervising the contractor who was building his villa on the other side of the mountain. "

"So are you a professional engineer?" the priest asked.

"Yes I'm a civil engineer with previous experience on infrastructure projects, building etc."

Donald saw a glint in the priest eyes.

"I see, that's good. I hope you don't mind me asking but could you find time to help with repairs to our village church? I have several small leaks in the roof and some of the doors need fixing. The church is very old. You can imagine in this environment the church has very limited funds. I could maybe pay you a small amount for your time, if that's okay?"

"No problem father I've got time to help. If you are able to provide the material don't worry about payment for my time. When would be the best time for me to take a look at what needs fixing?"

Father Gomez hunched his shoulders as he replied.

"How about tomorrow morning, or is that too soon?"

"Tomorrow morning will be fine. Do you mind if I come early? If I'm going to be climbing on the roof of the church, I'd rather do it before the sun gets too hot. Also does the church have a tall ladder or can I access the roof from inside the church?"

"Come as early as you wish. The roof can be accessed via the bell tower and there are walkways on the roof." Father Gomez replied.

"That's good. Okay I'll be there around 7.00am."

Father Gomez shook Donald's hand then got on his bicycle and rode off.

That evening after dinner Donald sat out on the front porch drinking a cold beer. He loved the smell of the evening air and the noise of the crickets buzzing. Occasionally a large moth would appear flying around the lantern. Donald watched the moth as it went around and around being drawn in by the attraction to the light. The atmosphere reminded him of the evenings he and Leela had when sitting outside at Falcon Ness. His heart felt heavy.

The next morning Donald got up early, had a light breakfast and made his way down to the church in the village. When he arrived the only person in the church was the cleaning lady. Donald smiled at her and she returned his greeting with a slight wave of her hand. She then started walking towards the back of the church and beckoned Donald to follow her. As he approached, she stood pointing towards a small hatched door. Donald realized this must be the access to the bell tower. The lady turned and walked away. Donald climbed through the door and proceeded to climb the ladder to the top of the tower. He stepped onto the roof and stood for a moment gazing at the splendor and beauty of the valley which stretched far into the distance. He looked in the direction of Falcon Ness but the hotel was hidden by large trees. However further down the mountain he could see the road to the village.

With a clip board in hand, Donald started the inspection of the roof. He could see several areas that had been patch previously. Whoever had carried out the previous repairs had done that great of a job. It took him just over one hour to finish his inspection. The sun was now beginning to rise higher and Donald could feel the heat starting to generate from the roof top. He stepped back inside the bell tower into a shaded area where he could complete his notes. He sat at a small table next to one of the windows so he could take advantage of the slight breeze at it passed through the tower. He took a drink from a bottle of water he'd brought with him. He lowered the bottle from his lips and looked out of the window. His heart missed a beat. In the distance he could see the lonely figure of Leela jogging up the road from the village to the hotel. As she did most days when jogging, she stopped halfway up the hill and sat on a wooden bench. She took a drink from a bottle of water then poured the remaining water over her head and shoulders as he'd seen her do so many times before. He continued to watch her as she stretched both arms above her head and clenched both hands together. He wanted to see her and be with her so desperately, but the time wasn't right, he needed more time. Sooner or later she would find out that he was back in the village and he would face that situation when it happened.

He made his way down the bell tower and stepped back into the church through the small door. He was dusting himself down when father Gomez approached him.

"So how does it look up there? Will you be able to fix the holes in the roof? I hope you can because this will save us from running around with buckets when it rains. We don't have a lot of rain here but when it rains it pours."

Donald smiled.

"Hello father. Well the roof doesn't look too bad. I've marked up the areas which need to be patched. This includes some areas that have previously been repaired. I'm not sure who done the previous repairs but with respect, they didn't do that great of a job. I've also put together a list of materials that needs to be purchased.

Father Gomez nodded his head. "I Understand. Thank you for helping out."
Donald detached the list of material from the clip board and handed it to Father Gomez.

"So father, when do you think you will have the material here? I'd like to get started on the repair program as soon as possible."

Father Gomez scratched his head and replied.

"Give me a few days and it will all be here. Oh by the way I have two part time volunteers who have agreed to help you. Let's just say they volunteered as part of their penance which is to help within the local community."

Donald smiled wishing to ask what misdemeanor the two volunteers had committed but decided to remain quiet. He shook hands with Father Gomez and walked back to the cottage.

There was an old BBQ pit at one end of the cottage porch that Donald had cleaned up a few days earlier. He'd decided to grill that evening, so he'd picked up some chicken from the village butcher. With a cold beer in his hand, he sat in the chair absorbing the smell of the chicken being cooked. The chicken took just under an hour to cook and about quarter of an hour to eat. It tasted good. He heard voices then saw a young man and woman walk hand in hand along the road. They both started laughing and talking loudly. It was obvious they'd been drinking that evening. Suddenly the man reached forward and grabbed the girl around the waist and pulled her towards him in a passionate embrace. The girl responded wrapping her arms around the young man's neck. Their kiss went on for a long time before they moved apart. Neither of them spoke. Instinctively the girl turned her head and looked across the road to where Donald was sitting. He felt a little embarrassed, so he waved his hand as a sign of a friendly gesture. The girl reacted by grabbing the young man's hand and walked over toward where Donald was sitting.

"Hello senor" she said in English with the hint of a slur in her speech.

"Hello" he replied.

"So senor what is your name? My name is Indira, and this is my friend Thomas." She continued to add.

"My name is Donald."

The young man had had a lot more to drink. He stood there for a moment trying to get his thoughts together.

"Yes. My name is Thomas and I'm Indira's boyfriend". He announced with pride.

Indira reacted with a look of mischief in her eyes.

"Boyfriend! did you say boyfriend? How many times do I have to tell you that you are not my boyfriend. We are good friends who enjoy each other's company. Okay?"

Thomas managed to retain his balance then slouched down and sat on the steps of the porch as he muttered something under his breath.

Indira walked over and sat next to Donald. She pointed her finger at Thomas.

"Don't take any notice of him, he's drunk."

Donald had a big smile on his face as he found the whole situation very comical.

Indira placed her hand on Donald's knee.

"So gringo Donald what brings you to this part of the world? Are you looking for a lovely woman? This is the place if you are. There's lots of them here and most of them are available."

"No I'm not looking for a woman." He replied lightheartedly.

With a puzzled look in her eyes Indira continued.

"So if you are not looking for a woman then what are you doing here? This is a very remote place to find a gringo like you here."

He knew his answer would puzzle Indira and most likely prompt another question, but Donald proceeded to give the answer which came to mind.

"I'm looking to find myself. I've been searching for quite some time. For a while I thought I had discovered who I really was… then the sky fell in."

"The sky fell in?" Indira repeated more as a question

than a statement.

Donald pattered the back of her hand which was still placed on his knee.

"That's an expression we use to describe an event in our life that is not good or when something bad happens." Do you understand Indira?

She nodded her head but still had a puzzled look on her face.

Donald decided to change the subject.

"So Indira do you and Thomas live in the village?"

"No, we live about two miles down the mountain. There is a group of houses, a few shops and of course three bars. Venezuelans are a nation of people who loved to drink, sing and dance. It helps us to forget about the life of poverty we lead. They say that in Venezuela the average married male gives his wife forty percent of his salary to feed the family and look after the home. He keeps the other sixty percent for himself and spends it on drinking and socializing."

Donald nodded his head and let Indira continue.

"Listen Donald tomorrow night we want to invite you to a party. It's an engagement party for my cousin. There will be lots of good food, drinking and of course music. Would you like to come? It's being held at the Como Cey restaurant starting at 7.00pm. Please say you will"

Donald smiled and thanked Indira for the invited but did not commit one way or the other.

Indira nudged Thomas.

"Come on Thomas……. it's time for us to go home."

Thomas stirred as Indira reached down to help him stand up. Donald stepped forward and moved over to assist. Thomas was now standing upright, but his head swayed from side to side. As the couple walked away Donald smiled to himself. She's right he thought, Venezuelans love to socialize and enjoy themselves. Maybe there is some merit to their crazy lifestyle of living for today and letting tomorrow take care of itself.

The next morning Donald left the house early so he could get started on the roof repair before the sun got too hot. When he arrived at the church the helpers were waiting for him. As he approached them, they both reached to shake his hand.

"Good morning gentlemen. Do either of you speak English?" he asked

The taller of the workmen responded.

"Yes we both speak a little English. We learned in working with the Gringo construction companies. My name is Amberto and this is Marco."

"I'm please to meet you both. I'm sure we are going to make a good team. When we finish let's hope that we will have not only pleased Father Gomez but also our Heavenly Father who is looking down on us. At the moment I could do with some divine intervention in my life."

Donald had a grin on his face. Alberto and Marco just looked at each other with a puzzled look on each of their faces.

The morning work proceeded better than expected. At around 1.00pm Donald advised the workers that they had finished for the day and he would see them the same time tomorrow morning.

He'd decided to eat lunch at the small restaurant in the corner of the town square. The smell of their cooking while he was working on the roof of the church had convinced him to see if the food was as good as it had smelled. Before he'd even ordered his meal, the waitress had placed a large glass of red wine on his table. She'd explained it was included in the price of the meal. He eased his chair back away from the table and stretched his legs. He took a drink of the wine which was smoother than anticipated. He called over the waitress.

Once a Chameleon

"Hello Senora, this wine is very good, does it have a brand name?" he asked.

The waitress smiled as she lightheartedly corrected Donald. "First of all, senor......with respect, I'm not married therefore I'm a Senorita."

They both laughed. She held the bottle in front of Donald and continued.

"The wine is from Chile. It's one of the best and cheapest wines in the whole world. Everyone in Venezuela loves Chilean wine, especially this particular wine. It's called Cato Negro. Or in English…. Black Cat. You like it? Here, let me fill your glass."

"Thank you, Senorita." Donald replied with a warm smile. There was something about this waitress that reminded Donald of home. It was a feeling of comfort and familiarity. Before the waitress walked away Donald asked her what her name was.

"My name is Camilla" She replied, "And what is your name?

"My name is Donald"

"Nice to meet you Donald, do you know what you would like to eat, or do you need more time?"

"Well I spent the early half of the day working on the

church across the street, I am helping Father Gomez with some repairs. Anyway, while I was up there, I kept smelling a delicious scent coming from this restaurant and I thought I should see if the food tastes as good as it smells, I'm just not sure what is was I was smelling. What would you recommend?"

Camilla was pleasantly surprised that this Gringo was helping out the local church as he clearly was not from this country. She made a note to ask Donald why he is in Venezuela before he left the restaurant.

"Yes, the food does taste as good as it smells I promise you!" Camilla responded with a wide smile across her face

"You were probably smelling the Chivo-al-coco, it's one of our most popular dishes so we always seem to be cooking it, would you like to try it? It's very good."

Donald was trying to decipher what Chivo meant in English. After the plane scare with Richard, Donald vowed he would pay more attention and try harder to learn the language. But just to be sure he replied...

"My Spanish is not good, but I think Chivo means goat in English right? Is this a goat dish?"

"Yes, it does mean goat, Chivo-al-coco is shredded goat meat that is slowly cooked with coconut milk and is served with mofongo, it's like a mix between a stew and a curry. It's a perfect dish for lunch and very popular during the summer here in Venezuela."

"I don't normally eat goat, but you make it sound so good I think I'll just have to order it." Donald replied with a nervous laugh.

"Its good to try new things!" Camilla replied. "I will go place your order in Donald, it should only take twenty to twenty-five minutes.

As Camilla walked away to take care of another table, Donald topped off his glass of wine. While he was waiting for his lunch order, he began thinking about how much he loved Venezuela, he loved how friendly all the local people were, he liked the weather, almost every day it was guaranteed to be a sunny day, he loved the food and the beer, but most of all he was beginning to like himself, at least the person he was growing to be in Venezuela. What was it about this place that made him so different?

Donald thought back to his married days and how his personality had changed since then.
He thought back to when Allison and he used to go out for date night. They used to go to the same restaurant, on the same night of the week, around the same time. Allison used to order the glazed salmon with Asparagus and broccoli, and Donald used to order fish and chips. The entire thing was so predictable and boring, neither Donald nor Allison would order anything

374

different. How odd thought Donald.

What stopped me from ordering something different? The fish and chips were good but not that good. Was Allison holding me back from trying new things or was I holding myself back? Could I have been a more adventurous person while I was with her? Donald realized his negative thoughts were beginning to spiral, luckily Camilla broke his thoughts when she brought Donald his lunch.

"Okay Senior Donald, here is your lunch." Camilla set the plate Infront of Donald and told him to be careful because the plate was very hot."

Donald looked down at his plate to see that Camilla was spot on when she described this dish as a mix of a stew and a curry. The sauce had a yellow tint to it which reminded Donald of an Indian curry, but the thick chunks of goat meat, onion and garlic gave it the perception of a stew.

Donald wondered if this really was what he had been smelling from church. He leaned forward over the bowl, just far enough so that his nose was caught under the steam that was coming from his plate. He closed his eyes and took a big breath in.

"mmmmm…. That smells fantastic!" he said to no one in particular

Camilla was standing next to Donald's chair waiting to see his reaction to the dish.

"I'm glad you like the smell, now let's see if you like the taste."

Donald Took his spoon and collected a piece of goat meat, some vegetables and as much sauce as his spoon could hold, bringing the spoon up to his lips he blew on it as to not burn his mouth.

"wow that's an amazing flavor! The texture of the goat is like silk that just falls apart."

"I'm happy you like it; I will let you eat your lunch in peace and come back to check on you in a little while." Said Camilla.

As Camilla walked away Donald continued to eat his lunch. He hadn't noticed how hungry he was until he began eating. It didn't take him long to finish his lunch or his wine.

Camilla came to clear the plate and ask if Donald wanted another bottle of wine.

"No thank you, one bottle is enough for me. Thank you for your recommendation, it was truly a great meal."

"well I am happy you enjoyed it."

Camilla wanted to find out more about Donald before he left so she thought she would take the chance now while he was full and pleased with his meal.

"I have been wondering what brings you to Venezuela. Especially to this little town? Asked Camilla.

Donald was starting to get tired of getting asked this question. Not wanting to show his emotions, he replied in a friendly manner.

"I came here to do some soul searching, I have been here some months now and have had a great time. This country is so beautiful, and everyone is very friendly."

Camilla was hoping to get more of a detailed answer from Donald but decided she better not push him.

"Yes, we Venezuelans are a friendly bunch." She said with a smile.
Donald couldn't help but stare at her smile, she had a beautiful smile, it was warm and full of genuine feeling.

"You have a great smile" Donald told Camilla.

"Thank you Senor Donald I like your smile too".

They both began laughing. If anyone were to look at their table, they would assume that these two people have been lifelong friends. Their conversation was smooth and pleasant, and their body language was very relaxed with each other.

"Speaking of being a friendly Venezuelan" Camilla Continued, "some of my friends and I are having a bonfire on the beach tonight, I would love it if you could join us? That is if you don't have other plans?"

It took Donald a few seconds to respond with an answer. One part of him wanted to just have a quiet night in, do some thinking about where he should go next. He came to Venezuela to do some soul searching but meeting so many friends on the way created more pleasant distractions that did not allow him time to really sort out his thoughts. On the other hand, he had met so many nice people and had shared his story numerous times that it was nice to get feedback, listen to what others thought about him and his situation. Then he remembered Indira's invitation to join her cousin's engagement party, that was tonight. He didn't want to be rude, but then again, he never told her he was going. Plus, he really enjoyed being around Camilla, it was like she had a physical effect on him, not a sexual one, but one that had the ability to drop his blood pressure. Donald wasn't sure if it was her voice, or her smile or just her aura in general but he wanted to spend more time with her.

"I would love to Camilla. What time and what beach should I meet you?

"I am assuming you don't have a car, so why don't I pick you up around 8:00 pm and ill drive us there."

378

"Great, sounds like a fun night. I have really enjoyed talking with you Camilla and I am looking forward to getting to know you some more."

"Me too" said Camilla

They exchanged phone numbers and addresses before Donald left the restaurant. He went back to the house, it seemed quiet, in fact it was so quiet the silence was almost deafening. It was at this point that Donald realized how much he appreciated Camilla's invite to have a night out. He decided to take a mid-day nap. Day drinking, especially red wine made Donald very sluggish and sleepy. He changed into his pajamas, closed the curtains, set his alarm for 3:00pm and laid his head down to sleep.

During his nap Donald tossed and turned, he was too hot, then he was too cold, he kept waking up worrying that he would sleep through the alarm. At 2:00 pm he laid in bed staring at the ceiling. He felt lonely. He started thinking about Leela. He wondered how she was doing and if he should call her or go see her. But how could he after the way he ended things? Donald felt ashamed and angry at himself. How could he do that to Leela? To her family? After everything they had done for him and everything they were going through.

After realizing that he was not going to get back to sleep Donald decided to get up. He made himself some coffee and sat on the couch in silence. He sat there for a long time, thinking about everything that had happened in his life up to this point. He left Allison because he was not happy with her, but he wasn't happy now either, in fact the only happiness he had felt recently was when he was with Leela.

After what seemed to be an eternity of thinking Donald finished his second cup of coffee and began to get ready for the evening.

Camilla Picked Donald up right at eight and drove them to the beach.

"I am really happy you decided to join me tonight Donald, I feel very comfortable talking to you, I think you might have a lot of good stories to tell." Camilla said with excitement.

"I really appreciate you inviting me, I have not been to a bonfire on the beach in Venezuela before. I really enjoy your company Camilla; you are very easy to talk too as well.

There was no sexual tension between Camilla or Donald. From the first time they conversed it had always felt like a close friendship. Neither of them felt judgment from the other.

As they got closer to their destination Donald could feel the temperature drop a little. The breeze had picked up and he could smell the salt from the ocean.

"My friends and I try to get together out here as much as we can, we like it better than in the town or in the city, its quieter, more peaceful with little distractions."

As soon as Camilla said these words she wondered if Donald would have preferred some place livelier. Although he was just as pleasant as he was at lunch, he seemed quieter, in need of a distraction.

"Well I mentioned to you earlier that I am in Venezuela to do some soul searching, so a low-key night on the beach, next to a fire sounds very appealing to me."

Donald's reply calmed Camilla's nerves. She could tell he had a lot of weight on his shoulders and would benefit from talking to someone about it. How could he not? What Gringo comes to Venezuela to soul search, most people go someplace closer to home. She thought.

As they reached their destination, Camilla put the car in park, grabbed a blanket and a cooler from the back seat.

"It's just a five-minute walk from here to where the fire is" she said

"Here let me help you carry something" Donald said as he reached for the cooler.

The air was thin, crisp, you could hear the sound of the waves crashing in the distance.

"what a beautiful night, it's amazing how many stars you can see when you get farther from town."

Camilla looked up to the sky and replied "I know, it's like this almost every night. The waves help drown out the sound of traffic, and the sky helps drown out the lights from the city, it really is a peaceful place to be, especially at night with few people being on the beach."

Donald could now see the fire Camilla's friends had started, there were only three other people there. As they approached everyone, Camilla greeted them with a hug and a kiss on both cheeks, she didn't hesitate to introduce Donald to her friends. Everyone spoke English which made Donald feel less out of place being the only one there over the age of thirty.

"Donald these are my closest friends; Pedro, Maria, and Edwardo." She said pointing to each person as she said their name. Everyone raised a hand to say hello. There was some small chit chat, the same questions Donald had been answering for most of his time in Venezuela. Where are you from? How long have you been here? Why are you here? They chatted about Venezuela and its culture; how different it was to the British culture. Donald told them about his son Richard, the places he had traveled too, and everyone shared a laugh when Donald attempted to convers in his broken

Spanish.

As the night continued the drinks were poured one after the other, before he knew it, Donald had a buzz, he relaxed and felt very comfortable around a group of strangers he had just met.

As he was staring into the fire, he heard Maria say;

"What time is it? Where is everyone else at?

"Oh, there are more people coming?" Asked Donald

"Yes, we have about seven other people coming but they normally don't show up until ten at night" replied Camilla.

This made Donald a little nervous, he thought it was just going to be a small get together, after all, he had just gotten comfortable with the people who were already here. Well Camilla seems like a good person with a levelheaded personality, I can't imagine her friends would be any different. Thought Donald.

"sounds great!" Donald said trying to sound as enthusiastic as he could.
Camilla noticed that there was an underlying tone in Donald's voice all night.

"Donald would you like to take a walk with me?" She asked.

"Yeah I could go for a stroll"

They both grabbed another drink, Donald put on his sweater and they started to slowly walk east of the party.

Camilla smiled and looked at Donald;

"You seem like you have a lot on your mind, I have been told I'm a great listener if you would like to share your thoughts.

Donald was not surprised at Camilla's observation; he had not felt like himself and she clearly could see it.

"I'm sorry if I'm not as chipper as I usually am, it's just that I do have a lot on my mind."

A part of Donald was happy that Camilla said something, maybe this was his chance to sift through his feelings and thoughts. Donald had been feeling so overwhelmed with everything that a deeper part of him was just waiting to pour out his thoughts to someone who wanted to listen.

"I won't bore you with the whole story. You seem like you have great instincts, so I'm curious as to what your opinion about my situation would be. The short story is that after many years of marriage to my wife Allison, I had started to feel like a chameleon in our relationship."

"Chameleon? How so?" Inquired Camilla

"I find that in most relationships people lose sight of who they are, their wants and needs because they are focused primarily on their partners. It's not a bad thing, but when you stop focusing on what your needs and wants are, you find that you end up living someone else's life. You blend in with what they want to do, and how they feel, and the focus on your own personal needs is no longer there. This kind of thing can lead to unhappiness, not just for yourself but for your partner and the relationship as a whole. Anyway, this is how I had felt for a long time in my marriage. Some months ago, I decided that I had to end my marriage, so I packed up my things and left to come here to Venezuela to find out who the person is that I lost."

"That's a very brave thing to do Donald, most people are afraid of change, they would have stayed in order to live in their comfort zone. I'm curious though, why did you choose Venezuela out of all the places in the world?" Asked Camilla.

Donald thought about this question;

"I am not totally sure, I remembered seeing something about Venezuela in a magazine some time ago. My wife and I used to always go to the same place for our annual Holiday, this year I wanted to go someplace new and warm, I guess Venezuela must have been in the back of my mind."

"I see. If you don't mind me asking how is your wife doing with you being gone so long? Have you talked to her at all?"

"Unfortunately, while I have been here, a few months ago, my son Richard flew here to notify me that Allison had passed away."

"Oh my gosh I'm so sorry Donald I had no idea!" Camilla said with a horrified look on her face.

"Thank you Camilla, as you can imagine the guilt I felt that my son had to deal with all of this on his own. I often wondered if this would have happened had I not left her."

"Donald you can't put that kind of weight on your shoulders, it was out of your control, that could have happened while you were at work, at home, or here, it's not your fault."

Donald nodded in silence, trying to keep his emotions from bubbling up to the surface. He didn't want to cry in front of Camilla. He was not good at hiding his feelings because Camilla noticed how upset he was and embraced him in a hug. They held each other for a minute or two before Donald lightly pushed away. He decided to change the subject and tell Camilla about Leela.

"I have had some good times here, it's not all been bad news. While I was living here, I had met a girl. Her name is Leela, she and I originally met at an airport in Florida. When I came here, I stayed at the hotel that is owned by her family. After a few weeks she came home, and we were reunited."

"By the grin on your face, is it fair to say this was a happy surprise?" Camilla asked this because she didn't want to assume anything like she had when she asked about Donald's wife.

"Yes, it was a great surprise. In fact, as I spent time there, I helped with some renovations the hotel was doing, and Leela and I grew to be close friends, and eventually more than friends. We fell in love despite our age difference. She had a way of making me feel like myself, but the best version of me."

"She sounds like a wonderful person; I'm beginning to wonder if she is the reason you seem so deep in thought all the time." said Camilla.

As Donald kept talking, Camilla felt like she was finally putting the pieces together. In her eyes Donald came here not only to escape a loveless marriage but to find himself and potentially someone who could share his newfound freedom.

"You are very perceptive Camilla. Yes, I have been

thinking about Leela for many weeks now."

"What happened between the two of you? I assume something bad must have happened otherwise she would be with you right now?"

"When my son came to tell me about Allison, he ended up staying for a few weeks with me in the cottage Leela's family had provided for us. He ended up going to Aruba with some friends I had met, as well as Leela's brother.

Camilla's stomach began to turn, she had really hoped this story had nothing to do with the plane crash that happened, she remembered it was a flight from here to Aruba. Why do I have to be so nosy!? She thought to herself. She decided not to say anything and let Donald Continue to tell his story.

"I am not sure if you heard but there was a plane crash a few weeks ago." He said glancing towards Camilla.

"Yes, I saw it on the news, what a terrible accident. Donald if this is too difficult for you to talk about please don't feel like you have to tell me."

"I appreciate you saying that, but I'm ok. Well that day, Leela and I were having lunch, and she overheard some people talk about the crash. When we got to the airport there was this big mix up with the list of people who were on it. Anyway, my son and one of the girls he was flying with, had been bumped off the flight list and had to take another flight.

Camilla let out a silent sigh of relief, she thought this story was heading into another direction.

"You must have been so relieved!" She said

"I was, but unfortunately that feeling didn't last long because Leela's brother was on that flight with the other female friend."

Camilla's stomach tightened again. Poor Donald, he has been through so, much she thought.

"When we got back to the hotel to notify her parents, they had already known, they were inconsolable. They began yelling at me, and I had already felt guilty that somehow, I had caused the situation. If I was not here, then my son would have never been here and Leela's brother would have never gotten on the plane. I panicked, there were so many heightened emotions I didn't know what to do... so I just left."

"I don't even know what to say Donald, you have been through so much in such a small amount of time."
Camilla didn't know what to say or do, how do you begin comforting someone who has been through everything Donald has.

"For a journey that was supposed to be peaceful it has been very stressful. It's like every time I feel that I am in a good place in my life, the other shoe drops. I left for a few weeks to think about everything, to get away from everyone. Every time I try and think about myself, I end of thinking about Leela. I came back because I have not made up my mind if I wanted to go see her again and apologize for my abrupt absence or if I should just leave it at what it was."

There was silence between the two of them for several minutes. Camilla was not sure if Donald was waiting for her response or tell him what he should do. She then asked:

"Do you believe in fate Donald?"

Donald was taken back by her question, "I am not sure, I have never really thought about it. Do you?"

"Yes, I am a big believer. I think that there are things in our lives that we have no control over. Yes we can make decisions but what those decisions bring us is not necessarily our choice. I think you were meant to meet Leela, and you were meant to go through all the things you have gone through. As horrible as they were, there is a reason that life gives us ups and downs. We learn from the unfortunate things in our lives, and we learn to enjoy the good things even more."

Donald nodded as Camilla was talking. He was trying

to figure out if he shared her beliefes in matter of fate.

"So now that you know part of my story, what do you think I should do? What would you do?" Asked Donald. He wanted to know what someone else in this situation would do, if only to ease his guilt for how he left things.

"Well I can't tell you what you should do because I am not in your shoes... but I will say this; somewhere in your heart you already know what you want to do. You just have not decided on it because a part of you is trying to rationalize your choice out of fear. I think you need to set the fear aside and listen to what your heart is telling you Donald. As I said, we all have choices to make in our lives but the unexpected, the unknown is the part that is out of our hands. Do you understand what I am saying?"

She looked at Donald and he looked puzzled.

"Okay, as an example, if you went to see Leela, she would either accept your apology and you have the potential to live happily ever after, or she does not accept your apology and you go home and meet someone else. You only have control over going to her, or not going to her, the rest is not in your control so don't let the fear of the unknown stop you from making the choice you already know you want too.

Donald Thought about this for a moment. She's right, I'm getting myself all worried because I don't know how Leela will react, but I won't know until I see her.

"Camilla, how did you become so wise at such a young age?" Donald asked smiling at her.

"I don't think I'm wise, I just think that sometimes the picture can be clearer when you stand back and look at it from a different point of view. I was once in a relationship that kept getting me into trouble, I didn't realize how wrong we were for each other until I talked it over with a good friend of mine. She gave me a new way of looking at it. I guess I just always remembered that it's easy to get in our own heads and complicate everything when we know the answer deep inside."

By now they had walked so far from the party that fire was barely visible and they decided to start heading back.

"Well enough of this serious talk, lets head back and enjoy the night." Said Donald.

"I really do appreciate you taking the time to listen to my stories, you have opened my eyes, I know what I have to do."

"No need to thank me Donald, I like listening to people's stories, and if I can help in any way, then that's just a bonus."

They laughed as they picked up the pace to join the

party. Once they got there, Donald met some of the others that had showed up. He had a few more drinks and tried to enjoy the party. After an hour and a half, he decided he was going to get a taxi back home. He had a plan on what he was going to do, and he just wanted to get it done with. The anxiety and constant wondering were making him feel crazy. The sooner the better he thought.

As he went to say goodbye to Camilla, he felt himself getting emotional, he wasn't sure if it was the lack of sleep, the alcohol, or the fact that he may never see her again that got to him.

"Camilla, I want to thank you from the bottom of my heart for letting me spend time with you and your friends. This has been a great night. If you ever need anything, please don't hesitate to reach out to me. Donald said as he gave Camilla a hug and a kiss.

"Thank you Donald, I will reach out to you, I am interested in how your choice plays out. It's been a real pleasure getting to know you. Have a safe journey home.

Camilla saw Donald off. Waving goodbye to him as he drove away in the taxi she wondered if she would ever see him again.

CHAPTER XIV

Newcastle England

Donald was looking out of his front window at two small boys playing in the yard. He was in a daze, staring at these children wondering when life starts to become so complicated. He couldn't remember the last time he had enthusiasm for anything like a child did with a new toy.

"Donald have the kids eaten their dinner yet?" Yelled a familiar voice from afar.

Donald didn't answer, he was in a trans and couldn't snap himself out of it.

"Donald did you hear me?" Asked Leela as she walked up next to Donald.

'Sorry love, no I didn't hear you, what did you say?"

"I asked if the kids have eaten yet?"

"Oh, no not yet, I was just about to call them inside"

"Donald you were supposed to feed them while I was on my run! Do I have to do everything on my own?!"

"Sorry Leela, its only thirty minutes past their usual dinner time, it's not a big deal."

"Yeah not a big deal to you! They need structure and routine at this age Donald, why do you make me always sound like the bad guy?"

"Edmond, Paul, come in and get cleaned up for supper" yelled Donald to his sons.

The boys came running in the house straight to the bathroom to wash their hands.

Leela and Donald set the table in silence. Leela had taken out some leftovers from the fridge for the boys.

"Do you want me to heat it up so you can take a shower?" asked Donald.

"No, I've done this much I can just finish it myself." Leela said in a cold tone.

"Donald, remember tomorrow we are going to the Johnsons house for dinner, please don't forget to call the babysitter."

"What? You never told me this before." Replied Donald

"Yes, I did, but what does it matter anyway, it's not like you're doing anything."

"It matters because you just assumed I didn't have

plans and that I would go." Said Donald in an irritated tone.

The kids came running into the kitchen, as to not argue in front of them, Leela only gave Donald a cold glare as if to say, *can't you just do it?*

"Okay" was all that Donald said before he left the kitchen. He went in his study and sat in his chair. Looking out the window he acknowledged how nice the summers were in England. It was nice being home again. Leela and him had been living in this house for almost ten years. How fast the time flies thought Donald.

He sat in his chair wondering when it all changed. He and Leela were so happy. The day after the Bonfire with Camilla, Donald went to Leela and apologized. It was as if their souls had been communicating, everything that needed to be said was done so through their eyes.

They were so in love, even her parents managed to forgive him and treat him like they did prior to their sons' tragic death. They were so happy for Leela on her wedding day. Donald had Richard as his best man, they had a beautiful wedding in Venezuela. All those happy moments, when did they stop? Thought Donald.

As he was watching the sun go down, he couldn't help but feel a familiar discomfort. It was as if a dark cloud of doom had hung over him. His heart felt so heavy. What did he not have to be happy about he thought? *I have a beautiful wife, two healthy kids, I live in a nice house, in a country I love, why can't I shake this feeling?*

As the sun fell behind the last house, it suddenly dawned on Donald, the feeling he felt was that of a Chameleon.